Mikael Lundt

ᚾᚨᚷᛚᚠᚨᚱ

NAGLFAR — Ark of the Gods

Imprint:
© Mikael Lundt, 2021
Published by:
Michael Gückel, Gartenstr. 15,
95191 Leupoldsgrün, Germany
Contact: mikael@mikael-lundt.de
On the web: www.mikael-lundt.de

Copy-editing & Proofreading: Sana Abuleil
Cover design: Michael Gückel

Printed and distributed by: Amazon KDP

1

Svea II mining complex, Spitsbergen, Norway,
1,400 kilometers north of the Arctic Circle
August 19

The smoke of the last blast had cleared. An odd smell with the scent of ammonia and burnt paper was all that still hung in the air. Vasily Petrov stepped into the tunnel and switched on his headlamp. He beckoned to his colleague, Leif Gulbrandsen, to follow him. Then, he turned on the bodycam attached to his jacket and started recording. Gulbrandsen was behind him removing the handheld radio from his belt and starting to report into it.

"We're going in," he said, releasing the talk button with a crackling noise.

The tunnel in front of them looked stable and was largely free of coarse debris. The precision of the blast still amazed Petrov. The new emulsion explosive, Fluktan C, had increased its level of perfection compared to what it was before. It produced 40% less smoke and dust, could precisely be dosed to a tenth of a gram, and its mixing ratio could be individually adjusted to the rock that required blasting.

Petrov knew that the geology of Svalbard was extremely diverse, with granite, gneiss, shale, sandstone, and lava in the strangest combinations.

So, it was a significant relief to be able to blast with such flexibility. And it worked! They were making faster progress than ever. Mining in the northernmost part of Norway, on the Arctic islands of Svalbard, was complex enough anyway. The equipment had to be perfect, otherwise it would very quickly become tedious. And digging for gold was pretty different from digging for coal, as had been done intensively here in the past.

Petrov walked to the end of the newest tunnel and examined the hole that they blasted into the wall. "This is strange," he grumbled, looking inside. He couldn't see much, but apparently a large cavern lay beyond the hole. It wasn't anything like what they had expected. But that didn't mean it was any less interesting.

Gulbrandsen came to his side with a powerfully bright flashlight. The wall on the opposite side of the cave became visible. "Well, that's not a mine," he noted.

"No, look over there!" Petrov pointed at carvings in the rock that covered most of the wall. "That looks like cave paintings or something."

Gulbrandsen reached for his radio again. "There's a cave here," he reported.

Petrov shook his head. This guy was surprisingly taciturn even for a North Norwegian.

Noise and crackling came out of the speaker. Then, a choppy radio message. "Repeat. Cave?"

"There's a cave here," Gulbrandsen said curtly, releasing the talk button again.

Petrov gave him a skeptical look.

Gulbrandsen pressed the button again. "There are drawings. We're going to move in to take a closer look."

Petrov nodded. "There you go. Now come on, let's go inside and examine the cave." He stepped through the hole as Gulbrandsen followed him with the flashlight.

The cave was undoubtedly of natural origin. There were no traces of digging tools, drills, or blasting. Petrov knew geology. He was not a simple miner; he was trained as an exploration specialist. This rock was pristine, untouched, except for the petroglyphs carved into the wall. The carvings had a noticeable red residue in each crack. Petrov knew the images must have been ancient— possibly thousands of years old. He had seen similar images before in Sweden and Norway, but were most prominent in the south. The pictures they were looking at appeared as though they were still in their original state. Were he and his stodgy colleague, Gulbrandsen, the first people to see them in thousands of years?

"What's up now?" grumbled Gulbrandsen, waving the flashlight in his hand. "Are we having lunch?"

Petrov turned away from the carvings, which depicted scenes of ancient Norse mythology and looked graciously at his colleague. "Yes, in a minute. I want to go over there first." He pointed to a tunnel left of the wall with the carvings. "There's a passage. I want to look at it. Hand me that radio."

Gulbrandsen answered with an unwilling grunt, handed over the radio, and followed Petrov. "Petrov here. We have discovered a cave with ancient petroglyphs and are now exploring another natural tunnel leading away from the cave. I'll get right back to you with details." He released the button and waited for confirmation. Nothing bit hissing and static noise came from the device's speaker. "There's probably something in the rock that's interfering with the signals. We should set up radio repeaters later."

"Got it," Gulbrandsen confirmed, taking the radio back.

"Okay, let's see what's in there. After all, we're still the reconnaissance team. Do you want to go ahead of me with the light?"

Gulbrandsen shrugged his shoulders and silently walked past Petrov.

The tunnel—leading slightly uphill—was a little too low to walk upright, but high enough so that they didn't have to crawl. A cold breeze much chillier than in the big cave came towards them. There were practically no major junctions; only a few bulges to the left and right of the passage. So, it was unnecessary to set markers on the way.

After about 50 meters, the path dropped slightly downhill again and they noticed more and more ice enveloping the walls and floor.

"Could get slippery," Gulbrandsen predicted. He stopped and pointed the light directly behind him.

Petrov held his hands in front of his eyes. "Stop blinding me, you moron!" he grumbled. Petrov heard a spiteful laugh from his colleague, then a scream. Suddenly, everything around them became gloomy. He blinked, trying to determine what was going on in the dark tunnel. "What's happening? Gulbrandsen!"

Petrov moved forward and turned his weak headlamp to all sides in a panic. There was a hole in the floor. From down below, he saw a glow. He heard somebody groaning.

"Gulbrandsen," he yelled downstairs.

"Shit!" was all that came from down there.

Petrov relaxed slightly. The idiot was alive. He must have broken through a layer of ice that had spread over an ancient shaft. Petrov estimated that it was probably three to four meters deep. At the edge of the hole, he saw rough steps carved into the rock. Then, he watched as

Gulbrandsen stood, wiped himself off, and held painfully onto his right side.

"Are you injured?" Petrov asked.

"My ribs are bruised! Dammit!" He paused and looked around, "There's something down here."

"Let's take care of it later. I'll get help," Petrov yelled as he turned around. Then, yelping came from below. "What is it?" he shouted into the hole. "Do you want me to come down?" Petrov stuck his head into the hole but Gulbrandsen was no longer in sight. It was obviously not just a duct. There was likely a cave down there. He couldn't tell how big it was from up there or what was inside. Gulbrandsen bellowed again, but this time, he sounded like an animal. His unnaturally loud screams echoed off the rock walls. and were

Petrov had goose bumps all over his body. He would not go down there. Nothing in the world could make him do that. He reached for his belt. Damn it, why had he returned the radio? He looked down the tunnel that was behind him.

Once again, he called into the hole. "Gulbrandsen! I'm going for help now. I'll be back. Just don't move."

He got a beast's grunt in response. The noise was closer. Then, he saw Gulbrandsen's face in the hole again. It glowed with anger. His eyes fixed on him like those of a predator. They were entirely red, as if the blood vessels inside had burst. Petrov gasped and jerked backward, banging his head on the low ceiling. The pain didn't matter though because horror was all he felt. He rushed through the cramped tunnel as fast as he could.

Though Petrov ran quickly down the tunnel, his thoughts ran even faster through his mind. What was going on here? He couldn't forget the terrifying expression that was plastered on Gulbrandsen's face. He looked as if he wanted to kill him—to strangle him with his bare hands.

Suddenly, Petrov heard angry roars and snorts behind him as his legs lunged him forward with an ultimate speed. The guy was climbing up the duct. "Shit," he mumbled. He knew he had to hurry.

As he continued forward, something grabbed him by the leg. and pulled him to the floor. Hard. Petrov screamed in panic.

Gulbrandsen dragged him closer. With brute force, he smashed Petrov to the ground, leaving him breathless. He stared into the horror that was about to devour him.

Gulbrandsen hit him in the face with his right hand as he incessantly bawled in a bestial manner.

Petrov wanted to raise his arms protectively, but Gulbrandsen threw himself on him and pushed him down with inhumane power. Then, he bit. Blood spurted from Petrov's carotid artery and covered the enraged Gulbrandsen from top to bottom with a red flush. Petrov became dizzy. His vision narrowed and his ears rushed. He didn't notice as Gulbrandsen stormed down the hallway and then on through the cave toward the mine.

He was smeared all over with blood and yet he was far from finished with his helpless victims.

2

In the sky above Svea II,
October 8

It was a stone's throw. Anika Wahlgren shook her head. No one takes a plane to travel a ridiculous 50 kilometers. Except there were no roads that led to where she was going. In fact, roads were exotic on the largely uninhabited archipelago of Svalbard.

The route from the capital, Longyearbyen, to Svea led over icy mountain ranges and, other than by plane, the terrain was almost impossible to handle, unless you were up for a life-threatening climb in Arctic conditions or a several-hour trip by snowmobile. Anika dreaded the thought. Her father would have enjoyed something like that, but he had also been a daredevil and a Northern Country fanatic. She shook off thoughts of him and focused her attention on the view of the untouched landscape below.

"Stunning, isn't it?" asked the pilot.

She nodded. "A fascinating view indeed."

The pilot had allowed her to sit in the cockpit, or, rather, had almost urged her to do so. She assumed he had just wanted to sit next to a young woman again. She was the only passenger on the Dornier 228 turbo-prop plane, which actually had room for 15 people plus cargo. The pilot had explained to her that this was a very reliable aircraft, in service all over the world, with excellent short takeoff and landing capabilities. Anika had only nodded and did not inquire any further.

Presumably, there was only one fairly short runway in Svea. She would soon find out—when the stone's throw came to an end. She could hardly wait, having already flown three and a half hours from Stockholm to Narvik and another two and a half hours from there to Longyearbyen. All in all, she had been on the road for almost nine hours and felt like she had been beaten to death. All she wanted to do was arrive safely and unload her 300,000 euros worth of equipment, which was stowed in the back of the cargo area. She hoped that the equipment had remained undamaged and would withstand the Arctic climate.

As snow-covered mountains and valleys passed below her, Anika wondered what exactly she was supposed to be doing in this place. What could they find up here? There were no early settlements on those islands and therefore little hope of significant archaeological finds. On the other hand, she had been forced to join the project—from the highest level. She had been promised a scientific sensation, exactly in her field interest: the Viking Age and early Scandinavian history. And to be honest, she needed a change from teaching at the university. Down there waited a big change.

The sun slid along the horizon as the pilot turned and headed toward the mining settlement of Svea from the south.

"Enjoy it," the pilot urged. "In three weeks, there will be no more sunlight at all. Then, it will be Arctic darkness here. But winter has its charms, too. You know, Northern Lights and such. If only it weren't for the storms.

"I can imagine. But I certainly won't be here that long."

"Alright, then. Just have them call me when you want to be picked up."

A road appeared in front of them. It led from the harbor at Kapp Amsterdam south of Svea up to the settlement. There were some low buildings, silos, containers, and rusty vehicles. Probably still the remains of the former mine.

She tried to imagine what it must have been like to dig for coal here—especially in winter. Deep in the mountain, there was only blackness: black coal and black rock. Outside, there was nothing but darkness for 24 hours a day. She looked at the low hanging sun once more. The golden rays made the ice-covered hills glitter. There was no doubt that with light, it was beautiful here.

"We're landing," the pilot announced. "Now you'll see what I meant by short-landing capability."

Anika tightened her parka around her and looked down the deserted runway. In the neighborhood, there were only a few tin huts and a snowplow. Behind them lay a fjord of the rough northern sea. The wind blew her blond hair into her face. It was freezing cold—minus five degrees Celsius. It was just 10 degrees Celsius back in Stockholm before she left for her trip. The weather was no surprise though.

The pilot began unloading the equipment from the cargo hold, and with relief, Anika noted that everything looked undamaged, even after three flights.

A large, bulky, black Landrover approached the runway from the settlement, stopping a few meters behind the plane. On the passenger side, a short, stout man with a thick, white beard emerged from the car. Anika knew it was Harry Stadler, the head of the research station. She remembered him from last week's video calls. At all three appointments, he had worn a coarsely knitted sweater in the typical Norwegian pattern. Today was no different. Red wool peeked out from under his gray jacket. The man's accent revealed that he was English through and through. Anika thought he looked even "cuddlier" in person. She couldn't describe it any other way: Stadler was the academic version of a teddy bear. She put on a smile and stepped toward him.

"Did our crash pilot bring you back down in one piece?" He cast a sly glance in the pilot's direction.

"You know, the stupid jokes cost extra, Harry," the pilot said tersely, removing the last crate from the cargo hold.

"He was very nice and knowledgeable," Anika commented. "I'm glad we get to meet in person now."

The two shook hands.

Meanwhile, on the driver's side, a tall man emerged and was standing behind Stadler. His hair was cut short—military style—and he wore some kind of uniform that didn't have any insignia. On his belt was a baton and a firearm. He stepped closer without a word and extended his right hand. "Øystein Sigurdson, I'm in charge of security," he asserted, squeezing Anika's hand. "Have you signed the documents?"

"Jesus, Øystein!" Harry retorted. "Just let her settle in first. She only just arrived."

"No problem," Anika replied, pulling a brown envelope out of her pocket. "I had plenty of time on the flight to read through your confidentiality restrictions. You'll see it's all signed."

Sigurdson took the envelope and nodded. Then, he made his way back to the Jeep, opened the trunk, and began loading the bags in.

"Fine, now that we've taken care of the formalities, we can get right to the nice things," Stadler smiled. "We'll quickly load up the equipment, then I'll show you around over there. You might also want to refresh a bit after the long trip."

"It's actually fresh enough for me here." Anika grinned at him. "A hot shower would be great."

Thirty minutes later, Anika had showered, thrown her clothes into the closet, and familiarized herself with her new site. The accommodations were reminiscent of a youth hostel: a gray-coated table, two worn chairs, a rusted metal wardrobe for clothes, and rough, dark brown curtains at the windows. She suspected the rooms had not been renovated and had been taken over directly from the mining company. The advantage was that only a quarter of the crew lived here, rather than the former 100 men that occupied the place. The bunk beds in the multi-bed rooms served as storage space now. Plus, Anika had a room just for herself. She would certainly be comfortable during her stay.

Anika left her room behind and made her way to the canteen. Harry had announced that he would introduce her to the other members of the research mission during dinner. She had to admit that she was curious who the jovial Brit might have gathered here. He had persistently kept silent about that until now—probably because Sigurdson had insisted on secrecy.

She walked between the low houses, mostly painted in dark red and white, and headed for a large, gray building. According to Harry, it had various supply functions other than housing the cafeteria and some of the staff offices. Her own office was located there as well, which Anika considered a plus. You could never go wrong with a space close to the canteen.

As she got nearer, she saw that a row of steel containers had been placed right next to the building, connected to the main house by a walkway. Some had antennas or satellite transmitters on the roof while others appeared like simple storage areas.

She opened the door to the main building and was met with a strong smell of meatballs and mashed potatoes. Did they cook Swedish Kötbullar especially for her?

She entered the dining room and looked around. A fat guy in a German national soccer team jersey came right up to her and grinned. "You must be Anika! Is Tommy coming, too?"

Oh, how she hated that! Whenever she met a German, they had to reference Pippi Longstocking because of her name. Where did this urge come from? Anika swallowed her angry reply. "No, my name is only spelled with one n," she clarified as neutrally as possible. Then, she shook the man's huge paw. "And you are?"

"Oh, sorry. I'm Björn."

"Björn? Like the fat bear?" She nodded toward his belly and put on a disarming smile.

"Well..." grumbled Björn, looking down at himself.

"Ha, now she's got you by your weak spot, huh? That was quick!" said a second man who had gotten up from the table and approached the two as they exchanged pleasantries. He was tall and slim and wore a hooded sweatshirt. Anika guessed that he was in his late 30s, approximately her age. He had brown, curly hair and small wrinkles around his eyes, clearly indicating that he liked to laugh. He also extended his hand. "I'm Matthew Grant, welcome to our Polar Party."

Anika had to laugh. "Thank you. I'm already very excited about the entertainment program."

"Come on over, dinner will be ready in a minute." He pointed to the back of the dining room where three large tables were pushed together. "And don't hold it against Björn. He's a fine fellow. This place attracts a special kind of person. Life is easier with jokes. You'll get used to it."

"No problem," Anika brushed off. "I have three brothers; I know how to fight back!" She followed Matthew to the table and sat down across from him next to a small,m black-haired Asian woman who appeared to be around 25. She poked listlessly at the cranberry compote that was on the table and looked up briefly at Anika, nodded, then continued poking away.

"This is Mi Chen, our measurement and computer genius," Matthew explained. "Social skills aren't her area of expertise."

"Hey, wait a minute," protested Mi. "I'm very sociable!"
Matthew laughed.

Then, Harry came out of the kitchen area carrying two huge pans of steaming meatballs. Joyfully, he put the pans down and disappeared back into the kitchen.

Slowly, the other residents of the settlement trickled in and took their seats at the table. Most of them gave Anika a friendly smile; some introduced themselves directly. She decided to make every effort to remember all their names.

Sigurdson was the last to enter. He walked to the middle of the room, turned right, and sat down alone at a small table. He was obviously not very social. But if she was being honest, she hadn't really expected him to be.

Matthew noticed her glance and smiled mildly. "Yes, our chief constable is not one for boisterous evenings."

Anika now looked back at Matthew and noted his tousled hairstyle. "Sorry, are you a surfer by any chance?"

He paused. "Yeah, I used to surf quite a bit back home in California. I still do it occasionally in my spare time—if I have any. But not here in the Arctic Ocean, of course." He laughed. "What made you think that?"

"The hairstyle. I know you shouldn't judge people by their appearance, but I've realized that I'm usually right about these things."

"We can sure use your intuition around here."

Harry came in with the rest of the pots and spread them out across the tables.

So, Anika was right. There was indeed Köttbullar with mashed potatoes and lingonberries. It was certainly not original, but she appreciated the gesture. Besides, she had never eaten anything prepared by an Englishman before. She hoped they wouldn't taste too British.

Harry raised a glass of red wine and looked around the table. "Here's to our new arrival and continued good luck. Dig in! I've been sweating blood and water in the kitchen to make sure it tastes authentic. Cheers!"

Anika suddenly found the environment really cozy. Even though she didn't know anyone yet and the arctic cold was lurking outside, she felt as though that she was in the right place.

After dinner, she said goodbye early as the long journey took its toll. Harry accompanied her to the door.

"That was a really nice evening," she offered. "And your Köttbullar were better than I suspected, too."

Harry nodded. "Thank you, I'm glad to hear that. I

think they were pretty good. Now, get some sleep. Tomorrow we'll get down to business. Come to my office first thing, and I'll explain exactly why you're here. And please forgive us for being so secretive before. There are certain people who insist on it. And it's for a good reason, too." He nodded toward the table where Sigurdson sat staring into a half-full glass of beer.

"He just takes his job as head of security very seriously, so that's good," Anika defended diplomatically, then said goodbye and retired to her room for the night.

3

For about two hours, Anika had been poring over the documents Harry handed her that morning to bring her up to speed on the project. They mainly consisted of photographs of petroglyphs, reports with references to other research, and some analysis of rock and pigment samples. Most of this was also found in the data collections on the station server, but Harry wanted to give her an initial overview this way. She had quickly come to the conclusion that they had done a clean job so far. She just wondered who had done them. If this was such a significant find—as one might assume—then why had she only now been called in as an expert? Apparently, there were already some findings. Who had created these documents? Harry? He was a historian and an expert in the field of early European history.

She looked at the photos of the mysterious petroglyphs spread out on the desk in front of her. Harry led the entire operation, and she doubted that he had had the time to explore the drawings himself. There was only one reasonable possibility. She had to have a predecessor. But who was it? And why had he not continued his work? An intriguing question, but Anika knew she should deal with the most important first. As soon as she had sifted through the documents, she was eager to go into the cave with the drawings herself. No photograph could replace the immediate experience of standing in front of a millennia-old testimony to history. She did not yet have a workable theory of how these petroglyphs might have come to be on an island that was considered uninhabited at the time. But as she understood it, that was an essential part of her task here.

She would be allowed to go into the caves in the afternoon, Harry had said. Her equipment would have to be down by then. Anika looked at her watch; it was shortly after eleven. One more hour and she would go into the cave.

At five to twelve, there was a knock on Anika's office door. Harry Stadler stuck his head in and grinned at her mischievously. Again, he wore one of his usual Norwegian sweaters and brown corduroy trousers. "Am I too late? I bet you're just bursting with curiosity." He waved a white plastic card in his hand. "This is your key. Please don't lose it or there'll be a big fuss. We don't need another one of those."

Anika stood up from her desk. "I'll guard it like the apple of my eye." She winked.

"Very good. Everything is ready. Shall we go straight over, or shall we get something from the canteen first?"

"I'm so excited I don't think I'll be able to eat anything now. And besides, I haven't digested the meatballs from last night yet." Anika grinned back just as mischievously and took her coat off the hook.

The entrance to the mine had been closed by a massive steel security gate, making it clear that something sensitive was being protected.

"There's the terminal over there. Why don't you try your card now?" Harry prompted. "Actually, you should be able to gain access without any problems."

Anika held her access card up to a stainless-steel RFID reader next to the door. A green light and beep signaled that her card was valid and authorized access. "Pretty modern for a mining facility."

"For a regular mining operation, this would indeed be unusual. We added this so we could guarantee a higher safety standard. You've met Sigurdson, after all."

Anika followed Harry inside the mine. The tunnels had been bored and blasted into the rock. In some places, they were secured with steel and wooden struts. On the left side, about ten meters away, were lamps fixated on the walls, bathing the tunnel in a yellowish light. But the warm light did nothing against the icy cold that seemed to penetrate the walls all around.

"What was mined here in the past? I read something about coal," Anika asked as they went deeper into the mine.

"That's right. This—or rather the Svea I mine next door—was the largest coal mine in Svalbard. But then the original mine was shut down," Harry explained.

"I read online that that was several years ago. Have they resumed coal mining recently?"

"No," Harry responded. "Not coal mining. You're correct; they gave that up years ago because the price of coal was just too low. It wasn't worth the effort up here in the north to do it. Coal can be mined much more easily and cheaply elsewhere."

"Then what were they looking for?"

"Test drillings have shown that there must have been deposits of gold, copper, and other metals here. A new mining company wanted to develop them with the capital of Norwegian and especially Russian financiers. But after these discoveries were made here, Norway decided to immediately ban further mining. Instead, we are here now exploring the secrets of this mountain."

"It's tremendously exciting. I'm happy to be a part of it."

"I'm glad. And we hear nothing but good things about your work everywhere."

Harry and Anika turned right into a branching tunnel. It was a bit narrower than the previous main passage, and it felt a quite damp.

"How long have you actually been here?" Anika inquired.

"About two and a half weeks," Harry answered. "But we were just setting up and getting ready the first week. It's all been so exciting that it only feels like it's been two and a half days rather than weeks." He paused and chuckled, ". All this excitement isn't actually good for my heart." His voice echoed strangely off the rough rock walls as he spoke.

"Do you really have heart problems?" asked Anika with a hint of concern.

"Yes, but I've had it for years. It's not really bad and I'm well-adjusted with medication. If something actually does go wrong, I'm in the right hands with Matthew. He's pretty overqualified for this mission here."

Anika nodded. "And he seems like a really affable guy to me, too."

"Oh, he is. And very attractive, isn't he? Pretty much all the female expedition members have already set their eyes on him."

"No, I really didn't mean it that way. I work professionally and would never mix business with pleasure," Anika clarified.

"It's okay; I was just teasing you." Harry pointed ahead

to where the hallway made a final bend. "Here we are."

Around the bend, another secured door came into view.

"Well, let's give your impatience a little satisfaction, shall we? Here you go. After you," Harry signaled.

Again, Anika held her access card up to the reader and the airlock opened. As they walked through, Anika immediately felt transported back thousands of years. Had it not been for the transport crates and the spotlights, they would have felt as if they had landed in the Nordic Bronze Age.

Anika stood open-mouthed in the middle of the cave and stared at the large-scale petroglyphs. These testimonies of a bygone era were as impressive as they were unusual. She knew of many rock carvings in southern Scandinavia. They were found almost exclusively on flat, glacially abraded stones, mostly lying down, but not on walls. Moreover, the richness of detail in this artwork was unsurpassed. It fit well within the framework of previous finds, but still seemed more sophisticated, as It was as if the creators had put in distinct effort for these drawings.

In the center of the largest scene depicted was a huge ship. It was by far larger than the usually carved small boats. The figures were also modified. It seemed to Anika that an attempt had been made to make women and men recognizable. There were six of each. In addition, there was another figure standing centrally above the others. It was clearly larger and depicted with rays around it. All in all, there were 13 figures, a large ship, and various smaller objects in between. The otherwise often depicted animals were completely missing. Around this large main drawing were several smaller effigies carved into the rock, which she was sure told a story.

Harry watched Anika smirk as she couldn't contain her amazement. Absent-mindedly and overtaken by fascination, she walked toward the drawings.

"Fantastic," she breathed, "Nowhere have I seen finds so well preserved." She stepped up to the wall and traced the indentations with her fingers. They were typical of this type of drawing—not very deep and traced with a reddish-brown color. "Really amazing. The color is only slightly faded, and the stone is barely weathered." She turned to Harry, beaming. "This cave is a fabulous stroke of luck."

"I know," he said abruptly. "But there's a downer." He pointed behind him. "The hole in the wall where the airlock is now is the result of a blast. Unfortunately, it destroyed some of the drawings. But I think there's still enough material for you to explore."

Only now did Anika notice the technician, Björn Lange. He had begun to take Anika's equipment out of the boxes and was setting up the first measuring devices.

"Oh, sorry Björn. Why don't you let me do it myself? The devices are very sensitive. It takes a delicate touch."

Björn looked at her in irritation for a moment, then shrugged his shoulders. "No problem at all. I was going to have lunch anyway," he grumbled, and a few moments later, disappeared through the airlock toward the mine.

Anika flipped the lid of the box in front of her and continued to look around the cave.

At both ends of what must have been a 200-square-meter cave, she discovered passageways. One was closed off with a smaller version of the access lock and the other was open. Light shone out. "What's back there?" Anika wanted to know and pointed to the lit passage.

"In my opinion—though it may be insignificant and invaluable—it is a burial chamber. It was discovered and uncovered only a few days ago."

"A burial chamber? Harry, you creep! Why didn't you tell me about this?"

"Oh, I certainly would have if you had been any more reluctant to join our little expedition."

"A burial chamber in a cave is unusual for that time. But probably everything outside was too icy to bury anyone. Are there bodies inside?"

"Yes. There is exactly what you would expect to find there: corpses, grave goods, and some everyday objects and artifacts. We didn't inspect the things further because we wanted to wait for you. We left everything as it was found."

"That's quite fantastic, Harry."

"I knew you'd like it."

"Still, for now, I'm going to dive into the petroglyphs here and complete the analysis and data I've done so far. That's why I brought my special equipment, after all. But before I do that, I have one more question: What's back there?" She pointed to the far end of the cave where the security door was built into the rock. "It looks like it leads to a high-security area."

"There's unsafe territory behind it," Harry responded sternly. "The passageways are at risk of collapsing."

"Did a boulder fall back there on the guy who used to fill this role before me?" asked Anika, looking at Harry expectedly. She waited for his reaction.

He very slowly pulled up the corners of his mouth and smiled.

Anika followed up with, "You didn't get the previous findings here from the cave yourself, did you?"

Harry swayed his head back and forth but didn't say a word.

"That's what I thought. So, I have a predecessor. Who was it and why didn't he finish his work?"

"You really are tremendously perceptive. Nothing can be kept secret from you for long, can it?" responded Harry.

"You're right about that! So, who was it?"

"Henrik Oddevold. But he was not killed. He had...how should I put it...psychological problems."

Anika nodded and looked at the drawings again. "Okay, that's enough explanation for me. For now. Henrik is a brilliant researcher, a bit old-fashioned, but immensely experienced. I'm glad he didn't have an accident."

Harry sighed. "It's tragic. I hope he gets better soon."

Anika wondered what exactly had happened to him. She knew would find out in due course, though, and was too intrigued by the drawings before her to pry any further.

She turned to the research director again. "Thank you, Harry. Thank you for having me!"

"I have to thank you. Now I'll leave you to your work." He dug a handheld radio out of his pocket and handed it to Anika. "Let me know if you need anything."

"Alright." She continued to set up her equipment.

Harry watched her do this for a few more seconds, nodded with satisfaction, and then sauntered out of the cave.

4

It was already late afternoon and Anika was sitting in her office in the main building of the settlement again. She had been processing the data from her first measurements for two hours. The visual analysis of the drawings had already been thoroughly fascinating, but it was all on the verge of becoming even more impressive. Anika entered a few commands and waited impatiently while the computer performed the complex calculations.

On her laptop's display, a three-dimensional mesh of thin, white lines slowly formed, gradually becoming denser and denser, followed by a gray texture.

She had taken half a dozen scans with the laser scanner in the cave and had now combined the data from all the scans in the computer to create one overall picture. The possibilities that this technology created were impressive. Now she had a complete 3D model of the entire cave, which she could explore virtually with virtual reality goggles if she wanted to, without even having to leave her office. That kind of gimmick wasn't the goal of her model, though. After all, she could go over there herself at any time and experience the drawings in person.

Anika used the laser to trace anything that couldn't be seen by the naked eye. The scanner scanned the walls to an accuracy of a fraction of a millimeter, revealing details that would not otherwise be visible.

Due to the extreme precision, Anika was even able to recreate the guidance of the tools used, could estimate how precisely the work had been done,, and what kind of tools were likely used in the process. With enough data, she could even figure out how many different artists created the work.

One thing she had already recognized though was that an area of the drawing seemed particularly accurate, almost as if more modern tools were used. This was practically impossible for the early time in which rock drawings like this were created. Or were these drawings more recent than they had all thought? Using precise techniques and technology, she would try to date them. Perhaps an analysis of the color pigments would help.

Still, the deviant area of the drawing was not the only mysterious thing. The whole existence of the picture so far north was a mystery. Such an early settlement on Spitsbergen had always been ruled out until now. It was assumed that the archipelago had been discovered much later. She did not give much credence to the theses that the Vikings had discovered what is now Svalbard in 1194. Their presence on the archipelago could not be proved and was generally considered rather improbable. In an Icelandic chronicle, the name "Svalbard" was mentioned, but the term, which meant "cold edge", could also have meant another island or the ice boundary.

Instead of Viking relics, here were these drawings that had very likely been created at least a thousand years earlier. Was it possible that the drawing itself told the story of its creation? She would have to take a closer look at all the partial images and try to put them in order. The riddle, which she was confident was hidden in the drawings, excited her immensely. This was a scientific sensation of the first order. She could hardly wait to learn more.

But on the other hand, there was this feeling of doubt. Was that all? Had they really been brought here for this— to the edge of civilization, to one of the most inhospitable places on the planet? And what was the purpose of the whole troop of scientists who were not working in the cave?

Why did the project need medics, geologists, physicists, computer scientists, all the technical staff, and even its own security company? There had to be more here.

A man Anika didn't know briefly from dinner burst into her office, interrupting her stream of thoughts.

"Is Torger here? Have you seen him?" he asked.

Anika looked questioningly at the man and feverishly wondered what his name was.

"Torger Hansen," he hitched impatiently. "Have you seen him?"

Anika slowly shook her head. The name meant nothing to her. "Who is Torger?" she asked with unmistakable astonishment in her voice.

The man offered no reply and disappeared from the office again as quickly as he had entered.

Anika got up and went after him.

The man seemed to be in a hurry. He stuck his head into the office next to hers and asked the same questions there, too. She heard a soft "no," and the man moved on toward the cafeteria.

"Shit," he grumbled.

Anika finally remembered his name. Lasse Iversen, one of Sigurdson's security team. He had been sitting at the front of the table last night and hadn't said much.

"Get ready for an emergency," Iversen said as he stepped into the cafeteria.

Anika entered behind him and saw that those present were quickly rising and heading for the exit. "What's going on? What's the rush?"

"Come with me for now," Mi Chen said, shuffling to the door with a coffee in her hand.

"Where to?"

No one answered.

In the hallway, Øystein Sigurdson met them with an expression even grimmer than usual. "He's nowhere to be found," Lasse Iversen reported to him. "Is he downstairs?"

"We're looking. Now, everyone go to the shelter immediately," Sigurdson ordered. He took a smartphone from his jacket pocket and typed something. A few seconds later, an alarm sounded.

Mi pulled Anika by the arm. "Come on, we better hurry up now."

Then, they all strode toward the exit.

Less than five minutes later, the entire scientific team gathered in a sealed-off structure that could be described as an oversized panic room or, better yet, a bunker. It had been fitted into a disused tunnel that ended in a dead end and was therefore only accessible from the outside—only if the door was unlocked from the inside. Once that was activated and the entire crew was present inside the bunker, the lock couldn't be opened from the outside unless with a charge of plastic explosives. The spartanly furnished room behind the thick, steel walls could accommodate all 26 people in the settlement if necessary. There were 21 present at the moment. In addition to the wanted Torger Hansen, Sigurdson and his three employees were missing.

Anika heard some of the others whispering. "Probably another one of those exercises," said one woman.

"Man, if they'd just let us do our jobs in peace!" one man retorted.

Anika sat down next to Mi and asked, "Who is this Torger Hansen. Some dangerous felon?"

"No, he isn't. But he's a nasty little eel, if you ask me. The way he always looks at you—that is, if he can keep his eyes high enough to make eye contact," she said as she rolled her eyes and shivered dramatically.

"But that's not why we're in here, is it?"

Mi smiled. "If it were up to me, we'd lock Torger up here, the old groper." She paused and sipped her coffee. "Okay, listen to this. Torger is a mining engineer—the only one of the former mining company's personnel still here. He was taken on because of his knowledge of the mining plant and machinery. He was lucky then; he was in the bathroom when..." Mi's voice trailed off.

Anika followed her gaze.

A status light on the wall had switched from red to green. Harry stood next to it at a terminal and nodded encouragingly to those present.

Three seconds later, Sigurdson entered the room and looked around sternly. He put an index finger to his lips and told everyone to be quiet. "My men and I have searched everything. Hansen is no longer here. One of the two snowmobiles is missing. We assume he took it."

"What's he doing out there? It's already dark," asked Stadler, who had joined Sigurdson.

"I have no clue. It's incredibly stupid to go out there now, and alone for that matter. I've sent word to Longyearbyen that a man is missing. We'll see what comes of it. If he doesn't show up by daybreak, they want to start a search. For us, that's an all-clear for now. You can go back to your work or go right to dinner or whatever you were about to do." With that, he turned around and left the bunker.

Harry approached Anika and took her aside. He had a tremendously serious expression on his face. "I think it's time I filled you in, even if Sigurdson protests. After all, you signed the confidentiality agreement. Shall we have lunch? Afterwards, I'll show you what all this panic is about."

"We might as well get started now," Anika responded curiously.

"No, believe me, you should eat beforehand. You won't be hungry after."

Harry and Anika had been sitting in a room that looked like a miniature version of a security center for about ten minutes, waiting for Sigurdson.

"I'm really sorry, that must have been pretty scary earlier, not knowing exactly what was going on. But we'll explain in a minute and things will make more sense," Harry assured.

Anika frowned and looked at Harry. What did she think he was going to tell her? "It's okay. I don't scare easily."

"That's good," Harry responded, making a sweeping motion with one arm. "This is Sigurdson's realm. He's certainly not the most likeable person in the world, but he does his job very conscientiously, and that's what counts for me."

As if on cue, Sigurdson entered and locked the door behind him. "Good evening," he said curtly. "So, you're really going to let her in on this so quickly?" he asked in Harry's direction.

"After what happened earlier, there's no point in keeping it a secret any longer, is there? I want everyone to be focused and not get bogged down in speculation, which is counterproductive."

Sigurdson nodded slowly. "That's understandable. And I support it. That is, if it works the way you think it will."

The corners of Harry's mouth twisted downward. "Now, let's stay optimistic, please."

Sigurdson sat down at a computer and logged in. Then, he opened another password-protected folder that contained nothing but a video file. He turned to Anika and looked directly at her. "You're ready?"

Anika nodded.

"Alright, let me just give you some context before we begin. This is a recording from a bodycam worn by one of the miners. The footage was taken the day the cave with the petroglyphs was discovered. You may have noticed that one of the branches out of the cave is blocked. What you are about to see happened beyond that door."

Anika felt a little queasy. Sigurdson's speech made her more nervous than she wanted to admit. She tried hard not to let anything show.

Sigurdson opened the video and projected it onto a large monitor mounted on the wall.

The shots began in a dim tunnel and the image was grainy and blurred. The glow of a lamp swinging around kept illuminating parts of the image. There was no sound, which made the recording seem even more surreal.

They watched as the cameraman stepped along the tunnel and finally into the cave with the petroglyphs. The second man was inspecting the cave. The other handed over the radio so that the cameraman could send a message. Then, he went ahead into the lower junction. The cameraman followed. The picture became even more choppy. For the most part, only the floor of the aisle could be seen. Obviously, the men had to walk bent over.

All at once, the second man disappeared. Then, the camera angle revealed a hole in the ground. Below, in the darkness, was the outline of a man. He struggled to his feet. Then, the frame panned wildly once more. When the hole came back into view, the man was no longer visible. After a moment, turned increasingly the man was seen frantically yelling in the hole, his face contorted in rage and his eyes bloodshot. Anika's hair stood all over her body. Even on video, it could clear that whatever was in his eyes was sheer hatred.

The image bounced up and down as the cameraman fled. There were only blurred shadows and streaks. But it wasn't long before the image abruptly slowed down. Then, suddenly and without warning, the man's contorted face filled with hatred showed up on screen once more. The attacker struck. The other man tried in vain to defend himself, but everything turned black at first, then red the next moment. The beast's angry grimace was covered in blood. A crimson gush splashed sideways, covering the lens and immersing everything in a blurry red-brown haze.

Sigurdson stopped the player and looked over at Anika. "After that, the guy went back through the mine, slaughtered six more men, and escaped into the ice."

Anika sat silently staring at the screen. "Whew," she finally said. "That's intense."

"Yes, and I'm sure you understand now that we place a

high value on safety. The shelter is the last refuge in case the situation gets out of control again."

Anika nodded. "No one has been down there since that day?"

"No, access is closed to everyone. We first have to find out if it's still dangerous. And to do that, we need more information. Before we do that, no one is going down there."

"So, you don't know what's down there? Or do you?"

"That's classified," Sigurdson responded promptly.

"Why did you bring me here if you're not going to tell me the truth?"

"To be honest, Harry wanted you here. I wasn't fully convinced from the start."

"So, please," Harry now interjected. "I think we should all pull together."

"Fine Sigurdson said. "To answer your question, we don't exactly know what's in the room. Not yet. But you're welcome to help find out."

Anika looked over at Harry who had a pained expression on his face. When he noticed Anika looking at him, he caught himself and changed the subject. Turning to Sigurdson, he asked, "Any news on the whereabouts of Torger?"

"Not yet. I just checked again. That's why I was a little late. I don't think we'll know anything until tomorrow morning. It's pitch-black outside. Either he made his way by snowmobile, or he broke down somewhere along the way. In that case, we shouldn't get our hopes up."

"Was he down there then, where..." Anika pointed to the screen, which still displayed the still image from the bodycam. "I mean, was he there?"

"As far as I know, no. But he hadn't been seen for at least two hours before he disappeared. In fact, we don't know what he's been doing since lunch or where he's been."

"We should probably work on that," Harry suggested.

"I've already arranged for surveillance cameras to be sent to us. But it will take some time."

Harry stroked his snow-white beard and looked urgently at Sigurdson. "I'm not particularly comfortable with the solution, but we can move on as effectively as possible." Then, he turned to Anika. "I'm sorry to see your first day of work end like this. If you need help processing what you've seen, contact John McFarland. He's a psychology major and very empathetic."

Anika put on a smile. "I think I'll be fine. But thanks." She paused for a moment. "You were right, by the way. I certainly wouldn't be hungry now."

5

> Tromsø, Norway,
> October 11

Morning fell upon the northern Norwegian coastal city of Tromsø in a dreary and oppressive manner. A drizzle fell from the cloudy sky as the weather outside sat at no more than four degrees. Torger Hansen looked through the window of the small breakfast café at Tromsø Cathedral, a wooden, Gothic church. The wood was a pastel yellow but appeared nearly gray in the pale morning light as the sky above shone through the windows. He drank a cappuccino while he waited near the clear, glass wall drawn from ceiling to floor. Soon, he would leave this cursed country behind where the sun hardly ever shone and where it was always far too cold for his taste. Torger had long since chosen Thailand as his future home, where it was much warmer and the girls were much more willing. That's where he would retire once he all of this was behind him. Forty-seven is a good age to stop working, he'd been telling himself. But first, he knew that the rest of the money had to be in his bank account before he could quit—and also the bonus he was patiently waiting for.

Torger clenched and unclenched his fist, trying to thaw his frozen fingers from yesterday's trip with the snowmobile. But he had fought his way through and was able to board the 6:00 p.m. flight from Longyearbyen to Tromsø on time and without much hassle. A night in the best hotel in town and an extensive stay in the wellness area had compensated him for the exertions for the time being. But that wasn't enough. If his clients were as keen as he assumed, then they would surely spring for something more. After all, he risked his life yesterday and quit a very well-paid job for this.

At 8:00 a.m. sharp, Torger spotted the sign they had agreed on earlier. A black sedan with tinted windows drove up from the south side of the road and stopped in front of the park. A man with a yellow umbrella emerged and walked towards the church. Torger finished his coffee, put enough money down on the table for the bill—with a reasonable tip—and left the café. He pulled up the hood of his jacket and sprinted across the street through the rain.

The church was silent that Wednesday morning. Not a single seat of the 800 that lined the church were occupied at that hour. As arranged earlier, Torger climbed up to the dusty organ and walked around to where the organist normally sat. Today, however, someone else was sitting on the white wooden bench. In fact, someone he was not expecting was perched in front of the instrument. He stopped abruptly.

"Don't be shy," the man offered in a Russian accent. He was tall and muscular, but scrupulously shaved and coiffed. His coat and suit looked like they had required him to fork over a hefty amount of money. His black leather gloves shone like new.

Torger overcame his fear for a moment. "I was expecting Viktor Nikolayev. Is he here?"

"He's busy."

"But...I have valuable information and I want to negotiate with him."

"Negotiate?" The Russian's tone was cold and sober. "What do you want to negotiate about?" He pronounced his words as if were talking to a maggot—a lowly creature that had wandered out of line.

Torger remained unperturbed. "The compensation," he said.

The man frowned. Then he answered almost indifferently, "I am authorized to arrange everything necessary."

"I would still prefer it if I could meet Viktor in person."

"I already said it couldn't be done. He's not even in town. And I don't suppose you'd want to fly to Saint Petersburg first." He paused for a moment and looked questioningly at Torger. When he didn't answer, he shrugged. "Then you'll have to talk to me."

"Alright, then," Torger agreed.

"First of all, do you have what we want?"

Torger nodded. "Yes. All the data I've collected so far, my access card, the codes, a detailed site plan, a list of employees, a list of security precautions, and some brand-new findings. I think my extra work is worth a little bonus."

The burly Russian eyed Torger for a moment. "Well, whatever. You'll get a markup if the data is as good and extensive as you claim. But I'll have to check it out first, of course."

"I need the money now. I have to disappear. They'll be looking for me in Norway."

"How much do you want?"

Torger thought silently for a moment and then decided, "Half a million."

The Russian smiled weakly. "That's twice the amount

you've already received. Don't you think you're being a little too greedy?"

"You are welcome to recruit another spy if I am too expensive for you." Torger realized that his tone had come off as arrogant. He bit his tongue. He knew better than to push it. "Well, we both know that's not an option," he added more calmly.

"Right," growled the Russian. "I'll arrange payment." He dug his cell phone out of his coat pocket and dialed a number. A brief conversation in Russian followed, then he hung up again. "The money is on its way to your account. Hand over the data, get out of here, and stay out of our way."

Torger reached into his jacket pocket and pulled out a USB flash drive. "It's got everything on it. But it's encrypted. You won't get the password until I confirm that the money has been received."

"Oh, I'm sure that won't take too long," the man said as he grabbed the flash drive from his hand, pocketing it and pulling out a white envelope instead. "This is the promised cash portion. 10,000 euros and 10,000 American dollars. Unmarked. I'm sure this will get you anywhere you want to go."

Torger tucked the envelope into his jacket and prepared to leave.

"Don't you want to count it while we wait for the transfer to go through?" the Russian asked.

"I'm sure the sum is right. I trust you."

"You can't trust anything or anyone. Count it, I insist." He fixed him with a relentless gaze.

Torger frowned. "Alright, if you must." He opened the envelope at the glue line, took out the bills, and began flipping through them. He was barely halfway through when he felt a strange dizziness and uncontrolled salivation in his mouth. "What is..." He glanced at the Russian who was sitting quietly on the organ bench, playing with a syringe in his hand.

"You've probably heard of Novichok, right?" he asked.

Torger shook. He had trouble staying on his feet.

"In the unlikely event that you do not know it, this may suffice as an explanation: It is a very potent nerve agent from the Soviet Union. There was enough on the bills to poison five of your kind. This..." he paused and flicked a finger against the syringe. "This is atropine. A simple but also very effective antidote."

Torger fell to his knees. His legs cramped and nausea overtook his very being.

"So, you give me the password and I'll inject you with the antidote. You have about ten minutes before it's too late."

Torger's mouth went numb. He swallowed a few times, then struggled to speak. "Pig!" he hissed shrilly. The word echoed strangely as he struggled to speak.

"Don't waste your precious time. Every second the poison spreads through your body, the damage gets worse, and the chances of recovery get slimmer."

Torger felt hatred, powerlessness, and increasing despair. He noticed how his body obeyed him less and less. "Good," he gasped, swallowing hard a few more times. "The password is 36a776xe." Then, he slumped to the floor and curled into a ball.

The Russian calmly typed the password into his smartphone. "Thank you very much."

"The syringe!" gasped Torger.

"Yes, of course," the Russian said in an emphatically friendly tone, setting the syringe down on the organ's music rack. "You can have it." With those words, he left, leaving Torger wincing and gasping for breath on the floor.

On Wednesday morning, Harry Stadler, Mi Chen, Björn Lange, and robotics specialist, Elvar Hauge, gathered in the central engineering control room of Svea II. It was cramped in the converted container and the air was stuffy. The installed ventilation systems were just as small as the electric heaters, which struggled against the icy cold that crept through the steel walls. But the assembled researchers had no sense of such trivial inconveniences that morning. They were about to make another major advance in their exploration of the mysterious cave.

"I am ready to initiate the rappelling process," Elvar Hauge announced without taking his eyes off the monitors in front of him for even a second.

"Go ahead, but gently, please," Stadler urged.

Meanwhile, Mi analyzed the data transmitted by the Cave Explorer's sensor system. That was the name they had given the modified robotic vehicle, which was actually developed for bomb disposal in rough terrain. Instead of explosive ordnance disposal tools, it was equipped with thermal imaging and infrared cameras, as well as countless probes and sensors, to be ready for any eventuality. They had already maneuvered the robot safely and without problems through the tunnels, testing that both camera images and measurement data were transmitted successfully and almost flawlessly. Now the hundred-thousand-euro device was about to be lowered into the cave automatically. There, it would hopefully provide more insights than the simple surveillance camera, which had so far only transmitted images from a distance. The images it had already shown were exciting, but the insights that could be gained from them were still limited.

"He's down now," Hauge updated. "I'll untie the line and pull it back in. Are we about to lower the spotlights and heaters?"

"Would be better," responded Björn. "Then, our friend can push it into position and turn it on."

"Okay, let's do it that way," Stadler confirmed.

Fifteen minutes later, three powerful LED spotlights on short tripods and two radiant heaters, each with a power of 11.5 kilowatts, were lowered into the cave as the robot tactically pushed and positioned them.

"There, that takes care of the dirty work," Mi grumbled impatiently. "Can we start collecting data now?"

Harry gave her an indulgent look. "You know we have to provide enough light and slightly higher temperatures first. The Explorer wasn't built to operate in glacial areas."

"Yeah, I know. I just want to finally have something to do."

"Okay, Elvar. Activate the sensors and move forward," Stadler ordered, now also turning back to the screens with curiosity.

The robot slowly drove further into the cave, which consisted largely of ice—clearly different from the tunnels and the cave with the petroglyphs. The heat emitters worked to melt the ice and expose cave walls or other objects.

The robot approached the only visible object so far. This, however, filled the entire rear area, creating a wall that partially protruded from the ice.

"Awesome," Stadler murmured. "Up close, the hull looks even more fascinating." He stared at the large central monitor, onto which the camera image from the Explorer was projected, making the object much easier to recognize. The screen clearly showed a ship stuck in the ice. It was difficult to estimate exactly how big it was, since the bow, stern, and upper superstructure were mostly hidden in the ice. Only one thing was clear: It was huge.

"What was it made of?" asked Hauge. "Can you tell by any chance, Harry?"

"I'm not sure. It almost looks like wood, but this structure is quite unusual. We should take a sample and have it analyzed at the lab. Can you take care of that, please?"

Hauge nodded. "Sure, that's what I'm here for."

Stadler turned around, "Mi, any insights from the sensor data?"

"No, all dead. Like a stone in a frozen lake. I'm only very faintly picking up the station WLAN signal on the antennas."

"Alright. Then we'll take the sample first," Stadler instructed.

Hauge moved the robot closer to the hull and unfolded a swing arm with a pointed pincer at the front end.

"Take an inconspicuous spot. We don't want to destroy any archaeological finds," Stadler said.

"Okay. I'll put it as low down as I can."

The camera image showed how the pincers on the gripper arm approached the rugged surface of the hull. Up close, the material no longer looked like wood. In a way, it seemed rather organic and yet simultaneously fossilized.

Hauge maneuvered the gripper in the lower third of

the visible area and touched down, as instructed. The robot instantly froze.

"Yikes!" shouted Mi suddenly from behind. "Now we're talking."

Stadler wheeled around. "What is it?"

"Signal spikes! Violent pulses on dozens of frequencies. Unclear exactly what it is."

Stadler joined her at the monitor.

"Look! It's subsiding, but there's still a pulsation."

"From the ship? Can you be a little more specific?"

"It's definitely coming from the ship. It's some kind of electromagnetic radiation. But I can't tell what it is yet. We need time to analyze it."

Stadler shook his head. "I mean, that's crazy. It's got to be a malfunction." He turned back to Hauge. "What about the robot? Is it malfunctioning?"

Hauge typed frantically on the keyboard. "I'm restarting the remote-control interface right now. Explorer is not responding. One moment."

They stared intently at the status bar on the screen.

"There, now everything is back to normal. I'm going back with the Explorer."

"Did he get anything?" Stadler inquired.

"I don't know, hopefully not. The best thing to do is get him upstairs and I'll have him checked out. We'll have to get the sample upstairs anyway."

Stadler nodded. "Let's do it that way." Then, he turned back to Mi. "Is the signal still there?"

Mi nodded. "Yes, weak. But measurable."

"Analyze it, please, and bring in colleagues as you see fit. This is a priority. Even if it was just a glitch in the sensors, I want to know what caused it."

"Eriksson and Ward could help me. I'll get right to work."

"And I'll let you know what's going on with the robot as soon as possible," Hauge added.

"Very well. Please send the sample in a sealed container to Juan Lopez in the laboratory. Have him check what kind of material it is. At 6:00 p.m., we'll discuss the situation. Let's get to work."

6

Anika hadn't slept well—not because of the brutal scenes from yesterday's video, but rather because of the mountain of questions that had piled up inside her. Until last night, she had assumed she was working on an archaeological project—an unusual one, for sure—but one that was nevertheless rather harmless. But what had happened to that miner meant danger. She couldn't help but agree with both Harry and Sigurdson: Safety measures were in order. If there was something lurking down there that could turn man into wild beast, then extreme caution had to be exercised. The whole thing sounded absurd—somehow like science fiction, magic, or the curse of the pyramids—but it was undeniable, nonetheless. The video was enough evidence for her to believe the unbelievable.

Anika thought of the cave drawings that hinted at mythological references. The rage she had seen in the man fit into this archaic world view. If she didn't know better, she would say that that bloodthirsty, distorted grimace belonged to a berserker—the myth of a warrior who fought mindlessly, felt no pain, and destroyed everything in battle. the berserker was not a new concept, even in serious research. But most respected scientists attributed the phenomenon to the consumption of psychoactive substances, such as mushrooms or certain other plants. She shook her head.

Were there some special mushrooms growing in the ice cave down there, whose spores had driven the poor man insane? Perhaps that was a useful theory. But she knew that was not her job. She was only meant to study the drawings. Matthew was a medical doctor, she recalled. Maybe he had an idea. She resolved to ask him about it later, when she had evaluated all the measurements from yesterday.

Anika sat down at her computer sipping her cup of coffee as she waited for it to turn on. While the computer booted up and loaded the standard programs, she wondered where to start. From where Oddevold had left off? Or all over again? Her predecessor had spent the two weeks he had been here making detailed descriptions of each drawing and measuring them traditionally. She certainly didn't need to do that again. But when it came to interpreting the pictures and placing them in their historical context, she preferred to approach the matter with an open mind.

Did the rock carvings possibly give a hint of what was in the other cave and what happened to the people there? Anika opened the 3D representation of the cave and overlaid the grid structure with the digital photos she had taken of the drawings. Now, the simulation started to resemble the original. Anika zoomed in and positioned the camera angle as if she were standing in front of the large central drawing. The ship in the middle of the figures was drawn extremely large—much larger than usual.

"Did you use it to sail here?" she asked quietly as she inspected the details. Anika knew that the large stone settings in Sweden, known as ship settings, showed that seafaring in the Baltic Sea had been a factor as early as the Nordic Bronze Age. But the Baltic Sea was far away from here. At that time, more people engaged in trade with other countries, which may have led individuals to embark on any dangerous crossings. So, why would the seafarers of that time set out for the most likely deserted northern Arctic Sea without knowing whether anything worthwhile was waiting for them on the other side?

The concept of religion popped into her head. People had always been willing to make completely irrational sacrifices for religion. She changed the picture frame as she pondered the thought and dragged the figures carved next to the ship into the frame. She looked at the larger figure standing in the center above the other twelve. What did those rays mean that were depicted all around? Was this figure supposed to represent some kind of deity or sorcerer? In her mind, she went through the usual Norse gods mentioned in the Edda. Was this supposed to be one of them, or was it something else entirely? A previously unknown or forgotten monotheistic god cult?

The mythological texts of the two parts of the Edda dated from the eleventh to thirteenth centuries and were thus much younger than common rock carvings. On the other hand, they were only the written record of long, orally transmitted sagas and legends. Who could say when and where they had originated? It was also possible that the stories had changed completely over the centuries. It was well conceivable that there had once been a fascinating personality named Odin or Thor, who was later believed to have superhuman abilities. Could such a figure have led the sailors up here? It seemed plausible. Still, the vague theory was still unsatisfactory. Why would anyone want to go to the land of eternal ice? "There's nothing here but death," Anika answered herself aloud as she dragged the chamber of death into frame.

Anika looked at the clock. It was almost eleven. Had

she been sitting in front of the screen brooding for so long? Harry was right, time was flying. She brought her coffee cup to her mouth, took a sip, and scrunched her face at the cold, black liquid. It was time for her to get a refill and pay Matthew a visit. She searched for map of the settlement online and looked for the medical complex. She memorized the way and logged out.

The medical department had its own small building. In addition to a classic infirmary, it also housed three adjoining laboratories and offices for the staff. Anika held her access card up to the reader and was admitted. It briefly occurred to her that perhaps she should have announced her arrival beforehand. She had no way of knowing whether Matthew would even have time for her. But now it was too late. She quickly made her way down the hallway, which was covered in the same oatmeal-gray linoleum floor as all the other buildings. As she passed, she read the signs on the doors: laboratories for material analysis and medical purposes, storage rooms. At the very back, a large, red cross was pasted on the white door panel, indicating that she had undoubtedly reached the infirmary. She walked up to it and stuck her head inside but no one was in the room. Anika looked around. She had expected better first aid equipment, but it almost looked as if they had tried to cram several specialist departments of a clinic into one room. "This is not the standard for research missions," she muttered, shaking her head. She recognized a swiveling X-ray machine, ECG, EEG, ultrasound, and much more.

"Do you like it?" a voice from behind her.

Anika winced and turned around, "Matthew, hi! I didn't hear you come in."

"It's an old thing. I like to sneak up and scare good-looking women." He laughed. "Can I help you, are you experiencing any discomfort or pain?"

Anika frowned. "Discomfort?"

"Well, this is the infirmary. People usually come here when they're feeling some sort of pain in their body."

"Yes, of course. Or—I mean, no. I don't have any discomfort or pain. Just questions for you if you have time."

"Sure, shoot," he prompted.

"Alright, first of all, what is it with Harry and these Norwegian sweaters?"

Matthew burst out laughing. "Those are the burning questions? Excellent!"

Anika shrugged her shoulders and smiled mischievously.

"It's a fair question," he teased. "I asked him the same thing on the third day. Harry is probably one-eighth Norwegian, hence the sweaters. Maybe he wants to emphasize his expertise in that area, or maybe he's having some fun with it. Oddly enough, not one of the ten full-blooded Norwegians here wears a sweater like that."

"Probably British humor," Anika said.

"Very possible! Okay, but seriously now, that's not why you came here."

"No. I wanted to ask you some other things, too. And after seeing how unusually well-equipped your department is, I think you might have answers."

"Yeah, I can't complain, the equipment is top notch."

"I take it you're privy to what's going on with the miner. Harry showed me the video yesterday."

Matthew nodded. "It's really disturbing. What do you want to know about it?"

"Does the term berserk mean anything to you?"

"I've heard it before, but I don't know the details. Help me out here."

"It's basically a myth that mainly appears in Norse tales, but under different names. It makes some appearances in the sagas of other cultures, as well. The berserker is said to have been a warrior fighting in a frenzy, who no longer feels pain or wounds and virtually mows down the enemy. I instantly thought of this myth when I saw the video."

"Sounds accurate."

"In any case, it's believed that the phenomenon actually existed. The theory is that these berserkers must have consumed certain psychoactive substances. And so, I was wondering if there might be something like that in this cave. Some kind of fungus or lichen or something. I know the Arctic climate makes it rather unlikely that anything would grow there, but then, there are the strangest vagaries of nature."

"I don't think that's a bad hypothesis. But you would have to take samples. Then, I can analyze them here in the lab. You should ask Harry. After all, you have to get everything approved here, especially when it comes to this cave."

Anika looked at him broodingly for a while.

"What is it?" Matthew wondered.

"I don't know. It's just a feeling. I'm used to always being on top of everything and ahead of everyone else. But somehow, I have the impression that everyone else knows more here than I do. I only get what's already been filtered."

"Don't worry about that. They're a little particular

about secrecy. But I'm sure they're not hiding anything significant from us. Look, they showed you the video and brought you up to speed, so that shows trust, right?"

"You're probably right." She paused and pondered his words for a moment. "Well, anyway, I think the miner's behavior would be best explained by a psychotic episode."

"You don't have to convince me," Matthew smiled. "Do you want me to ask Harry? I have to give my status report later anyway."

"No, I'll do it myself. I have a few more questions for him. What kind of status report do you have to give him, by the way? Are we all required to turn something like this in? I wasn't told anything about it."

"No, no. This is about the infirmary. Basically a formality. I just have to report how many patients there were there, whether unusual physical or psychological symptoms occurred, and if someone seriously injured themselves, and the like."

"I see. And have you been busy?"

"Other than giving out a lot of cold sprays and headache pills in the last week, nothing special. But the onset of winter is entirely to blame for that."

"Then please give me a package, too." Anika held out her hand, her palm facing upward. "Because my nose is already tingling."

Viktor Nikolayev was casually sitting in the treatment chair of the best manicure salon in Saint Petersburg. A neat, Asian woman was filing the nail on his right index finger with the utmost precision. Viktor knew the procedure by heart, the sequence of the various tools, and the effect of the individual lotions. He went to the manicurist at least every two weeks because a well-groomed appearance was never to be underestimated. Clothes made the man; shoes made the man, and perfectly groomed hands made the man. Besides, he wasn't getting any younger—he had to admit that to himself. He thought about the small wrinkles he had discovered on his forehead and around his eyes. He had turned 50 last month and had no intention of just submitting to decay. After he had taken care of urgent matters, he resolved to make an appointment for a consultation with the plastic surgeon.

Boris Karlov was set to arrive that evening and hopefully report that he had resolved everything to his satisfaction—though Viktor knew satisfaction was relative. The bankruptcy in Norway was still gnawing at him. He felt anger boiling inside him again when he thought about how he had been booted out. What were those stiff government bastards thinking, taking away his prospecting license? After all he had invested! And just when they had struck rich, gold deposits, too. He hadn't even been able to remove the 200 ounces that had already been extracted from the mountain. It reeked of intrigue. Viktor had nothing against intrigue; he just hated it when he wasn't the mastermind.

And these cowardly excuses! What did the few mine workers who had died in the alleged rampage matter? It was ridiculous to use that as a reason and continue working in the mine.

But one could also learn something from it. The way they were behaving could only lead to one conclusion: There was something there of even greater value than gold. And it was his. He had found it. And if what his spy had already told him was true, it should be a good deal. He recalled the video that showed the crazy miner. Maybe he should get back into the arms trade with a new ace up his sleeve? And even if, contrary to expectations, the find didn't sell, this was no longer a question of business, it was a question of honor. And the Norwegians had offended this honor. They had made him look like an idiot though he was the richest man in St. Petersburg and the third richest oligarch in Russia. No one did that with impunity. His former competitors could certainly tell a lot about how vindictive he could be, whereas most of them had nothing to report at all.

The manicurist switched to his left hand and applied the file. Viktor took his smartphone out of his pocket and called up the picture Boris had sent that morning. It showed an artifact in the ice cave at the end of the mine. It had to be a ship, but what was it carrying? Viktor concluded that he would find out what was in it and take whatever it was. Then, those moose-heads would see who was in charge. They would beg to have the artifact returned to them. And that's just what Viktor wanted.

Viktor put the phone back in his pocket and put his hand into an oil bath that the manicurist set up for him. Viktor felt the liquid penetrate every pore, making his skin supple. His hands were those of a pianist, even if he did not master the instrument. He played on the keyboard in the global market and didn't worry about getting his fingers dirty. After all, there were cheap slaves for almost everything. And for the trickier matters, there were expensive but highly effective specialists. Money was the least of his worries. The Svalbard operation would cost him a lot—that much was already clear. But the reward would certainly be hard to express in numbers. A grim smile crept onto his face. It was his turn and they would regret having betrayed him. He would make sure of it.

He looked again at the petite Asian woman who was massaging his left hand and grew increasingly aroused. With his free hand, he waved his bodyguard over who had been silently standing behind him in a corner of the treatment room. He came closer and Viktor whispered something in his ear. Then, the brawny man disappeared and quietly closed the door on his way out.

He raised his left hand and stroked the woman's cheek who was sitting in front of him. Very kindly, he would now ask her to expand her range of services.

7

The central engineering control room was gradually filling up. It was shortly after 9:00 a.m. and at that time, according to the shift schedule, work began. Harry stepped through the door with Mi and nodded to Sigurdson, who had taken a seat in front of one of the computers. Mi sat down in the second row at her usual place and immediately typed away on the keyboard.

"Is Hauge not there yet?" asked Stadler, addressing Sigurdson. "Are there still problems with the robot? He completely disassembled it yesterday, didn't he?"

"No, the Explorer is being brought back to the scene right now," Sigurdson explained, switching the view of the monitors. Images from two surveillance cameras appeared. They showed a section of the corridor and the entrance to the ice cave with the winches installed. "In a moment, the robot should come into view," Sigurdson declared, pointing to the left half of the monitor.

Elvar Hauge came through the door, nodded to everyone, and sat down next to Sigurdson. He started the controls, then turned to Harry. "We double-checked every system yesterday. There's nothing wrong with the robot. We can send it back in and take new measurements."

"So, there was no interference?" Stadler probed.

"At least none that could be tracked. The robot was already working fine again when we brought it up."

"But down there it was malfunctioning."

"There's no question about that."

"So, I think it would be good to find out why."

"Well, it could be the signal," Mi interjected.

"So, it really did come out of the ship?" huffed Stadler.

"I'm 100% sure of that. We lowered separate antennas while the robot was inspecting. The measurements show that the signal was still there. I just checked again. Now it's gotten weaker and has almost disappeared."

Sigurdson turned and looked directly at Mi. "You still haven't answered one thing for me. Is it dangerous?"

She shrugged her shoulders. "It's definitely unusual. I ran various analyses overnight. I haven't been able to determine anything. I haven't even been able to find a pattern in the way the signal was behaving."

"This is unacceptable," growled Sigurdson. "What do you mean you haven't figured anything out yet?"

"Hey, we've only just started. You can't expect us to uncover all the secrets in one night," Mi shot back.

"I don't think he meant it that way," Stadler defended, raising his hands placatingly. "We'd all like to know what's in the ship, right?" He paused. "And we all want to find out if it's dangerous. Arguing about it isn't going to get us anywhere."

Elvar Hauge turned back to his controls. "The Explorer is in position. Shall I lower it?"

"Yes, please begin. And from now on, all telemetry will be recorded without gaps," Sigurdson ordered.

"Already made arrangements for that," Hauge confirmed, watching as the robot was lowered on the winch.

The camera image showed that the heaters had already thawed the ice in the cave.

"Explorer is being decoupled," Hauge reported.

"Good, maybe now we'll get a clearer picture of what's

going on. Move in a little closer, but not as close as yesterday. Then, start the measurements." Then, Stadler stood and walked toward the door. "I'm going over to the lab and asking for the results of the sample analysis from yesterday again. Juan should be finished by now."

"We're holding the fort, chief," Mi Chen said, sinking back into her screen.

"Okay, move forward a little bit, but gently," Sigurdson repeated.

Stadler took his jacket off the hook and disappeared out the door.

As Anika walked through the mine tunnels at 9:00 a.m., Elvar Hauge, a technical specialist, met her halfway. She remembered the first evening at the station, when the formerly reserved Norwegian had started reciting poems after dinner. They sounded like ancient Norwegian works, at least to half of those present who understood anything at all. As a Swede, Anika understood Norwegian with relative ease, but to Americans like Matthew or the German Björn Lange, it probably only sounded like gibberish. She wasn't a big fan of poetry herself but had to admit that Hauge had made an effort to select powerful works that expressed images of impetuous nature and overpowering feelings. She had not been able to attribute any of the poems to a known poet and was surprised when Hauge explained that he had written them himself. She would not have expected such a strong lyrical streak from a robotics expert. She greeted him and continued toward the cave. Hauge nodded briefly and scurried past. He was obviously in a hurry.

When Anika came to the large cave with the petroglyphs, she found it abandoned. She was all alone with the millennia-old evidence of a journey whose purpose was still unknown. With one finger, she stroked through the depressions and walked along the wall toward the burial chamber, her fingers brushing lightly against the walls as she moved forward. So far, she had kept her curiosity in check and had not even risked a glance inside. But today, she felt an urge to look more comprehensively. And so, Anika pulled a pair of latex gloves out of her bag, slipped them on, and wore her goggles. Ancient tombs were unpredictable, and personal protective equipment of any sort couldn't hurt.

Everything had been left as they had found it. So, she remembered Harry's words on her first visit in the cave. Who had discovered the chamber? She still didn't know. Surprisingly, Oddevold's records didn't contain anything about it. Perhaps he wasn't able to get around to it before he... She paused and thought about what might have happened. She made a mental note to ask Harry about that, too.

Anika stepped through the opening into the chamber. Immediately, she felt something was strange but couldn't quite put her finger on it. She turned her gaze toward the corpses, noting how well-preserved they were, likely with permafrost, thus giving them a mummy-like appearance. Otherwise, only skeletons would have been left behind.

She counted the bodies lying in recesses directly in the walls—six to the left and six to the right, each in two rows above the other. Altogether there were twelve, as the picture behind her represented. She concluded that these must be the people who, according to the drawing, had come to the island.

Anika went a little further into the narrow room, in

which there was hardly any room for more than three adults to stand in a row. Further back, in smaller niches in the rock, some art and everyday objects made of metal, stone, and wood were placed: a statue, a bulbous vase, an amulet, and a knife.

"How did you even get here?" she murmured into the dead silence. She shook her head.

Once again, she looked around thoroughly, noticing something wrong with the niches in the rock. Anika bent down and brushed her fingers over the stone. The edges were smooth, and the openings were cut to fit the bodies exactly. There was no way these niches could be of natural origin. Someone had created them. But who? And how? Who had buried these people? All twelve were dead. Had the last one put himself in his niche after burying the others? Had they all laid down here together to die? Had it been some kind of ritual suicide in honor of the ominous deity hovering over the twelve people draw on the stone image outside? It was all plausible, but practically impossible to prove. And even if it were, it didn't explain why there were no tool marks of any kind on the niches. Another mystery.

Anika suddenly remembered Harry's words. She remembered how he had raved during the first video conference that this was the discovery of his life and that it would be the discovery of her life as well. She had seen unbridled passion in his eyes and heard the enthusiasm in his voice.

The professor seemed so familiar to her, even though they hadn't known each other very long. Anika thought of Harry like the grandfather she never had. She often imagined him reading her stories about foreign people and faraway lands back when she was a child. Her own paternal grandfather died early of cirrhosis of the liver. Her father explained to her that the old fool had not been able to keep off the booze. And her maternal grandfather was a grouchy old grump who raised reindeer far up north in Sweden and whom they had virtually never visited.

She shook off the memories and thought about her task again. The grave raised enough questions for her to investigate. She wondered if her predecessor, Oddevold, had also asked himself the same things. Did he even get a chance to look at the tomb? Or—and this thought worried her a bit—had finding the burial chamber led to his collapse in the first place? In any case, he hadn't made any notes about the tomb.

Anika went back out into the big cave with the drawings. She urgently needed more information—more pieces for her puzzle. The overall picture was fragmented; it was just a big, confusing pile of parts that, on their own, were not very meaningful. But she felt that something significant would emerge should they all be combined into something bigger.

She turned around again and searched the drawings. Her gaze lingered on the larger tunnel opening with the airlock she had come through half an hour ago. Harry mentioned that parts of the drawings were damaged in the blast. And indeed, smaller parts of an effigy were still all around. But there were more than a few artifacts and hard-to-read lines that were invisible. No one would be able to deduce the actual content of the picture.

Anika moved closer and inspected the artifacts at the edge of the drawing. Two looked familiar. She thought she had just seen them in the smaller niches of the burial chamber. Apparently, the blast destroyed the very image that depicted the creation of the burial chamber, which was a major setback. But perhaps she could learn enough anyway. In any case, she would talk to Harry about the discovery of the burial chamber and probe for any information he might have.

Anika looked over to the smaller lock that led into the cordoned-off area. She thought of Elvar Hauge, who had come toward her earlier. What had he been doing in here? As a robotics specialist, he would hardly be interested in cave drawings or mummified corpses. He must have come from the forbidden passage back there, which Harry claimed was in danger of collapsing. That had clearly been a lie—perhaps to distract her. But it fed her suspicion that something was still being kept from her.

Maybe Hauge placed a robot to descend into the cave where the poor miner had gone mad.

Anika felt a slight resentment rising inside her. The longer she was here, the more questions piled up. She was fed up and wanted nothing but answers. She would confront Harry and insist on knowing all the details. And today, she wouldn't be brushed off like she was yesterday when he didn't have time to talk about sampling. She would ensure that he'd give her his full attention, no matter what it took.

The north wind drove hard, grainy snow through the settlement. Anika pulled the thick hood of her parka over her head to keep the grains from trickling down her neck. This was the nastiest kind of weather—half sleet, half snow, plus a wind that felt like it was pushing the temperature to minus ten degrees. It was a foretaste of the brutal Arctic winter. And Svea was still in a relatively sheltered part of the island.

She had left the mine entrance behind and was walking down the main street toward the cafeteria building. Halfway there, she saw Harry Stadler disappear into the medical complex where she had visited Matthew Grant earlier.

She followed him, shook off the snow, and stepped into the building. She heard Harry's voice from further back in one of the labs and listened attentively. She couldn't make out much through the door, which was only open a crack. She only picked up scraps like "sample" and "further analysis." Then, someone shut the door from inside.

Anika thought for a moment. Should she just go in? What was the name of the scientist who worked there? Anika only remembered that he was Spanish. Was it Ramón? Anyway, the guy was way too tanned to be working in the Arctic. Anika decided to wait and meet Harry on his way out. She went to Matthew's office across from the lab and knocked.

"Come in, whoever you are," she heard Matthew's friendly voice echo from inside.

She opened the door and leaned casually against the doorframe. "Morning, Matthew," she greeted. Then, she nodded toward the hallway and asked, "Are they analyzing samples over there yet?"

"I honestly don't know what Juan is working on, but he was here forever yesterday. And again this morning, even before I came. Apparently, they were doing a reconnaissance of the cave. From what I've heard, there must have been some kind of glitch. That's why Harry was so grumpy." He stood and came over to her. "But we can check back in a bit to see what's up with your samples. I'm sure he can't say no to that adorable smile of yours."

"Well, it didn't help yesterday."

"No, no, I'm quite sure," Juan said, folding his arms in front of his chest. "You had me flown in from Spain because I'm the best in the field of material analysis, right?"

Harry tilted his head and sighed. "Of course, I didn't mean it that way. I just can't understand how such results come about."

"I can tell you. The results are based on flawless, scientific testing methods. I've performed all tests twice with different subsets of the sample. There is no reason whatsoever to doubt the results. The material is a very special composite. On the outside, it looks like wood—you're right. In fact, it also has a kind of organic surface, only with a quite unusual nanostructure. Inside, however, you'll find a mixture of polymer and metals. It's an alloy that I've only been able to partially break down into its components."

Harry nodded slowly and thoughtfully. "Good work, Juan. I really didn't mean to offend you. I appreciate your expertise. Please try to find out some more about the basic substances. And please don't talk to anyone about it for now. I'll discuss the situation with Sigurdson, then we'll have a conference with everyone."

"Of course, I'll keep the results confidential."

"Thank you. Keep me posted if there are any new findings."

Outside Juan's lab, Anika and Matthew were already waiting for Harry. He stopped. "Is this a robbery?"

Anika put on her most charming smile. "Morning, Harry. I wanted to tell you about my theory. Maybe you have some time today?"

"I knew you were persistent. Alright, I've got five minutes," Harry said.

"Okay, I'll be brief. I believe that this tragic incident with the miners was the result of a psychotic episode and that there are psychoactive substances in the cave that triggered it. It could perhaps be some kind of fungus. That's why I want to have samples taken from the walls and floor as soon as possible."

"A psychotic episode? I didn't know you knew anything about psychiatry."

"Not really. And certainly not in detail. But I have studied the berserk myth. And when I saw the video...well."

Harry nodded. "Agreed, I'll have samples taken and then we'll talk more. But now is not a good time. I have to get back over to the control room."

Anika and Matthew looked at him questioningly.

"I know you want to know more, but I don't have time now. There will be a meeting with everyone later. But before that, I need to clarify a few things. Alright?"

"Yes, of course. There's no rush. We can work on other things," Matthew explained, looking at Anika.

"We can. Only it might be more effective if we had all the information," Anika said with a hint of sarcasm.

"I know," Harry replied apologetically. "Just a little patience. I'll let you know tonight at the latest." Then, he walked past the two and left the medical department.

Anika looked after him. "I wonder what they were talking about in there."

"Let it go. We'll just get on with our work."

"Speaking of work," Anika said to Matthew. "Do you feel like dissecting some mummies? Maybe we can find out what the people in the burial chamber died of."

"Do you really think there are that many possibilities? My guess is that they simply starved to death. Nothing grows here, after all. And I wonder if we'll find out much with the condition they're in. But as far as I'm concerned, I'd be happy to open one of them up and do some research."

"Wonderful. Let me go over to the burial chamber and document everything with photos, then we can transport one of the bodies here."

"Alright, let's do it that way. I'll request the help of two technicians," Matthew decided and went back to his office.

8

Harry knew what was about to come. As soon as he had told Sigurdson about the results Juan had unearthed, he would question everything: the scientific direction, the mission objectives, and the schedule. The problem was, Harry couldn't even blame him. They hadn't found what they expected to. But he couldn't possibly keep it from Sigurdson. After all, they were both equal in mission leadership.

Harry walked through the canteen building to the very back, where the passage to the control room was. He opened the door with his access card and stuck his head inside. "Is everything going according to plan so far?" he inquired.

Sigurdson and Hauge looked over at him. "Measurements are running now. So far, everything is within limits," Hauge reported.

"Very good. Can you take samples of the walls and floor later? We want them for biological analysis. Anika Wahlgren has a theory worth checking out." Harry looked directly at Sigurdson. "Can we talk privately over there?"

Sigurdson nodded, stood, and followed Harry two rooms down into the security center.

"What's up?" asked Sigurdson, taking a seat in one of the chairs.

Restlessly, Harry paced up and down the small room. "Findings. New, confusing realizations. And we need to talk about how to deal with them."

"Well, let's do that."

"You and I both know that we have to make major decisions together," Harry began. "This is officially a purely civilian and international research expedition. I'm not naive, though. I realize that secretly, the Norwegian government has some say, as does the military. You are the liaison, although you belong to a private company. And I know you aren't just here to protect us from polar bears."

Sigurdson listened to everything silently, then cleared his throat. "What are you getting at?"

"I think the focus has to change. This is no longer a purely archaeological mission."

"In what way?"

"There are probably no gold coins or scrolls in that ship. There's technology in it. But it's not just this signal that we picked up, which is obviously not from a malfunction. There's more. Juan analyzed the material of the hull. It's a man-made product. He says it's a highly complex alloy with an organic coating. And now I'm wondering how dangerous these things might be."

"So, it's a military case now?"

"No, we're nowhere near that," Harry responded. "We just need to be careful. We need more time to do our work. It's not like we have any pressure. If we don't get anywhere, we can always call in the army, though I don't know how that would work. You know as well as I do that the archipelago is demilitarized territory."

"Well, good, since we're talking so openly and honestly right now, then I think it's important to mention that I already know there is technology down there."

Harry looked at him in wonder.

"We found Gulbrandsen. Quite a while ago, actually."

Harry's mouth opened, but he didn't make a sound.

Sigurdson continued. "He had splinters of the material under his fingernails. The analysts say it's a technically complex product. That's why the huge budget for this mission was approved in the first place. You don't think we're going to put on this circus here for some cave drawings and an artifact of some sort in an ice cave?"

"Well..." Harry swallowed. "I had assumed that..." his voice trailed off.

"That's beside the point, though. We still have the same goal. We want to know what's down there. And we want to know what it does to people."

Slowly, Harry nodded. "Where is Gulbrandsen's body? Can we get it here? Maybe Matthew can do an autopsy to find out more."

Sigurdson swayed his head back and forth, thinking. "If it serves the cause, then I'll arrange it."

"So, are we going to keep doing what we're doing?" asked Harry.

"I don't see what's wrong with that. But you must realize that I have the last word. You don't have to like it, but I'm sure you'll see that it's better that way in the interest of safety."

"Maybe you're right." Harry paused and sighed. "I want us to fully brief Anika Wahlgren. I think she can make a crucial contribution. She's not a technical idiot like Oddevold; she thinks in interdisciplinary terms. And that is exactly what we need. I would like to have her at the meeting tonight."

Sigurdson frowned. "I'll think about it," he said, standing. "Now let's get back to the control center, or there'll just be unnecessary talk."

While Matthew prepared for the autopsy he was going to perform on one of the bodies from the burial chamber, Anika browsed through relevant literature on the early Nordic Bronze Age and the handling of mummies. She was pleased with the direct satellite connection that gave her unhindered access to all relevant research databases and libraries via a VPN internet tunnel. It was as she had suspected. A tomb like that hadn't been discovered before and she couldn't find any evidence of a settlement in Svalbard that existed more than a thousand years ago.

Over the past hour, she had read a lot about the discovery of the famous glacier mummy, Ötzi, which was found in 1991 at an altitude of over 3,200 meters in the Ötztal Alps. At around 5,300 years old, it was considered both the oldest and the best-researched mummy in the world. At some point, even the stomach contents of the Stone Age man had been analyzed and it was possible to find out what he had last eaten.

Anika counted on the fact that she and Matthew could also perform such analyses on the corpse from the burial chamber. First and foremost, she was interested in the cause of death and the actual age of the body. She didn't know how well-equipped the infirmary's lab and material analysis were, but Anika thought Juan might even be able to determine the age using the radiocarbon method.

She snapped her laptop shut, took it out of the docking station, and headed back to Matthew. The clock read 1:30 pm. There was still enough time to gain some insights before the scheduled meeting with all the senior scientists at 5:00 p.m.

When Anika returned to the infirmary, the sight before her way quite bizarre. On the steel autopsy table, the cave mummy lay in the harsh light of two LED spotlights. It looked out of place—like a foreign body in the sterile environment of the medical department. Unlike in the comparatively dim cave, every detail of the corpse was recognizable. Its leathery, gray-brown skin stretched over bone and internal organ remains. The eyes were non-existent. A few teeth protruded crookedly from the dried lips. The body appeared completely emaciated but was still recognizable as human.

Anika walked around the body and looked at it from all sides. From what she could see, it was a man. What secrets lay hidden in these mortal remains? Had it been right to take him out of the burial chamber? Was it right to cut him open? Anika knew these were moral and overly sentimental questions. It was impossible to determine any semblance of right or wrong in this context. She only knew that it was necessary.

Matthew walked out of the lab in the next room and greeted her warmly. "Hey, good of you to come. Everything's already set up. I just finished taking some X-rays. They should be ready in a minute. It's best if we look at them first before we take samples," he suggested.

"Sure, whatever you think is right. It's my first autopsy, you know."

"I don't do it all the time either," he added. "I prefer live patients. Although the dead ones don't complain about injections."

"I don't like injections either," Anika said with a smile.

"Good to know. Come on over. There's a big monitor where we can watch the footage."

"No light desk or anything?"

He shook his head and led her into the lab area. "No, those things have long since been phased out. X-rays are digitally scanned these days. So, you can zoom in and magnify details. I hated poring over some blue-black film with a magnifying glass. Digitalization has made diagnostics much easier, after all."

They sat down in front of a large screen and Matthew pulled up the images of the mummy. "I've taken pictures of all the major areas: head, chest, abdomen, one arm, and one leg. If you want anything else specific, we can add more pictures."

Anika shook her head and silently studied the photographs. The bones looked well preserved. The skull looked intact, so obviously the man had not been bludgeoned or otherwise violently killed. Everything was in place, just as one would expect.

Matthew pointed to the arm. "Here, look. It seems like the bone was broken once and healed crookedly."

Anika moved a little closer and squinted her eyes.

"I can magnify it, as I said," Matthew explained with amusement.

"Yes, please. There's this little light spot down by the wrist. It looks like a thick grain of rice or something."

Matthew zoomed in. "Hmm..." he grumbled. "Looks like a glitch. Or..."

"What?"

"It can't be."

"What can't be?"

"Bright areas like this are usually caused by metal. Implants, screws, things like that."

"That would be really strange."

"Yes, probably a defect in the X-ray film or the scanner. I'll check the exposure."

Matthew stood and took an X-ray film out of the scanner. He turned on the room light and held up the film.

"Back to the roots after all," Anika joked.

"Yes. Looks like it."

"So?"

"It's also on the film. And it looks like there are very fine structures in the object. It looks too artificial to be a mistake. Let me scan the film again at the highest resolution and maximum dynamic range." Matthew put the X-ray back into the digitizer and made some inputs on the PC next to it. Two minutes later, the image appeared on the large screen. Now, the object was even easier to see. Matthew placed a digital scale next to it and took a measurement. "It must be about four millimeters long and just under two millimeters wide." He zoomed in. Structures resembling a ransacked box full of building blocks became visible inside the object. "What the heck is that?" muttered Matthew. He stood and walked out into the main room of the infirmary. Anika followed him curiously. From a box, Matthew pulled out two pairs of latex gloves and handed one to Anika. Then, he approached the body, pulled the gloves on, and palpated the right arm at wrist level. "There's actually something there, just under the skin in the tissue. Feels hard."

Anika approached the table and ran a finger over the spot to examine it. "What could it be?"

"Let's take a look," Matthew said, pulling a small mobile table with medical tools toward him. He took a scalpel from the tray and placed it against the forearm. Very slowly, he cut into the tough skin with the knife. "Nurse, pass me the forceps, please," he said, extending his hand toward the tray.

Silently, Anika handed him a small pair of stainless-steel pliers with flattened ends and watched anxiously to see what he would pull out of the arm.

Matthew pushed the tip of the pliers under the skin and felt around a bit before grabbing it and gently pulling out the object. It shone strangely silver in the spotlight. Matthew held it up and looked at it from all sides. "Looks like a precious metal—platinum or palladium maybe."

Anika frowned. "That's completely impossible. We're talking about the Bronze Age!"

"Bronze it definitely isn't," Matthew said succinctly, placing the object in a small metal bowl on the small table.

"I can see that, too, you expert! I just don't get how that got in there."

"It's good that we can already rule out bronze. We'll get it checked out later, okay? Should we take more tissue samples right now, now that we've already started cutting it open?"

Anika finally turned away from the bright silver implant. "Yes, please. I need bone material for age determination. Do you know if Juan can do radiocarbon testing?"

"Phew, I'm not sure. That's quite an elaborate process. But from what I can tell, he loves a challenge. If necessary, we'll have to send the samples to Oslo. In three days, we'd have results."

"Okay. I'd like tissue samples, too, and if we can, let's examine the stomach and find out what he last ate"

"Alright. You'll have to help out though. I actually don't have a nurse here."

"That's what I'm here for. I want to be there anyway. You know I'm unspeakably curious."

Matthew laughed. Then, he reached into the lower compartment of the tool table and pulled out goggles and face masks. "Better put these on. It might get a little dusty when we get the bone saw going."

"Alright, doctor. Nurse Anika can hardly wait."

Henrik Oddevold gazed rigidly upward. He was literally glued to the white structural panels of the hospital room ceiling. Whether he was aware of them—whether he was aware of anything at all—the doctors couldn't say with certainty. Their patient had been in a kind of waking coma for over a week. His vital signs were completely within range. It was almost as if he was asleep. But his brain activity was at an unusually high level. This still puzzled doctors at Oslo's Ullevål University Hospital. A medical explanation for his condition could not yet be determined. What was even more perplexing was that the man even seemed extremely fit and healthy for 65. They had previously searched for some sort of infection or injury, but even that was in vain. It was as if his body and mind had been decoupled in some unknown way.

One morning, his eyes twitched wildly back and forth, indicating hope for improvement, but it was premature. Soon, he was staring motionless at the ceiling again, no longer reacting to any external stimuli—not to pain or temperature changes. Even his pupils showed no significant reaction to light. The patient's puzzling case was certainly an ideal subject for a doctoral thesis, but it wouldn't heal him. There was simply no knowing what to do with him other than wait for his condition to change on its own. He was physically stable so far and could be fed by a stomach tube, but the doctors weren't satisfied. Especially since no one told them how their patient had become unconscious in the first place. They had no idea if he had come into contact with an unknown substance or if he had been exposed to any other influences. They didn't even know his name. They only knew that the instructions came from the very top and that they had to keep quiet about the patient and his condition. There would have been nothing to reveal anyway.

So, the days passed during which Oddevold outwardly did nothing but stare at the ceiling, day after day, night after night.

9

At 5:00 p.m. sharp, most of the station crew gathered in the mess hall. Nothing but blackness penetrated through the windows. Outside, night had long since fallen and the thermometer showed temperatures just below double digits. The 20 or so researchers and technicians sat spread out at the tables and waited for Harry Stadler and Øystein Sigurdson to begin the meeting.

Anika and Matthew sat together at a table and had a small, black plastic box in front of them. In it—hidden from prying eyes—lay the silver implant from the mummy. After its surprising beginning, the autopsy had been rather unspectacular. They were now waiting for the samples to be analyzed in the laboratory. They had even gone back into the burial chamber shortly before the meeting and checked the wrists of the other mummies. At least five other corpses had such implants in their arms.

Anika was eager to tell Harry about this discovery, but she knew she shouldn't spring it on him. She would wait and see what he had to say first.

At last, Stadler and Sigurdson stepped through the door and set up next to each other on the long side of the room. There, they could be easily seen from anywhere. "Good evening, everyone. It's nice to have a chance to bring everyone up to speed today. I don't want to keep you from dinner too long either. I know we're having lasagna today and, more importantly, tiramisu," Stadler explained.

Approving murmurs traveled through the room.

"Okay, so why are we here? First, because we're trying to solve a mystery that's thousands of years old. Second, because we want to know what happened here a few weeks ago and if it's dangerous for us, too. And third, we are here because we are explorers, and it is in our nature to pursue the unknown and want to discover new things. And, dear comrades-in-arms, it seems to me that we will be challenged, especially in the last area. You are all experts in your field, but we need to work together. We need to encourage exchanges, even more than we do now, so that we can make progress. At the same time, we have to be very careful." Stadler looked to Sigurdson.

"We, as expedition leaders, agree that security and discretion must be our top priority. And that everything discussed here remains confidential for the time being." He paused and looked at every participant in the group, as if to enter a silent contract with each. "I think we understand each other," he finally concluded.

"Alright, now let's get down to the nitty-gritty," Harry announced. "We've made some findings down in the ice cave that I'd like to inform you about. And just a heads up, I don't think it's what we expected."

Anika fumbled with the plastic box that lay on the table in front of her.

Matthew squinted down and put his hand over it.

"Sorry," she whispered.

Harry continued to speak, unimpressed. "Whatever exactly is down there, it's nothing historical in the strict sense—nothing that fits the time period it's supposed to be from. It's technologically advanced. We've picked up a signal from inside, but we haven't been able to decipher it yet. And we've taken samples of the material. It's made up of a mixture of organic, metallic, and polymeric components."

Chatter echoed through the hall as some shook their heads in disbelief while others started whispering.

Harry raised his hands. "I'm going to ask for a moment of silence, please. I know this sounds unbelievable, but we've tested everything several times. That's why we've been withholding this information. But now there is no doubt at all. We have to all brainstorm how we're going to deal with this situation." He looked again at Sigurdson. "We also agree that we will proceed with the utmost care because these findings don't change the goal of this mission. We are always open to your ideas and comments."

Silence spread through the room after Harry finished.

Then, Anika raised a hand. "Harry, if I could just cut in for a second."

Stadler nodded at her. "Please."

Anika stood. "First of all, I am glad that you are now enlightening us so comprehensively. For me, as a latecomer, it was a bit difficult to see the connections. It's much clearer now. And second, Matthew and I can contribute to this mission directly." She held up the plastic box. "We examined one of the bodies from the burial chamber this afternoon and came across similar inconsistencies."

"In what way?" echoed Harry.

"In this small box is an object that we took from the forearm of a dead man. It is apparently made of metal and has a complicated structure inside. It must contain some kind of technology."

Harry raised his eyebrows in surprise and walked over to her.

Anika took off the lid, revealing the shiny, silver implant. Other researchers also stood and came closer to look at it. "As far as we have been able to verify so far, more of the mummies have this under their skin."

"Fascinating," Harry breathed. "I'd like Mi to take a look at it. If it contains technology, it may be possible to analyze it."

"Sure, she can have it. I would just like to stay updated about any findings related to this," she said.

"Yes, we are all playing with our cards on the table. We've come to the conclusion that the previous incremental secrecy has done more harm than good. We need to share as much information as possible if we are to move forward. Don't we, Sigurdson?"

Sigurdson nodded weakly. "As long as the information doesn't leave this settlement, I can live with that. And remember, we monitor internet traffic." He threatened vaguely.

"Alright, that's it for today. We'll have another meeting in two days to bring everyone up to speed. Let the information sink in first and get back to me if you have something on your mind."

While the others gradually went to the buffet, Harry turned to Anika. "By the way, we've taken samples from the walls and floor as we discussed. They've already been turned in for analysis. We should know by tomorrow if there's anything there. However, after what we've discovered these past few days, I'm doubtful we'll find anything."

Anika nodded. "Yes, it could be a dead end. But then at least we'll know for sure. I also think that the burial chamber may provide more information for us." She paused for a moment. "Perhaps it would be helpful if you could also tell me how it was discovered in the first place."

Harry sighed, "I honestly don't know. Oddevold must have discovered it. He was alone in the cave for hours, studying the drawings. And in the evening, we found him there unconscious. The passage to the burial chamber had suddenly appeared. I have no idea where it came from. Oddevold had an artifact in his hand that must have come from the chamber. He probably wanted to compare it with the drawing, so he took it outside. But we didn't have a chance to ask him. After two days of being unconscious, he finally opened his eyes, but he was out of it. We couldn't do anything for him here and had him flown out. As far as I know, his condition remains the same."

"It must have been some kind of waking coma. I haven't seen anything like it," Matthew explained. "I did a neurological exam on him with McFarland. The EEG showed that there were sparks of activity in his brain, but outwardly, he seemed as rigid and mute as a block of ice."

"That explains why I didn't find anything about the burial chamber in the records," Anika said. "He never got around to writing anything down."

"Yes, that's correct. We inspected the burial chamber and couldn't find any source of danger. We put the artifact back in the empty recess."

"After everything we've learned since then, it would probably be appropriate to examine these pieces more closely, as well," Anika said. "It's possible they also contain some technology that could be responsible for Oddevold's condition."

"That's an excellent idea. Coordinate with Mi and report back to me as soon as there is any news." Harry looked toward the kitchen area with the food counter. "Excuse me, I need to get some lasagna before it's all gone. I have the hideous tofu burger from yesterday to make up for."

Boris Karlov sat in a rented luxury loft on the top floor of a building in downtown Tromsø that offered a fabulous view of the hills, which were gradually becoming silhouettes in the burgundy twilight. Below, the lights of the city were sprawled out like a glittering carpet. Karlov had little appreciation for the beauty of it all, though. He rummaged through the files searching for posters of his troops one last time to memorize all the new faces and names. Karlov was pleased with his team members. It was always impressive what an amazingly wide selection of mercenaries they had. Both in his home country of Chechnya and in other parts of the former Soviet Union, there were plenty of well-trained and battle-hardened men. He was free to put together the team of his choice and, as usual, had largely trusted his gut feeling. Karlov mainly chose men with whom he had already successfully completed a mission with once. Reliability and efficiency were extremely important in his business—as was discretion. He hadn't had to compromise on the core team in any way. The budget Nikolaev gave him would not only comfortably cover everyone's pay—and lavishly do so, for that matter—but it would also allow him to pay himself a nice bonus. After all, he had gotten his hands dirty in Tromsø. During that situation, it occurred to him once more that his boss, Viktor Nikolayev, probably had one or two screws loose. There were much simpler and yet effective methods to get rid of someone. The fact that he had insisted on the nerve agent, Novichok—stuff of the devil—was insane. But it wasn't his place to question the one who was throwing around bundles of money. And if he thought about it, it might have been a clever move after all, because all the evidence would point suspicion at the Russian secret service. And the investigators would be at a loss as to how a Norwegian drilling technician could be linked to the FSB. Besides, Karlov knew that he still owed Nikolaev. After all, he had supplied weapons to Chechnya, which ultimately saved him from a lot of trouble he would have otherwise faced.

Karlov pushed aside thoughts of the dead Torger Hansen. The guy was no longer important. He had obtained all his information, deciphered it, and even found it highly useful. Now he knew how they had to proceed to make the mission a success.

He pulled out a bag of dried bison meat for a snack. It was an old habit from his army days. God knows he could afford to be more culinarily fancy, but he had become so accustomed to the taste that he couldn't help himself. He ate the jerky like other people ate potato chips. He knew he had traded in his camouflage clothing for an expensive suit, but that didn't make life any less risky—certainly not when working for Nikolaev.

Karlov still had three files on the table in front of him. They were the tricky candidates—the ones he didn't know personally, but who were indispensable to the mission. These three were part of the submarine's planned crew—another of Nikolaev's insane ideas. There were relatively few suitable candidates who had submarine experience. Karlov was not entirely happy with any of them, but he knew that he had enough other loyal men on the team.

Karlov looked at the clock that read 6:52. At 7:00 p.m. sharp, it would be time to inform all team members of the task and assign them their respective duties. He flipped open his laptop and pulled up a window for an encrypted video conference to take place. Another window displayed the contents of a folder. In it, he had packed all relevant data from Torger Hansen's encrypted archive, as well as his own findings. He wanted his crew to be prepared. They needed to know the facility like their own living room and needed to have an overview of all security systems. For the latter, Karlov had already tracked down hacks and vulnerabilities on the Darknet and even had hackers develop custom attack methods. None of the systems installed would pose an insurmountable obstacle for him and his men. Karlov had also placed this data in the briefing folder so Yuri Chenkov could familiarize himself with it; he was the squad's technical expert and would surely prove valuable this time, as well.

He started the video conference and ensured that all twelve selected team members were already waiting for him to begin. As ordered, they were all connected via encrypted streams. "Good evening, men!" roared Karlov, looking grimly into the web cam. "It's that time again. We're going on a mission. And the mission we have ahead of us is a tough one—I can tell you that. But the rewards will be all the more bountiful. Everyone who works for us can count on the usual bonus for successful completion. I know you don't really need this incentive, but this time, we are going to Svalbard, and it may be rough up there. In a moment, I will send you all the briefing material in a coded archive. Keep it confidential. We'll go through everything together. And remember, we leave Severomorsk in 36 hours. Be there on time. If not, the boat will leave without you, and you can forget about your payment. I hope we have an understanding."

Karlov heard a twelvefold "Yessir!" echo from the loudspeaker. He loved the sound of obedience. "Alright, let's get going!"

10

It was a quiet day at the research station. Anika had slept like a rock and woken up much too late. Now, she sat in the deserted canteen and planned for the day. She was going to start by catching up on all the results. She had a lot to work through and would certainly be out for half the day exchanging ideas with her colleagues. There were all kinds of analyses to discuss about the cultures created from the ice cave, the samples from the tissue, and the contents of the mummy's stomach. Additionally, she needed to analyze the bones to determine the age and figure out more information about the implant they had found.

The age determination results weren't expected before late afternoon. Juan had been abundantly coy about tackling them at all. He explained in a theatrical tone that he would have to improvise and that this was not really his thing. But Anika made it clear that she didn't want to wait three or four days until they could do an analysis in the lab in Oslo. If Juan was only half as good as he claimed, he would certainly be able to do it.

However, it was hard to predict how long it would take Mi Chen to find out something solid about the implant. She only hoped that the measurement technology would soon reveal more about the mysterious object.

Anika stepped to the window of the canteen and looked outside. Today, the weather seemed unusually mild. It was still, almost windless, and not a cloud covered the sky. The thermometer read around zero degrees. After the sometimes-lush snowfalls of the last two days, Anika felt it was a welcome respite. But if she had correctly interpreted the forecast on the notice board in the hallway, it was only the proverbial calm before the storm. The weather report predicted an extended period of bad weather. "Potential storm warning" was written under the report. That was presumably why another supply flight was announced for today. Anika looked over at the emptied buffet. She was hoping for fruits and vegetables more than anything else. The menu could definitely use more freshness. She finished the last sip of coffee, put the cup on a mobile cart with dirty dishes, and left the cafeteria.

Mi made a disgruntled face. Without taking her eyes off the monitor, she reached into a bag of gummy bears lying on the table next to her. Unhappily, she realized that it was already empty. She groaned and reached into a drawer to pull out a candy bar. She had already been sitting in her lab since 6:30 a.m., poring over the data from yesterday's cave exploration. Now, two and a half hours later, she was still trying to piece together the measurement results. If she didn't have candy to get her through it, she would have thrown in the towel long ago. The data stubbornly refused to reveal its secrets. Mi got in the habit of looking for patterns and tracing an internal logic. She knew from experience that there was actually almost always something like that in the data and she had a knack for uncovering such things and making connections where other people only saw noise. But this time, all she saw was noise, too. Mi detected no pattern in the signal emitted by the object in the cave. Of course, that could be because the data was faulty or incomplete. It could also be that she was still looking at it from the wrong angle. Or it could be because this signal was completely random and coincidental. The third option was still extremely unlikely for her, because what would be the point of generating and emitting such a signal in the first place? Everything pointed to the fact that an intelligence was behind it—an intelligence that didn't fit into the historical epoch from which the cave drawings and the artifacts seemed to originate.

Was this really more appearance than reality?

She found it particularly sobering that she could not take a look behind the facade. And she meant this in the literal sense. The heat radiators had exposed a much larger area of the ship's surface. Mi guessed it probably wouldn't be long before she could get a comprehensive view of the vehicle that lay buried there in the ice. But it was still just the view from the outside. All the technical measures they had taken to get a look inside had failed. Infrared scanning and analysis of all wavelengths of visible light, even into the ultraviolet range had failed. Radar, terahertz waves, EM measurements, and detection of radioactivity had also failed. Everything only resulted in unbearable noise. It was as if the object was shielded by an invisible cloak of lead, concrete, and steel that swallowed everything they threw at it. But it wasn't like that. It didn't swallow everything. The object even gave off something after coming into contact with the robot. Now, the mysterious signal, which randomly changed wavelengths and amplitudes, had all but disappeared. It had reacted to the robot's touch the way it had reacted to contact with the miner back then—and with the fatal consequences documented on video.

Mi knew whatever was down there was not a dead object. It was aware of its environment. It was interacting.

And she would love to find out how. And what or who it was doing it for.

Mi's gaze slid over to the silver implant that Anika had given her last night. It could be the key. The shiny object lay under the microscope. She had only been able to take a brief and not very detailed look at it so far and would have much preferred a scan with the so-called compact CT device. But the power supply of the device, which in reality was not quite so compact, had burned out, and the replacement part was days overdue. Supplies in the far north were nowhere near as extensive as in the research strongholds where Mi previously worked. Still, she hoped that the spare part would finally arrive with the next delivery so that she could look inside the mysterious part.

At 9:15 p.m., Harry interrupted her musings with a visit to the lab. Mi immediately recognized that he had resumed his old persona: friendly but demanding. She knew ambition lurked behind the jovial English façade. Harry had high expectations of his employees, and Mi didn't want to disappoint him under any circumstances. But that was easier said than done.

"Good morning, Mi. How is it looking?" asked Harry, sounding as casual as if he were inquiring about the weather.

Mi didn't know how to respond. It looked messy; she couldn't present him with what she had set out to do—what he expected her to do. "Good and bad," she answered. "Good is that we were able to collect a lot of data. Bad is that it doesn't make sense."

Harry sighed and sat down next to Mi at the computer. "Let me see!"

Mi opened some windows with the measurement

results in parallel. "I've tried just about every trick I could think of. I can't get a clear picture of the inside. It's almost like walking through dense fog without glasses. Everything is gray on gray."

"I was afraid of this, to be honest. The first measurements were already useless. My hope was that you might be able to find something. Is the signal still there?"

"One moment it's there, the next it's as if it's been erased. As if it were shifting in phase and erasing itself with interference at irregular intervals. But, if it were interference, there would have to be a pattern in which this phenomenon appears. I haven't quite figured out how this signal is constructed. Also, it's almost gone now."

"Hauge swears that his robot and measuring devices are working properly," Harry offered. "Is there any reason to doubt that?"

"No, I believe him. I checked some of the instruments myself. And my antennas up here picked up the same thing when the signal was that strong for a short time."

"Seems to me we're not supposed to know what's behind this strangely textured ship's wall any more than we're supposed to know what this signal means," Harry concluded.

"It almost seems that way. Then again, why would it send out a signal? It seems like it's trying to attempt communication."

"You are absolutely right. But the frustrating thing is we don't understand it. Or we're misinterpreting everything. What if this signal is a warning?"

"Interesting thought," Mi agreed.

"Well, as interesting as it might be, we can't prove or disprove it."

"So, if that really is a ship down there, how could it have gotten into the ice here?"

Harry twitched one corner of his mouth, making a smacking sound. "I've asked myself that same question. It's a mystery how this ship could have even been transported so far inland."

"Maybe the waves brought it over?

"Not likely."

Mi leaned back in her chair and looked at the ceiling. "What are we going to do now? We've exhausted all methods."

"Thoralf suggested drilling into the hull," Harry said. "But I don't think that's a good idea. Remember what happened the last time we just briefly touched it?"

"The robot stopped responding," Mi answered. "Whatever is in there could cripple our technology."

"That's a huge risk and danger," Harry said. "Sigurdson isn't thrilled about it either." Then he nodded toward the microscope. "What about the implant?"

Mi shook her head. "I haven't had a chance to examine it more closely. The CT is still broken."

"This afternoon or tomorrow morning at the latest, the new PSU will arrive with the supply flight."

"That's good. I had Matthew give me the X-ray data and I can at least confirm that there's some kind of technology in there, but I'd need a much better resolution to say more about it."

"Very good. Connect with Anika for a moment. I have a feeling she can help us solve this puzzle. Maybe she has a perspective that can complement yours."

Mi nodded. "Sure. I'm always open to cooperation."

"Great!" Harry patted the table with his hand and

pushed himself up out of the chair. "That's the way I like it. Always think interdisciplinary." He disappeared from the lab, satisfied.

Matthew Grant retrieved the cultured samples from the lab's incubator and spread them out on the table in front of him. Even at first glance, he saw that none of the six dishes showed a true match. There were minimal traces of growth in two of the dishes, but these were almost certainly due to contamination. Either they had occurred before the sample was taken or they resulted from carelessness during processing. Grant had seen this kind of thing hundreds of times; he knew what typical germs and fungi were floating around in the normal ambient air. And he knew they could easily settle on sample dishes and swabs. Everything seemed normal. He also wasn't particularly surprised that there were no special microbes in the ice cave. In fact, that would have been quite unusual.

Still, it was too early for disappointment; the day was young and there were more promising analyses to come. He put the samples back in the cabinet and went over to his work area with the analysis equipment. His options on the station were limited—he was aware of that. But he wanted to do his best to evaluate the tissue samples.

There was a knock at the door and Anika stuck her head in. "Hey, any progress yet? Do you want me to help you out again?"

"Sure, come on in. So far, we don't have anything exciting. The samples from the cave are all negative. No exotic fungi or bacteria. Nothing that isn't floating around the canteen."

"I see. And the tissue?"

"I'm in the process of doing that right now. But I have to say that we have to limit ourselves here to microscope analysis and a determination of basic building blocks such as proteins, fats, and the like. We don't have the equipment here to do DNA testing. In Oslo, they could do detailed molecular biology tests, including electrophoresis or PCR tests. The lab there could do a comparison with the DNA database. That would help determine what plants or animals they ate."

"That sounds good. Then why don't we send some of it there? I heard there's a plane coming today that could take the samples. Until then, we'll see how far we can get on our own."

"That was my thought, too. I'll set that up later." Matthew slid a glass slide containing a small portion of the stomach contents into the microscope and adjusted the magnification. "Do you want to go first?" He took a step away from the microscope to make room for her.

Anika stepped closer and looked through the double eyepiece. "Hmm..." she muttered, "I don't know. Looks to me like that awful pudding they served yesterday at lunch."

Matthew laughed. "Well, only this pudding is probably more inedible. Let me see it, please."

Anika slid to the side and Matthew looked silently into the microscope for a while. Every now and then, he adjusted the magnification factor and moved the slide back and forth. Then, he sighed and looked up.

"What is it?" asked Anika.

"I don't really know. I don't claim to be an expert, but from everything I've read, this isn't normal. This mass is actually completely homogeneous, like the pudding."

"But 2,000 years ago, people didn't know pudding,"

Anika said. "People ate fish, meat from wild animals, primal grains, and that sort of thing. That's pretty well researched."

"But there are no meat fibers here, no grain husks or bones. Nothing like that at all. It's as if the meal had been pureed, which of course doesn't make much sense."

"Can we find out what it is?"

"I'll put a sample into mass spectrometry. That at least gives us a general idea about whether there's anything unusual in our pudding. I also have some reagents and equipment that I can use to roughly determine fat content, carbohydrates, and protein content. That's about all I can do here. We'll have to hope that the DNA analysis reveals more."

"Riddle upon riddle," Anika muttered.

"We'll figure it out. I'll prepare the sample right away and put it into the device. It'll take a while, though. Do you want to come back later?"

"Yes, I'd love to. I also have some catching up to do which I can work on in the meantime. Juan just said that he would at least need until tonight to do the age determination because he first had to rebuild an apparatus. Then he cursed something in Spanish. I don't think he's enjoying the action."

"Oh, let him be. He's a little temperamental. But he's doing an excellent job. So, we'll talk again this afternoon?"

"I'll be back here at two, is that okay?"

"Perfect."

11

Øystein Sigurdson gritted his teeth and stared at the e-mail he had just deciphered. It came from the military branch of the Norwegian Intelligence Service. The sender had marked it confidential and encrypted it with Sigurdson's personal crypto code. In the past, he had received such messages frequently. But that was during his active time overseas. He had hoped to leave all that behind and was tired of the nerve-racking service as an agent. This assignment was his chance to take it easy for once, up here at the proverbial backside of the world. But disaster seemed to cling to him. He skimmed the e-mail once again.

> "Torger Hansen found dead in Tromsø. Poisoning with agent from the Novichok group confirmed. Circumstantial evidence points to Russian involvement. Increase in security measures at Svea II site recommended."

This was news that Sigurdson would have preferred to do without. But it would have been an illusion to believe that the escaped Torger Hansen simply wasn't a fan of the weather. He had other motives. And now he had been professionally poisoned. Sigurdson wondered what this meant. What had he revealed about their efforts here—and to whom? His instincts urged him that the situation was about to get dicey. Soviet warfare agents, after all, could not be bought at the supermarket. Developments indicated that they had an adversary with significant resources and needed to respond. He needed reinforcements before it was too late. With his three staff members, he could do little if push came to shove. He needed to talk to Harry as soon as possible and convince him to agree to a significant increase in security personnel. If necessary, he would violate the security regulations and inform Stadler of the contents of the message. If he did that, Sigurdson knew he would be forced to comply.

Mi came shuffling into the cafeteria at around 3:30 p.m. with a grumpy face, grabbed a croissant, and sat down next to Anika, who was drinking her coffee by the window with her laptop open on her lap. Outside, it was already dawn and the sky was changing in the most fascinating colors. The spectacle had been keeping Anika from her work for over half an hour. She turned to Mi and watched her silently for a while, chewing on the pastry and looking outside.

"It's getting dark," Mi grumbled, "again."

"Well, I guess that's how it is in the Arctic," Anika responded succinctly, shrugging her shoulders.

"I know. Doesn't bother me. But when it's dark, the plane doesn't come. We don't have lights on the runway. And that means I won't get my spare until tomorrow."

"And I won't get my fresh fruit," Anika said.

"Who wants fruit when they can have delicious croissants like this?" Mi laughed and held up the greasy pastry. "They'll keep for nine months and won't taste a bit worse than they did on day one. Isn't it a miracle of food engineering?"

"Do they taste good on day one?" Anika asked.

"No." Mi laughed again. "But you know, devils and flies and stuff. I need tons of candy when I'm thinking. It's fuel for my brain."

Anika nodded. "Are you getting anywhere with your analyses now?"

Mi sighed. "Not really. Well, with the analyses, yes, but I can't figure out the results. I haven't been able to examine your implant yet, either, because the damn power supply on the CT machine burned out."

"This is the spare part you're waiting for?"

"Right. And it was supposed to be here a week ago. The care up here is really substandard."

"Tomorrow it will come for sure."

"Ha! Harry's been telling me that for a week."

"I'm sure he's doing the best he can."

"Yeah yeah. I know. I'm just frustrated because I don't have any useful results yet. How's it going for you?"

"Confusing. I analyzed the mummy's stomach contents with Matthew today."

"Oh, that must have been disgusting." She put the half-eaten pastry away.

"Well, it's okay. You can't be squeamish about it."

"So, what did they eat? Croissants?"

"No. Not what you would usually expect, either. They had some kind of mush in their stomachs that couldn't be determined in detail. But the strange thing is that, according to Matthew, it was absolutely nutritionally balanced. The proportions of protein, fat, and carbohydrates were pretty much in line with what nutritionists recommend."

"So, nothing like Stone Age diets?"

"Bronze Age. And no, the stomach contents are

completely atypical. They should have had meat fibers and cereal remains in their stomachs."

"I can see we're in the same boat. It's all very mysterious."

"You're right about that. Say, do you want to go to the cave together tomorrow? I want to do some more research there. And now that it's clear that there's some kind of technology at work down in the ice cave, why don't you check with your gauges to see if there's anything hidden there, too?"

"Sure, I'll come over right after the morning tech team meeting. I have a mobile setup we can use."

"Great, I'll bring you a Swedish chocolate from my emergency ration for your brain. Tastes good from the first day to the last."

"Deal," Mi said as she stood. "I'm going back over there. I have to calibrate some equipment."

Anika stood as well. "Alright. I'll see where Juan is with my age determination."

"Have fun," Mi hollered as she already begun to walk away.

15 minutes later, Anika stood in front of the door of Juan Lopez's lab. There, she found a one-page computer printout. At the top, he had written Anika Wahlgren in red felt-tip pen. It was obviously the results of the age determination analysis. At the bottom, a yellow sticky note hung to the sheet. Anika plucked it off.

"Migraine. Need to lie down. Juan," it read.

She took the printout off and stuck the yellow slip of paper back on the door. She skimmed the lines of the report: Calculated age: 2,000 years, +/- 200 years tolerance.

That was the first result, which turned out exactly as she had expected. But since all other findings and indications didn't quite fit into her theory; it still did not bring her any closer to answers. She needed more data, more clues. And she would have to trust her intuition even more, which was exactly what she planned to do when she explored the cave again the next morning.

Harry Stadler had a sinking feeling in his stomach. He had been sitting in Sigurdson's security center for ten minutes listening to the security chief's dramatic lecture. He still wasn't sure what to make of it. After all, he knew Sigurdson well enough to know that he was not prone to exaggeration and generally presented things as factually as possible. He was a man who had probably seen it all and had no reason to get worked up over trivialities. And it was this fact that probably worried Harry the most. If Sigurdson was so insistent about something, there was probably every reason to be.

"Harry, it's like this," Sigurdson stated. "I pulled some strings and found out more about the whereabouts of Torger Hansen."

"What strings? Anything I should know?" asked Harry.

"Don't be naive, Harry. I have a military past. In fact, I was in the secret service."

"Are you still?"

Silence.

"No," said Sigurdson after a while. "But it doesn't matter at all. Trust my experience and instinct. Does Novichok mean anything to you?"

Harry tilted his head. "It's a poison. It was all over the news when they murdered that dissident."

"Yes, it's a poison. A warfare agent, to be exact. The devil's stuff."

"And Hansen died from that?"

"There's no doubt about that, unfortunately. And when someone goes so far as to poison one of our employees, then we can be sure that danger lies ahead."

"Torger was a spy? Is that what you're saying?" clarified Stadler.

"I don't know what exactly he was. Maybe he was just a stupid stooge. But he played a dangerous game. And he lost. His teammates pushed him out of bounds."

Harry sighed. "That's tough. And I don't understand why anyone would take such measures. We don't even know what exactly is down there. Why is someone risking it all and walking over dead bodies to find out what we know?"

"That's a fair question. It all looks like it was done to get rid of a spy who became troublesome. But it doesn't quite make sense. What's the motivation behind it all? I don't understand why they coldcocked Hansen so publicly. That doesn't really point to a foreign intelligence service. There are more discreet ways of doing something like this. But it could be that they deliberately wanted to create a false trail. Still, it is beside the point. All I know is that we have to take action."

"So, you need more men?"

"Better trained men. I need better armed men."

Harry took a deep breath and exhaled again, as if trying to calm himself down internally. "Soldiers?"

"Not officially. We know the rules, after all. I can contact some former colleagues who could help us."

"Hold on. We have to think this through. Most of the

people here are scientists, just like me. They might be hesitant to be surrounded by heavily armed troops. And I don't want to jeopardize the research mission."

"I understand that. Your people aren't used to eating breakfast next to machine guns."

"For heaven's sake, Sigurdson!"

"A joke, forgive me. I have a rather dry sense of humor."

"That's not dry. Your jokes have a desert climate." For the first time, Harry saw something like a smirk on Sigurdson's lips. "You think that's funny?"

"No. Of course not. So, what is it? Can I call for backup? I hope you know I'm going to do it anyway. But I'd rather see us agree on the issue."

Harry nodded. "Yes, go ahead. But no more than five people. And please tell them that this is a civilian operation. Tell them to stay in the background."

"They're all professionals, don't worry. We can also disguise them as technicians if you like."

"That would be fine with me. The main thing is that they hide the machine guns under their jackets." Harry rose and walked toward the door. There, he turned once more. "When will they be here?"

"In two to three days at the latest. Until then, keep this between us, please."

"Good, keep me posted." Harry left the container and headed for the exit. He needed some fresh air. The talk of ordnance and guns angered him, but he knew there was no alternative to Sigurdson's suggestion. At most, he could call off the whole operation and send everyone home. But that was not an option for now. First, he wanted to know what they had stumbled upon here.

12

Anika entered the cave with the petroglyphs that morning feeling differently than before. After yesterday's analyses and the undoubted realization that this mission involved at least as much technology as archaeology, she looked at the human remains in the cave from a new perspective. It seems as though she had to look behind the images. They were only a fragmented projection of what had happened here long ago.

Anika planned to do that today, not only figuratively, but also quite literally. She opened one of the transport boxes with her technical equipment and took out a heavy construct with two rollers at the front and a holding bar at the back. The labeling identified the device as a RadWave L600 cavity radar. Anika had specifically requested it before leaving Stockholm so that she could use it to non-destructively search for voids in the floor and walls. She had a premonition that there might be more to discover in this cave and burial chamber. She approached the section of the drawing that, according to the laser scan, had been particularly finely crafted. The image was probably meant to reflect some kind of disaster or catastrophe. Some of the figures were drawn lying down, with wild lines above them that might suggest a storm. Additionally, the larger figure that hovered above the others in the main painting was also depicted again, but now amid those lying down, carrying an object in her hands. Anika thought it might be a bulbous vessel or a large stone.

Anika set up the cavity radar in front of the section of the wall with the drawing and programmed it to scan vertically. Then, she connected it wirelessly to the laptop and opened the measurement software. She created a new project and started recording. Slowly, she traced across the wall in single lines from left to right, starting at the bottom and overlapping each strip as specified. Anika knew that the software would calculate a coherent image from this and mark any anomalies in it.

It took about twenty minutes to record the entire area and another ten to analyze the data. Then, the results were in. Anika looked at the highlighted areas. It appeared as if there were a cavity behind the object carved into the rock that carried the larger figure. A narrow channel led out of the calculated image. Anika compared the image on the computer screen with the actual image on the wall. From this, she estimated the direction in which the channel was likely to continue. She was sure it led straight to the burial chamber.

She stepped closer to the drawing and tapped on the object depicted. It sounded hollow. A small amount of dust trickled down. Anika frowned. Intuitively, she pressed on the object. It crunched and the entrance to the burial chamber closed as if it had a mind of its own.

"Oh my!" exclaimed Anika in amazement.

The passageway was so perfectly sealed and camouflaged that no one would ever think another room was hiding behind it.

Anika pressed again and access was released.

At that moment, Mi entered the cave with a large, plastic box. "Wow, what was that?" she asked, fascinated.

"Some mechanism. I just found it with this." Anika

pointed to the radar device next to her. "Oddevold must have found it by accident, too, and that's how he uncovered the burial chamber."

"Does it work mechanically?"

"I don't know."

"If it's electronic, we're about to find out." Mi set the box down and began taking out the measuring equipment stowed inside. "But I'm not getting my hopes up; I've taken measurements in here before, after Oddevold collapsed. There was nothing."

She put some of the pieces together to form a device that served the same purpose as a compass. The construct had differently shaped antennas in all directions and was attached to a 1.20-meter telescoping handle. Just above the handle was a small monitor that would display the signals being received. Mi tapped a few times on the apparatus' touch display. "I need to calibrate the whole thing to block out the background radiation," she explained. "It'll just take a moment. Then, we'll see if anything here is giving off electromagnetic radiation."

Anika watched Mi work away for a while. She operated the technology as if she had done nothing else for decades—yet she was probably not even 25. "Tell me, Mi, how did you end up here anyway? I mean, I hope this doesn't offend you, but I expected someone your age to have interests far different than tracking down cryptic signals in a cave at the ends of the earth."

"Harry asked me to come along. We met at a university in London, where I studied physics and digital engineering. And yes, I was one of three female students, in case you were wondering."

"I can imagine it's pretty much a male domain. There's

also considerable testosterone excess in archaeology, but probably not as blatant as in physics."

Mi shrugged. "I honestly never cared about it. I just do what interests me. It's always been that way. I had a hard time in school because I couldn't muster any enthusiasm for most subjects. But in science, I was always the best." She checked the status on her antenna monitor and entered another command. The device emitted a short beep, followed by a longer one. "And you? I've heard you're the Viking expert, so to speak," Mi smiled.

Anika laughed. "Well, that's probably an exaggeration and an understatement at the same time. My area of expertise is early Nordic history, including the Viking Age. That's only a very small section. But it's true, I've always been interested in this period, even as a child. While my classmates were setting up dollhouses, I was launching little homemade dragon boats with my father."

"Sounds cool to me. I wish my dad would have taken an interest in me. But anyway, let's start the measurement now."

Anika stepped aside and made room for Mi.

She took a few steps toward the wall and ran the antenna rod along the surface, watching closely to see if the readings on the display changed. Nothing. There was not a tiny blip. She looked at Anika and shrugged apologetically. "Just as I thought. No signals."

"Maybe in there?" Anika pointed at the entrance to the burial chamber.

"We can try. But don't you dare close that door! I don't feel like sitting in the dark with a dozen dead bodies."

"Oh, they won't do anything," Anika said, smiling. "But I'll come in with you just to be on the safe side."

Mi made a face. Then, she walked over to the entrance of the burial chamber as Anika followed closely behind. Still, the display showed nothing but random noise.

With the meter, she scanned all the bodies and the walls. Nothing. Finally, she scanned the artifacts in the back. Nothing. "Well, it was worth a try. But there doesn't seem to be anything here."

"We must be doing something wrong," Anika concluded.

Mi frowned. "You can't really go wrong with this. The measurements are foolproof."

"That's not what I mean. I'm sure the measurements are correct."

"Then what do you mean?"

"I don't know." Anika looked around. "We're missing something."

"I don't see what that could be."

"Do you know what artifact Oddevold had taken with him into the cave?"

"I think this carved wooden stick, but I'm not entirely sure."

Anika stepped closer to the objects standing in the alcoves. "These things must be here for a reason. Maybe Oddevold was on the right track, but did something wrong?"

"Yeah, you could say that. His brain is now Jell-O."

Anika gave Mi a reprimanding look.

"Sorry. It's the truth, though."

Anika walked out of the burial chamber and Mi followed on her heels. Anika stood in the middle of the cave and searched the petroglyphs. She compared the artifacts with the images of the cave drawing. After a short time, she had discovered them all spread out on different effigies on the wall. "It's a mystery."

Mi looked at her skeptically. "Oh, come on."

"Yes, I know. That doesn't sound extremely scientific. But tell someone that you found metallic implants in a thousand-year-old mummy. He'll think you're nuts, too."

"If you ask me, this has long been a case for Erik van Jänike."

Anika laughed. "You're right. The old UFO hunter would have had fun with this." She fished a pair of latex gloves out of her pocket and slipped them on, retrieving the bulbous vase from the burial chamber and using it to approach the image of the large creature, behind which lay the opening mechanism of the burial chamber. The closer she got, the more obvious it became that the objects were very similar. "If my brain is about to be Jell-O, get me to Oddevold and put me in a bed next to him."

Mi screwed up her face. "Do you think this is a good idea?"

"No."

Mi's meter suddenly beeped. She looked down at the display. "Aha! Something's happening!" She walked up to the artifact. "That's not it." Then, she held the antennas toward the wall. "It's coming from in there."

Anika took a step closer.

"Okay, this is serious. The signal strength just doubled," Mi reported.

Together, they took another step toward the wall.

"Doubled again."

After the next step, no more measurement was needed. The stone that Anika had pressed earlier to open the burial chamber moved by itself. It slid inward and then flipped upward. Anika peered into the opening. "There's something in there." She held out her hand.

Mi grabbed her arm and held her back. "Don't! Whatever this is, it's giving off quite a bit of radiation."

She paused in mid-motion. Then, she nodded. "You're right, of course. Let's be careful." She fetched the lid of a transport box and a folding ruler. With it, she fished the hidden object out of the opening and set it down on the ground, lid and all. Anika was immediately captivated by it. The dark gray, shiny stone was slightly larger than a mango. It looked as if it was made of smoked glass. To Anika, it seemed as if wisps of smoke were drifting very slowly beneath the glassy surface. They were hiding something. "Do you see that, too?" she asked Mi.

Chen nodded. "Crazy. Something's moving."

"Yeah, and what's behind the smoke?"

Both bent a little closer and stared into the dark interior of the stone.

"They're runes," Anika answered her own question. "They shine silver, although this smoke swallows almost all the light."

"Can you read it?" asked Mi.

"I'll try. Hold on." Anika looked intently into the stone for a while, waiting for the runes to emerge from the smoke. "That's..." she breathed.

"What?" inquired Mi.

"It says Loki."

"Loki?"

"That's the name of a god from Norse mythology. Loki, of all things, the most mysterious and strange of the so-called Aesir."

"It makes sense, doesn't it? As mysterious as this all is."

Anika emptied the transport box that matched the lid and put it over the stone. Then, she closed the box on all sides with the latches. "We should take the stone to your lab."

Mi nodded and began packing up her measuring instruments. "I've got better instruments over there. Maybe I can figure out what this thing is emitting. Somehow, I think it's similar to the signal from the ice cave. But I want to make some comparative measurements before I theorize."

Mi and Anika had just left the airlock at the mine entrance when they heard the rattle of an airplane overhead. Anika recognized the small plane she had landed with just the other day. It seemed like yesterday to her. But so much had already changed since then. She had discovered so much and none of it was what she had expected.

Anika watched the pilot steer the plane through the light flurries and increasing wind. The plane set course for the runway, which was out of sight behind the houses. "Must be our lucky day," she said to Mi, who was standing next to her, pulling her hood up over her face.

"I hope so! We better hurry up; the weather is getting worse." She walked ahead toward the settlement.

Anika averted her eyes from the dancing snowflakes in the sky and followed behind her. The quiet nights were likely over now. The unnerving whispering of the wind would follow her back into the night and into the days to follow.

If it weren't for the candy wrappers lying around, Mi Chen's labs could have been mistaken for a sterile clean room. All the instruments were lined up on spotless tables and shelves and all the equipment—without exception—appeared to be in top condition. The CT unit, however, was switched off and standing in a corner with its side panel open.

Mi placed her transport boxes with the measuring equipment on a shelf against the wall.

Anika placed the box with the stone she had just found on a countertop in the middle of the room. "Oh, I promised you something," Anika remembered, pulling a 200-gram bar of chocolate with whole almonds in it out of her jacket pocket. She held it in front of Mi's nose.

"Nice to have people to rely on," she replied with a grin, grabbing the tablet. "Now we're ready to go."

Anika carefully opened the latches of the transport box and placed the lid on the table. They both looked at the stone, which had lost none of its fascination in the bright light of the laboratory. On the contrary, they could see the swaths floating around inside and the glittering runes even better than they could before.

"Do you feel it, too? This attraction? I feel like I can't take my eyes off it," Anika mentioned.

"Yeah, it's nuts. And kind of worrisome."

"Where should we start?" asked Anika.

"I have no idea. I've never seen one of these things, let alone examined one. I don't even know exactly what it's supposed to be. I suggest we somehow try to record the signals it gives off. Who knows how long it'll emit them for."

"Back there, you said whatever it's emitting reminds you of what comes out of the ice cave, right?"

"Yes, exactly. It's really similar to the signal that came

we detected in the ice cave before but has since disappeared. After the robot touched the ship's wall, it suddenly became stronger and interfered with our technology. But gradually, it diminished."

"What was that signal?"

"I have no idea. I couldn't analyze it exactly. It's erratic—it comes and at irregular intervals. It's like it's overflowing with interference that can't actually be measured. And that's what seriously frustrates me. But maybe now I can find out more about these signals and work on this object in under controlled conditions. I think I'll be more successful in finding something."

"Do you think it's dangerous for us to be this close?"

"What do you mean?"

"Well, look at it. This is clearly something powerful. Do you think it's dangerous that we're this close to it?"

"Potentially. Especially when you think about what happened with Oddevold. Or with the miner in the cave. Even the robot we sent down there stopped responding for a short time. So, it's obviously affecting humans and machines alike, which is pretty amazing. But if we were affected, we probably would have felt something by now. And we can't yet conclude the extent of the signals are similar."

While the women discussed their next steps, the technician, Björn Lange, drove into the laboratory with a small cart. He had loaded up a heavy cardboard box and sat it in front. "Morning, girls," he grumbled. "Here, at last, is the gem you've been waiting for, Mi."

"My power supply! Great. Just in time. We can put it to good use now and analyze our artifacts."

"Should I install it right away?" asked Björn.

"If you have time. I can do it myself if you're busy, though."

"I'll do it, I didn't come here to push a handcart." Björn put the cart next to the CT machine and lifted the box. "Will certainly take a while. I have to remove the old power supply first and familiarize myself with the machine," he explained. "Let's hope it doesn't burn out again." He winked at Mi.

She gave him a venomous look. "You better watch out; I'm going to lose it if this thing doesn't work."

Björn chuckled to himself and started screwing around with the CT.

Mi took some equipment from the shelves and began to set up a measuring apparatus. She set up several antennas around the stone and connected them to evaluation units. Meanwhile, Anika looked around the lab and spotted the implant under the microscope. She peered through the eyepiece. "Did that thing give off any signals?" she asked Mi.

"No, nothing. It could be that it's a purely passive component or that the battery is dead. It's hard to say. But when Björn gets the CT fixed, we'll take a better look."

Björn gave a grunt and stood. "I'll be back. I need more tools," he grumbled.

"What?" Mi asked. "I have a whole arsenal here."

"30 TORX screwdriver. The dumb version with the hole in the middle. Do you have one of those?"

"I'm sure I do. Let me look," Mi answered as she disappeared into a small storage room next door.

Meanwhile, Björn looked at the measurement setup that Mi had constructed in the middle of the room. He stepped closer and inspected the antennas, catching eye of the stone. "Where did you guys get that? It looks amazing."

Anika turned her head as Björn reached out to touch it. "No! Björn, don't touch!"

It was too late. The stone was already wrapped in Björn's fingers, but Anika's screams startled him enough to make him withdrew his hand. "What?" he asked in a panic.

Mi jumped into the room and stared at Björn. "What did you do?"

"Nothing. Nothing happened at all. The stone is undamaged. I just wanted to touch it for a moment. I don't know why."

"Damn it, Björn!" Mi said, clearly agitated. "That could have went downhill fast." She looked back and forth between the technician and the stone several times. "You're okay?"

"Yes, everything is fine. Absolutely nothing happened."

Mi handed him a TORX screwdriver. "Here, this should fit. Go ahead with the CT. And don't touch anything else, please!"

Björn nodded. "Sorry. I didn't mean to mess anything up."

"It's alright. I'm just relieved nothing happened."

Less than two minutes later, Elvar Hauge burst through the door. "Mi, come with me! The signal is back, but its twenty times stronger. The robot is going crazy, and so is all the technology around it."

Mi cast a startled glance over to Björn. Then, she looked again at the stone. She hadn't noticed it before, but it now seemed to glow faintly from within. Finally, she looked at Anika. "Close the box, please. And let's all get out of here for now."

13

Mi and Anika followed Elvar directly to the engineering control room in a hurry.

Anika stood at the back of the room, trying not to get in anyone's way, but watching attentively to everything that was going on as Harry paced up and down the room like a caged tiger. Mi and Hauge jogged from computer to computer, calling out the status of each system to the other. They were checking connections, analyzing incoming data, and trying to get the robot, which was running in circles down in the cavern, back under control. Sigurdson sat quietly on the sidelines, watching.

Anika appeared spellbound as she watched the video image that flickered incessantly across the large monitor. While the robot rotated around its own axis, the mysterious ship that seemed to be the trigger for everything repeatedly came into the picture. For a brief moment, Anika thought she could make out characters, but the video was too shaky to be sure.

Mi, meanwhile, was sitting at a computer in the second row, hastily typing commands. "I was able to save the transmitted measurement data," she reported.

Harry joined her in the back and looked over her shoulder. "Well?"

"I'm analyzing it right now. But Elvar was right, the signal strength is much higher now. It's radiating up here."

"Hurry up a little, please," Sigurdson urged. "We need to know if there's any danger."

"I'm going as fast as I can," Mi shot back.

"Hauge, what about the robot?" Harry asked. "Why don't you turn it off?"

"I'm going to try to completely reset the controller. It'll take a moment at most."

The image on the large screen was still rotating. But all of a sudden, it became still and the camera focused on the hull. For the first time, Anika was able to get a clear view of what was lying down there. The heaters, which were visible on the left and right, had cleared so much surface from the ice that the curve of a ship's hull was visible. Anika had never seen anything like it. The ship looked huge. The hull was iridescent in an unusual beige-red-brown and it didn't appear to be made of wood. Then, she recognized the runic inscription at the very edge of it—it was just barely clear of ice. She blinked, moved closer to the monitor, and read.

ᚾᚨᚷᛚᚠᚱ

She silently moved her lips, then breathed the words. No one took any notice; she was drowned out by the excited conversation Hauge and Harry were having. "Naglfar," she said again, shaking her head. This was completely insane.

"I've got something," Mi shouted, drawing attention to herself. "I think it's a message that keeps repeating. Some discrete reading, maybe, or some kind of tracking device that communicates a position. Now that the signal strength is higher, the signal isn't completely disappearing, but there's some interference, just as I suspected."

"What is interfering with it? Do we know anything new?" Harry was desperate for answers.

"It seems that an analog interference is modulated over the digital values. Or it's two different signals that are overlapping. I can't quite conclude that yet, but I'm still concerned. I've been wondering for a while: What if this signal caused the miner to go crazy? We were safe because it was very weak at first and didn't reach anyone outside the cave. But now..."

"Part of our research mission, of course, is to find out exactly what triggered the miner's horrible reaction," Sigurdson calmly confirmed.

"We shouldn't forget Oddevold either," added Mi. "We don't know exactly what happened to him but I think it's becoming clear that this wasn't a random breakdown."

"We took all the necessary safety precautions to prevent anyone from going down there again without proper clearance," Sigurdson explained. "We had no way of knowing there could be any danger outside the cave."

"No, no one could have predicted this. And we're learning every minute," Harry agreed. "It's fortunate that they at least finally recovered Gulbrandsen's body. I've asked Matthew to do an autopsy on him in the next few days, and maybe that will yield some new information."

"And one more thing," Mi interjected. "As I said, the signal initially weakened after it first appeared, but now it only seems to be getting stronger."

Sigurdson rose from his chair and approached Mi's workstation. He looked at the readouts on her screen for a while. "Keep analyzing and find a way we can shield or neutralize the radiation—just in case it really is what's triggering the mental problems."

"I can't make any promises, but I'll try."

Anika cleared her throat. "Speaking of new discoveries," she said, "I know it may not be as spectacular as this signal, but I've also discovered something."

Everyone turned to her in surprise, as if she had appeared out of nowhere. "Anika, please, speak up. What is it?" asked Harry.

She stepped forward and pointed to the far corner of the painting, where the runes were visible. "I assume you can read this, Harry?"

Harry stepped forward and looked at the characters. "You've got to be kidding!" he said. "Naglfar?"

"That's what it says. In the oldest known runes," Anika confirmed.

"The ship of the dead from Norse mythology that is mentioned in connection with the end of the world: Ragnarök?" asked Harry, already knowing the answer.

"Well, I know that sounds pretty impossible. Downright insane. But we must remember that this is mythology. Tales and legends that were passed down orally for centuries before they were written down in the form we know now. Who knows what they originally meant. And Ragnarök doesn't necessarily mean the end of the world. In Old Norse, it means something more like the fate of the gods," Anika explained.

Sigurdson stepped closer to the large screen. "You're saying that's a ship of the gods?"

"I don't know. But just earlier, I made a discovery with Mi in the cave with the petroglyphs that seems to make sense."

Sigurdson looked back and forth between Mi and Anika. "What is it?"

"An artifact. A strange stone, to be exact. And there are runes in it, too. It says Loki. In one part of the Edda, the Völuspa, it says that a god named Loki will hold the helm of Naglfar. He will drive it to the battle between giants and gods. But as I said, these are all myths—there's no solid historical evidence." She pointed to the picture and shrugged. "So far, at least, there hasn't been any."

"This stone," Mi spoke, "it may have amplified the signal. I've taken measurements. It's definitely giving off something. I haven't been able to make any comparisons yet because..." She faltered. "Björn Lange touched it."

"And you're just mentioning that now?" Sigurdson said, clearly irritated.

"Sorry, I got carried away with all this. And nothing happened," Mi apologized. "We sent him to the infirmary."

Without another word, Sigurdson left the control room.

"Let him be. He's a bit tense," Harry said calmly. "Björn is okay?"

"He said he didn't feel anything," Anika replied. "But right after that, Elvar came and explained that everything was going crazy here."

"Right," Hauge agreed. "It came out of the blue. We were just scanning the ship's perimeter with terahertz waves and radar to find out how much was left in the ice and where the cave walls ran. Then, wham, the robot started spinning. And the data transmission exploded."

Harry nodded. "Okay. So, something down there has woken up. But none of us have become bloodthirsty beasts yet, and none of us have slipped into comas like Oddevold. That's a good sign for now." He turned to Mi. "Investigate this stone, but proceed with extreme caution. Try to find out how it's connected to the ship."

"I'm doing the best I can," Mi assured, "but I could use some help. This isn't just a technical problem." She looked to Anika.

"I'm in," she replied without hesitating.

Sigurdson found Matthew Grant and the ward psychologist, John McFarland, together with Björn Lange in the infirmary. They were in the middle of the examination and were just connecting the technician to the EEG device.

"What's the update?" asked Sigurdson with unmistakable urgency in his voice.

"Everything is fine so far," Matthew said calmly. "We've already run almost all the standard tests. Pulse, respiration and all reflexes are normal. Blood pressure is a little high, as usual, but nothing to worry about."

"Now let's see if there's a neurological disorder." As he spoke, he rubbed his right earlobe. McFarland always did it when he talked to Sigurdson. He wondered if the psychologist was aware of this quirk. "But even without an EEG, he looks perfectly normal to me. I don't think we're dealing with a case like Oddevold's. He had, after all, collapsed immediately."

"It's better if we get to the bottom of this," Sigurdson said, looking over at Björn Lange as Matthew applied the final electrodes of gel to his scalp.

The technician was sitting on a treatment chair and looked rather unhappy. Sigurdson eyed him attentively. "What were you thinking, anyway, touching an artifact that you don't recognize, not knowing if it's potentially dangerous? What exactly happened in the lab?" he snapped.

"I...it...," Björn stammered. "I'm terribly sorry, I wasn't thinking. But this object somehow attracted me. I don't know. I didn't even want to touch it. But suddenly, I saw my fingers reaching out toward it. And then Anika screamed, and I immediately pulled my hand away. I swear I don't feel any different. I feel the same as before."

"Well, I think that's enough questioning for now," Matthew urged. "We want to calmly complete our examination, and after that, you can continue to grill and reprimand him for all I care." He looked over at McFarland, who had taken a seat at the EEG monitor. "All set?"

"Yeah, we're good to go. I'll start the recording," McFarland said.

They spent the next few minutes writing the EEG data, and Matthew asked Björn a few more questions along the way to check for brain activity. When the measurements were complete, they all sat together in front of the screen and looked at the results. McFarland had also loaded Oddevold's EEG onto the screen and was comparing the two recordings. "I don't see any worrisome similarities here. Oddevold's EEG was unusual in many ways, whereas Björn's looks quite normal. It is as it would look in me or anyone else. The other results are also those of a completely healthy and not traumatized or otherwise injured person. I think this was a false alarm."

Sigurdson raised his eyebrows. "Are you sure?"

"Yes," Matthew and McFarland echoed in unison.

"If I had any concerns..." Matthew continued, "...I would voice them immediately. But from a medical standpoint, I can't find anything that points to any sort of mental malfunction."

"Psychologically, too, he seems fine. I think he's genuinely sorry for what happened," McFarland added, nodding at Björn.

He smiled sheepishly.

Sigurdson once again looked at everyone in the group. "Alright, gentlemen, you are the experts. I'll trust you, then." He turned back to Björn. "And in the future, be more cautious! We're dealing with things here that none of us can fully understand yet. And the last thing we need is mindless action."

"Yes, of course, I understand. I already explained that it really wasn't intentional."

"Alright. Then go to your quarters now. Call it a day and get to work in the morning."

"Eat something and then lie down," Matthew recommended as he began to pluck the electrodes from Björn's head. "But as soon as you feel any change, any pain or other symptoms, you come here right away. In the middle of the night if you have to. Press the emergency bell; the alarm goes straight to my room. I don't want any nasty surprises," Matthew said, patting him on the back.

14

Henrik Oddevold sucked in a hissing breath. Then, he jolted up in his hospital bed. He tore off the taped sensors and pulled out his stomach tube. He jumped out of bed. The nurse holding the IV fell to the floor with a clang and was dragged behind him until the band-aids on his wrist finally came off and the needle was torn out of his vein. Blood trickled down his fingers. He felt no pain. His mind was foggy. He ran through the nighttime hallway of the clinic, staggered, caught himself again, and kept running. Startled by the noise, a nurse came running out of the wardroom, saw Oddevold, went back, and raised the alarm. Through the window, she saw her patient rush past, arms flailing, eyes wildly darting. At the corridor intersection, he turned indecisively in a circle a few times and then ran to the left.

Two orderlies rushed out of the elevator at the end of the hall and ran after him. They grabbed Oddevold by the arms, but the man seemed to have developed superhuman strength; he tore himself away, lashing out. The nurses could hardly cope with the situation. The night nurse drew up a syringe with a double dose sedative. She hurriedly approached from behind. At last, the orderlies wrestled Oddevold down and held him as best they could, as one of them placed a knee on his back so the nurse could insert the needle. Oddevold reared back, flailing, screaming like an animal. But gradually, the drug began to take effect as it traveled through his veins. He curled up, puffed heavily, and breathed ancient word fragments that no one understood. Then, he gave up. His eyes closed and he sank into unconsciousness.

Ward physician, Dr. Dahl, rushed over and knelt beside Oddevold. He felt his pulse. "Normal," he announced after a moment, then turned to the nurse. "What happened?"

"I don't know, doctor. Suddenly, he ran down the hall as if stung by a tarantula. Up until then, everything was normal. I sedated him, but who knows how long that will last."

The doctor nodded. "Take him to the room; we need to examine him. Make sure he doesn't get peritonitis. This is a concern if the feeding tube hole doesn't close. Nurse, page Dr. Saaqi. He may have to operate on the patient tonight."

Anika tossed and turned in her bed. She had been trying to find peace for hours but hardly succeeded. The wind outside was getting stronger and stronger. After a few minutes of dozing, she woke up again because it was howling outside, or the wind was whistling through some cracks.

But it was not only the wind whose sounds prevented her from finding sleep. It was also the events of the day, which had her completely overwhelmed and lost in thought. Her mind kept drifting off, turning in circles trying to draw a logical connection between everything they've uncovered so far. But still, none of the pieces seemed to fit together. She had a hard time connecting mythology and technology. But the evidence for both was lying on a platter in front of her. She just had to interpret them correctly. At some point, they would fit together, and it would suddenly click. At least that's what she hoped.

Suddenly, another sound mingled with the howling of the wind. It came from upstairs on the second floor of the building in which she was housed. First, there was a thumping, as if someone had fallen out of bed. Then, she heard footsteps. Anika sat up and listened. Who was being so noisy in the middle of the night? She looked at the alarm clock. Half past two in the morning. The footsteps got closer. Anika pressed her ear against the door. Strained, she listened outside. Was someone having a conversation at this time of the night? A deep, humming voice uttered sentences that she could only understand with difficulty. Was it Old Norse? The words sounded like Icelandic, but even more raw and unpolished. She opened the door a crack. The dim, orange light in the hallway was just enough to make out outlines. Someone was coming down the stairs. Then, she recognized Björn. He shuffled through the hallway as if dazed, his eyes open and staring straight ahead. Again and again, he muttered cryptic fragments of sentences.

"Sleepwalking," popped into Anika's head. It was a phenomenon that had been heard of dozens of times, but that hardly anyone had ever experienced themselves. She wasn't sure what to do. Supposedly, it was dangerous to wake up sleepwalkers. Or was that much-cited nonsense? In any case, she had no desire to confront this bear of a man. Even more so with the knowledge of what had happened to him today. She couldn't exclude the possibility that he had been influenced in some way.

Quietly, she closed the door again and put on her jacket and shoes. She waited quietly until Björn passed her room, then slipped out behind him and ran toward the back exit. She had to get Matthew and McFarland. This was surely a case for the psychologist!

Anika left the apartment building through the exit on the back side and landed in the middle of a knee-deep snowdrift. It was terribly cold. The wind ruffled her hair and she first had to get her bearings. It took her a few seconds to find her way in the snow.

Then, as quickly as she could, she ran around the house and made her way through the estate. She saw Björn stagger out the front entrance of the apartment building and make his way toward the mine. Her mind raced. What should she do? She could hardly stop him. She had to sound the alarm. Björn was dressed only in boxer shorts and a short t-shirt. He didn't even have shoes on. In this weather, he would freeze to death.

She wondered if Matthew had mentioned where he was billeted. Then, it popped into her head. It had to be the building right next to the infirmary. He said he wanted to be ready to go at a moment's notice in case there was an emergency. First, she ran to the infirmary because she had seen an alarm button in there the other day. But she realized she hadn't taken her access card with her. She cursed and ran on to the next house. She knocked on the door as loud as she could, ran to the side, and banged on all the windows.

After a few seconds, Matthew stuck his head out. "What the hell is going on? Oh, it's you, Anika. Is there an emergency?"

"Yes, you must sound the alarm and get Sigurdson. He and his men have to catch Björn. Right now, he's running toward the mine. I think he's sleepwalking or something.

He's not in his right mind. And if we don't catch him soon, he'll freeze to death."

"Okay," Matthew said curtly and disappeared into the room. A moment later, an alarm siren sounded. Matthew came out of the front door of the house carrying a black doctor's bag. "They're on their way!" he called out to Anika. "Show me where he went."

The two walked through the blowing snow the way back through the settlement, past Anika's apartment building, and made their way toward the mine entrance. "There's no way he'll get into the mine. I hope he doesn't get lost somewhere," Anika said with concern.

"This guy's big. We'll find him," Matthew agreed.

A Jeep with a small snowplow in front roared up. Anika and Matthew jumped to the side. The car stopped next to them. "Get in!" yelled Sigurdson, accelerating just as they both got in the car.

A rifle was leaning on the passenger seat.

"You're not going to shoot him, are you?" asked Anika, startled.

"Yes, I am," Sigurdson said calmly. "With a tranquilizer dart."

As quickly as the weather permitted, they dashed along the road. After a few meters, the massive figure of Björn Lange came into view.

Sigurdson turned the car and lowered the passenger window. He raised the rifle and took aim, which was difficult in this wind, but Sigurdson was a skilled marksman. The rifle also had laser target acquisition. A red dot appeared on Björn's back. Sigurdson fired. Björn jerked briefly, turned his head around, and howled. He shouted ancient-sounding words into the wind.

"It didn't work," Sigurdson said in horror, and set about inserting a new dart.

"What's he yelling about?" Matthew wanted to know.

"Something about war and winter and the end of the world," Anika responded. "I can't understand it entirely. It must be some ancient form of Nordic."

Meanwhile, Björn approached the car from the front, making him out of the line of fire. With his bare fists, he punched dents in the hood.

Sigurdson pushed open the passenger door and jumped out of the Jeep. He ran around the car and gained a few meters of distance, then he started up and shot again. He hit Björn in the chest. He howled once more before finally collapsing.

Matthew got out of the back and shouted, "Everyone help! We need to get him to the infirmary now before he's completely hypothermic!"

With their combined efforts, they loaded him into the back seat of the Jeep. Anika and Sigurdson went to the front while Matthew accompanied Björn in the back. Then, they drove back to the settlement. AltohughAlthough Björn was out of it, he continued to utter barely audible, unintelligible gibberish.

"Is he having hallucinations? Or are they nightmares?" asked Anika.

"I don't know. I haven't seen a condition like that. The fact that you had to give a sleepwalker two rounds from a stun gun is odd, but the fact that he still won't quite rest is even odder. My goodness!" said Matthew, shaking his head.

Sigurdson, meanwhile, radioed to his men that the immediate danger had been averted but that they should take up positions at the infirmary.

A few minutes later, Björn was lying strapped down on a couch in the infirmary. He was dazed but kept turning his head back and forth. Monitors on the left and right recorded his vital signs. His pulse was much too high for someone who had just been sedated, and his blood pressure was also significantly elevated. Björn's eyes were closed, but his pupils wandered restlessly behind shut eyelids. Every now and then, he mumbled a word or made a grunting sound.

John McFarland lifted one eyelid and shined a light into it, then switched to the second. "Barely any pupillary reflex. He's out of it. But still, he's so restless. Incredibly peculiar."

"You had just concluded that everything was perfectly normal with him a few hours ago" challenged Sigurdson, who was standing about six feet from the bed with the stun gun ready to fire.

"Yes, I did. You saw the results yourself," McFarland replied.

"We still can't figure out what triggered it," Matthew said.

Dissatisfied, Sigurdson ground his jaws so that his defined cheekbones stood out even more than usual. But he remained silent.

Matthew turned to Anika, who—along with Harry Stadler who rushed over—was also standing a few feet away. "What was he mumbling earlier on the drive? It almost sounded like a poem."

"Pretty disjointed stuff. It also reminded me of a hero's song," she explained.

"He must be under some foreign influence," Harry said. "Björn certainly doesn't speak ancient nordic, at most a smattering of Swedish. And besides, he's a technician, how would he know those ancient verses?" He shook his head. "It must be the contact with this stone."

"Or the signal from the ship," Anika added.

"Or both," Harry offered.

"The more pressing question for me is what to do with him," Matthew said. "The storm keeps getting stronger and we certainly can't get a pilot to fly him out."

Sigurdson gave a low growl. It sounded almost as if a dog had been deprived of its bone. "We'll all stay here for now. You're right. The weather report predicts at least three days of storms. We won't get any supplies in that time either." He looked sullenly in Harry's direction.

He didn't elaborate, but said succinctly, "We have everything we need here. And as long as this weather prevails, we'll keep to ourselves here." He turned to Matthew. "Do what you can for him. You have an excellent ward dispensary, don't you?"

"Of course. After the incident with Oddevold, I ordered some stuff. I've already talked to John; we want to try Lorazepam to stabilize him. The drug has a number of neurologically beneficial properties. And if that doesn't help, we have a few more options. But for now, we'll just wait for the night to see how his condition develops."

"My men will take turns standing guard here. I'm not taking any more chances," Sigurdson said, then left the room to give instructions to his associate in the hallway.

"Well, I guess you and I will take turns here," Matthew told McFarland, receiving a nod in response. "Everyone else might do well to get a few more hours of sleep; we'll have plenty of time to get back to work tomorrow."

"I'm scheduling a meeting for 8:30 after breakfast in

the canteen so we can bring everyone up to speed," Harry explained, nodding goodbye to the others. Then, he left the infirmary followed by Anika.

15

Anika sat alone at the table during breakfast. She would have liked to eat breakfast with Matthew, but he was obviously still with his patient. So, she eavesdropped on the conversations happening one table over. Word had long since spread about Björn's nocturnal tour. To her left, geologist Linda Janssen was discussing the matter with a colleague whose name Anika couldn't recall.

"Is it the pressure of the mission? He's been here since the beginning," Janssen asked.

"I don't know. So far, he's been completely normal. Very even-tempered. A pleasant guy. For a German, even very funny. You've gotten to know him a bit, too," the man said.

"But why would someone run out of the house at night in just their underwear and then hit a Jeep?"

"Not a clue. That's totally nuts. But I'm telling you, it has something to do with that damn thing down there. We're lucky it only damaged the Jeep and not us."

Linda looked at the man, startled.

At that moment, Harry Stadler came in the door. "Good morning, colleagues!" he said in an emphatically friendly manner. "Some are probably wondering why we're meeting today. And others are probably already making their own assumptions. So, I'd like to put a stop to all speculation right away." He looked around the room, as if waiting for a response or agreement. Then, he continued. "First of all, there is no reason to worry. We have taken all precautions.

Lange woke up this morning, healthy and in good spirits. He cannot remember why he went outside last night. We currently assume that it was an extreme form of sleepwalking. Today, he will remain in the infirmary for observation."

A murmur traveled through all the employees present.

Harry continued regardless. "We also have many other things to discuss. So, I'm going to bring you all up to speed on the findings now in hopes that you'll be able to continue working as effectively as possible." Harry reported on yesterday's findings and analysis, the hypotheses, his plan for the next few days, and the expected weather.

Anika's thoughts slipped away in the meantime. She wasn't able to get any rest last night and was therefore exhausted. She tried not to let it show. But it wasn't just the lack of sleep. It was partly a nagging doubt that she and Mi weren't to blame for what had happened to Björn. They should have been more careful.

Only now did she realize that Harry had fallen silent. She looked up and found him still standing against the front wall next to the entrance. He suddenly seemed disoriented. She immediately stood and rushed to his front. Others also approached, including Elvar and Mi.

"What's wrong? What's wrong, Harry?" urged Anika, touching him on the shoulder.

He peered in her direction as if he didn't recognize her. Then, he blinked a few times. "What?" he asked.

"Are you okay?" Anika asked.

"Why wouldn't I be? What's going on?"

"You seemed completely disassociated for a moment. We were worried," Hauge answered.

Harry shook his head. "I was just in thought. Maybe too

little sleep." He earned skeptical looks. After a moment, he nodded slowly. "I'd better get over to Matthew's, just in case. We've covered all the essentials, after all. Now get to work."

"I'll come with you," Anika said. "I want to check on Björn."

Half an hour after the meeting, Mi screwed the cover of the CT unit back on in her lab. After yesterday's incident with Björn, she had to do the repair herself. Replacing it had not been a big deal—only the weight of the power supply posed a challenge for the petite Asian. But she was used to pushing through and doing things herself if necessary. She knew she could only rely on others in the rarest of cases.

Mi packed her tools in a suitcase, and took it to the storage room next door. She returned with a transparent, plastic box containing Loki's stone. She positioned it together with the box in the CT device and switched it on.

With a loud whirring and rattling noise, the machine booted up and performed a self-diagnosis. A connected monitor showed its progress. The device was working perfectly again. She could finally begin the analysis.

"It must have been a restless night in general," Matthew said to Harry and Anika, who had arrived at the infirmary. He pointed to his open laptop. "I received a message from the hospital in Oslo. Oddevold took a little trip last night, too. He stormed through the hallway and had to be subdued by two orderlies and a nurse. They sedated him. It also appears that he has come out of his coma. Only he doesn't remember anything. He doesn't even know who he is anymore. Or, to put it another way, he seems to think he's someone else entirely. The doctors are having a hard time understanding what he's saying." He looked at Anika.

"Does he also mutter Old Norse phrases?"

"Seems like it. Just like Björn." He pointed to the curtained-off area behind which someone was snoring. "He's gone back to sleep. I guess the trip was a little draining after all. And I gave him another dose of Lorazepam, which makes a lot of people sleepy. But he's doing well again. He just, as I said, has no memory of his nighttime hike."

"What is going on?" asked Harry. "Is this triggered when a person comes into contact with these artifacts?"

"Anything is possible. I can't tell without exact data. I really hope Mi can provide me with something later. I have asked her to send me all the results."

"Harry might also be affected," Anika said.

Harry waved it off. "But I didn't touch anything, and I know who I am!" he protested.

"No, I didn't mean it that way. But earlier, you looked at me as if I was a complete stranger."

Harry shook his head. "I..."

"I'm just saying," Anika added. "Safety first, to quote Sigurdson." She paused. "There could be some kind of interaction between this radiation from the ship and the artifacts. It's possible that touching them amplifies the effect, but it could also be there without direct contact."

"We should definitely give Harry a thorough checkup. It won't hurt," Matthew suggested.

"I'm fine. I just had a brief blackout earlier. That's all," Harry explained, then sat down on a treatment table.

"I'll leave you men to it then," Anika said wished them all goodbye.

Mi removed the lid of the plastic container that held the stone—carefully and without touching the artifact itself. She also wore thick rubber gloves for safety. Once the stone was perfectly in place, she started scanning through the computer tomograph. The machine made creaking and tapping noises, slowly moving the specimen table forward, which was supported by a rail.

Mi eagerly awaited the results, but the screen remained black, as if there were nothing to analyze. She frowned. Did the device have a malfunction that the self-test didn't detect? Had she possibly assembled something incorrectly? That was unlikely. The power supply should not have any influence on the function of the imaging process.

Mi stopped the scan and removed the tray with the stone sitting on top. She lifted the pad and the stone and placed a handheld radio on the sled instead. Then, she started a new scan. After less than two minutes, she had a perfectly reconstructed image of the device in the computer. All the details of the inner workings were effortlessly visible. So, the scanner was working completely normally.

Once again, Mi pulled up the saved image of the stone. Nothing. Not the slightest data, as if the tray had been sent in empty. That had to mean that the stone was deflecting all radiation. The results of the scans from the ice cave came to her mind. It was almost like the ship. This one also refused to reveal its secrets. It was like trying to look into a black hole from which not even light could escape. But these artifacts differed from a black hole in the sense that signaled leaked out of them.

Mi reached into a tray next to her and took out the small box with the implant that Anika had given her. She knew that this one wouldn't be so uncooperative. The X-ray that Matthew had taken already showed a rough picture of the inner workings. Analysis of the image under the microscope had shown that it lacked contrast and had a certain blurriness enveloping the entire image, but Mi had suspected this might be due to maladjustment of the X-ray apparatus. This had, after all, been built for large-area images of people, not for analyzing technical implants the size of a grain of rice. She placed the small box on the CT carriage and started a new scan.

She attentively followed the progress. She expected something to appear on the screen in just a moment. But as soon as the X-ray beam hit the outer edge of the implant, the device emitted a shrill sound. Mi looked into the tube but could see no defect or other reaction. The image showed the implant as a completely white surface with no structure. It was the exact opposite of what had just happened to the stone. This thing absorbed all radiation. Mi restarted the scan with increased power. Again, a shrill whistle, then a flash inside the device. She winced. There was a discharge and she heard a sickening splutter that gave her goose bumps. Then, there was a loud bang as acrid smelling smoke came out of the device. Mi quickly pressed the emergency stop button. The CT machine fell silent, but the emanating smell made it immediately clear that this time, more than just the power supply had been damaged. This was a disaster. No matter how she spun it, the technology they found here was absolutely incompatible with theirs. Mi stood, turned the fan power to maximum, and walked over to the window. Outside, the wind drove thick snowflakes past, the sky a little more than a gray soup that would soon turn to black. And when she thought about the storm warning that had come in, she felt sick to her stomach. They were trapped here. They had been more or less before, of course, but at least it hadn't been so obvious.

She forced herself to take a few deep breaths, then walked over to her laptop and began compiling all the results so far. She uploaded the data collected to the station's share server and sent a link to Matthew. Maybe someone with a completely different perspective would figure it out. She hated to admit it to herself, but she was getting tired of it all. She had had high hopes for the CT, but it had been a complete failure.

She went back to Loki's stone and looked at it half perplexed, half reproachful. "What are you hiding? What's the point of all this?"

Silence filled the room as the smoke from the CT slowly dissipated through the ventilation. Without receiving an answer, Mi put the plastic cover back over the artifact and carried the box into the storage room.

16

"Your physical condition is absolutely impeccable considering your age, Harry," Matthew praised, removing the cuff attached to the blood pressure monitor from his patient. "Heart sounds, respiration, and blood pressure are all fine, so I gather you are taking your medication as prescribed?"

"Right on schedule, as prescribed," Harry confirmed.

"I'd like to do another EEG, if I may?"

"I'd rather get right back to work; I've been sitting around here long enough."

Matthew gave him a wry look.

Harry sighed. "Fine, let's go."

Matthew led him over to the EEG and asked Harry to sit in the treatment chair. Then, he picked up a bundle of electrodes and a tube of special gel that improved skin conductivity. He hurried to wire Harry up, then started the measurements. "Won't take long, I promise."

Twenty minutes later, the examination was completed, and Matthew released Harry from the infirmary. He sat down at his computer and began to evaluate the data. He retrieved all the comparative measurements made so far from the dossiers and also opened Oddevold's data recently transferred over from Oslo. It was time to systematically look for similarities or a common inconsistency. He knew that this approach would not yield meaningful results for all measurements because individual patients had been in different states of consciousness when the EEGs were taken but still, he placed the patients' measurements side by side. First, he searched the EEGs for alpha waves, which occurred at rest with eyes closed and formed something like the basic rhythm of the brain. He could find no gross irregularities here. He moved on to beta waves, which normally occurred with eyes open and mental activity. Again, these results were completely normal in most EEGs. Except in Oddevold's case. He already knew that the EEG he had taken here after his collapse was unusual. Despite Oddevold's unconsciousness, parts of his brain had shown pronounced beta waves, but more importantly, strong gamma waves in a frequency range above 30 hertz. Matthew knew these kinds of brain waves usually occurred during heightened attention in a focused state and not during unconsciousness. In contrast, the theta and delta wave patterns, which were typical of fatigue and deep sleep, were underrepresented. Matthew had not examined these two waves further because of the dominance of the other types. Perhaps he should do so all the more meticulously now. He set some parameters in the software to show only the data from the electrodes that had picked up the slow delta waves and enlarged their display. It became apparent that it had possibly been a mistake not to analyze the EEG in detail right away. But he had assumed that extensive neurological examinations would be performed in Oslo and had relied on that.

Matthew zoomed in on a section of the curve even further and spotted strange peaks in the course. Again and again, they protruded from the leisurely crests and troughs of the waves. They jutted out like sharp-edged stones from a surging sea. Using a ruler, he measured the distance between two peaks in relation to the frequency of the brain waves, which fluctuated between one and three hertz in the EGG. This corresponded to one cycle of oscillation. He stored the value. Then, he measured the next distance. It was exactly twice as large. The next swing came after three times the distance. Matthew continued with the measurements and read off the values: five times the distance, seven times, eleven times, thirteen times, then regular, singular distance measurements again.

He leaned back in his chair and looked at the monitor, which displayed a table of the measurement results. Once again, he reviewed the distances. They were exact multiples of each other. And not only that—they strangely corresponded to the first seven prime numbers.

Matthew shook his head in disbelief. That was basically impossible. How could these signal spikes be generated by a human brain at exactly these mathematical intervals? The spike itself was also far too high of a frequency to occur naturally in a brain. There had to be an outside influence. And Matthew didn't have to think long about where it might have come from.

He loaded the other EEGs into the software and applied his filters. For the measurements that did not contain slow delta or theta waves, he also set a frequency filter exactly to the frequencies of the wave peaks that he had determined to mask out all other parts of the spectrum. The result was clear. All the EEGs, including the one Harry had just taken, showed the same patterns. Jumpy spikes at the intervals of prime numbers.

He had to show Mi. Then, he remembered that she wanted to send him data. He opened his email and found the link to her collected results. He downloaded the recordings of the signals and looked at the waveforms.

They seemed familiar in a strange way. Almost like...

"Figured it out yet?" he heard a voice behind him. He turned around. It was Mi, standing casually in the doorway.

"Hey, Mi! Come on in. I just downloaded everything."

She came closer and sat down next to him.

"Did you check this data for prime numbers?" asked Matthew.

"Prime numbers?" Mi echoed, perplexed. "In what way?"

"Whether there are any in the signal."

"It's hard to say. It's very complex. Without concrete clues, it's impossible to figure out."

"What if I give you the exact number sequence and a frequency range?"

Mi looked at him as if he was about to pull a rabbit out of a hat. "You're serious?"

"Look," he said, switching back to the EEG viewer software. "I've analyzed the EEGs of all the patients. They show erratic spikes in the spacing of the first six primes and that's in a frequency range between 3.8 and 18.4 kilohertz."

Mi stared at the waveforms and nodded slowly. "Wicked. Now that's progress. Let me get on the computer." She slid to the keyboard and downloaded an analysis program from the server, which she installed on Matthew's laptop. Then, she pulled in the recordings of the signals and applied her own filters in the program that matched Matthew's specifications exactly. It took a moment for the computer to do the calculations and present the results. Mi eyed it suspiciously. "It doesn't make any sense, I'm afraid. It was a good try, though."

Both stared at the monitor.

"But..." stuttered Matthew. "I was sure there had to be

something. Those rashes in the brain waves aren't natural. They must be coming from outside!"

Mi tapped her right index finger nervously on the tabletop. Matthew could tell she was brooding. "The other way around!" she said suddenly.

"What?"

"Frequencies and spacing."

Matthew looked at her, perplexed.

"Wait." Mi typed some commands and started the analysis again. After a few seconds, there was a result. "There it is!" exclaimed Mi. "Your prime numbers are included. They correspond to the frequency jumps, which I couldn't identify exactly. So, they're not defined intervals, like your brainwaves, but specific shifts in the spectrum."

Again, she typed something, and the display changed. "If I filter it out, this is what we get."

Critically, he looked at the displays. "Looks like an EEG."

Mi nodded. "Yeah, just higher frequency if I'm seeing this right. The waves look pretty darn similar when you adjust the scale."

"So, I think we have some initial evidence that the incidents are related to this signal." Matthew looked back and forth between the various representations of waveforms. "Well, so far, so good. But what does that mean now? Is there some kind of technical mastermind inside the ship that's giving off these signals?"

"Interesting notion. But until someone goes inside that ship, we'll have to settle for speculation. All the measurement techniques we've used give the same result. We can't get a picture of the inside. By the way, this also applies to the stone that Anika and I found yesterday. The implant that you discovered was a total failure. It wrecked my freshly repaired CT when I tried to scan it."

"How so?"

"I have absolutely no clue. All I can say is: flashes, ruckus, smoke. All we're left with is your X-ray, and I'm afraid it's pretty blurry."

"I see. But I don't think Sigurdson and Harry are going to let anyone down there. Especially not now that we've proven that these signals have a direct effect on the brain."

Mi nodded. "I agree. And who would be dumb enough to go down there at the risk of some obscure radiation frying their brains?"

"That's richly rustic language for someone with a degree in physics," Matthew remarked, smiling. "Is there any way we can technically neutralize or shield ourselves from these ominous brain rays?"

"I don't know. It's possible. But I can't say if it would do any good."

"Why?"

"You showed me the EEGs earlier. The one from Oddevold is from this morning, if I saw correctly. He's more than a thousand kilometers away."

"Right, that's strange. But there must be something else behind it. His condition was much more extreme than Björn's or Harry's." Matthew pointed to the partitioned area behind which Björn was still snoring quietly.

"Okay. I'll think about if and how there can be a technical solution, but maybe you should also consider a medical one. Just in case."

"Already on it. As soon as Björn wakes up, I'll do another EEG and check if the medications I gave him help against the influence."

"I'll go over and report to Harry," Mi said, rising. "Good work, colleague. This interdisciplinary approach isn't so bad after all."

Mi found Harry at Sigurdson's security center and when she entered, it was clear that she had walked in on an ongoing argument. Both men made an obvious effort to dispel this impression immediately. But their ears and faced were turning red from anger.

"Yes, come in, Mi. What is it?" asked Harry in a rather unfriendly tone.

"I didn't mean to interrupt, but I just came from sickbay. Matthew and I have made some progress analyzing the signal."

Harry's expression, which had been strained a moment before, brightened a little. "What is it?" he and Sigurdson asked in unison.

"Very succinctly summarized, the waves resemble brain waves, only at a higher frequency level. The whole thing is also modulated with a sequence of prime numbers. Or superimposed. I can't say for sure about the latter yet."

"Brain waves?" asked Sigurdson incredulously.

"Yes, not only that. We have analyzed the EEGs, from Oddevold, Björn, and also from you, Harry. In all of them, there is an image of the signal. Or rather a reaction to it. It's in all the EEG recordings."

"There you go!" said Sigurdson. "This signal is affecting people and making them unpredictable. Harry, we have to take action." His tone had become sharper again.

Harry shook his head. "Surely we can't keep everyone locked in their quarters outside of working hours!" He suddenly sounded angry again.

"I don't like it myself," Sigurdson argued. "I'd love to get all the personnel out of here, but evacuation is impossible in this weather. And I can't get more men either!"

"I understand all that. But now think about it. How do you know if your people are immune to the effects of the signals? They are probably just as influenced as any of us. And they're carrying guns! In my opinion, we should keep all the weapons safe until—and if—anyone else goes crazy."

Mi looked helplessly back and forth between the two men, who were now threatening to drift into an argument. "If I might interject for a moment..."

Sigurdson and Harry looked at each other silently for a while, as if carrying on the argument with glances, then turned back to Mi.

"I think it we should stay calm and find a solution. Matthew is looking into whether a drug will help right now. And I want to try to make the signal useless with a jammer."

"A jammer?" asked Harry.

"Yes, a jammer that superimposes the frequencies of the signal, rendering it harmless. I don't know if it will work, though. The frequency pattern is complicated and probably not perfectly replicable."

"Risks?" asked Sigurdson curtly.

Mi shrugged her shoulders. "It is completely unknown how the signal is created and what causes it to be emitted. I would only operate on the symptoms, not the causes. If there are concerns, then I won't."

"We have to keep all options open. Construct a transmitter like this and get everything ready, but don't activate it without me..." He faltered and looked to Harry. "Without us giving the go-ahead."

Harry nodded. "And until then, we should all remain vigilant and watch for any unusual behavior. The situation is confusing enough as it is. I'll send a memo to everyone later."

"Okay, I'll get right on it," Mi announced. "Oh, and by the way, the CT is broken again. Blew out while analyzing the implant. I think it might be a good precaution to take the artifacts back to the cave. Just in case they amplify the signal somehow."

"A sensible suggestion," Sigurdson said. "But it would probably be even better if we got them as far away as possible. I think one of the abandoned tunnels of the old coal mine would be safest."

"Agreed," Harry said.

"I'll send Ove Holm to the lab right away and have him take the stuff there," Sigurdson explained.

"They are already boxed, so there is no direct contact," Mi said.

Sigurdson nodded appreciatively.

Meanwhile, Harry rose and went to the door. Before he stepped out, he turned around once more. "So, this meeting has ended well, after all. And I apologize for raising my voice just now. It's unlike me. Maybe it's the stress."

Sigurdson raised a hand placatingly. "We are all under pressure, including me. So, I can only agree with Mi that everyone must make an effort to stay calm until we find a solution or see any improvement in our current situation."

17

Murmansk, Russia
October 14

Viktor Nikolaev's private jet landed at Murmansk airport at around 10:00 p.m. local time. A black stretch limousine was waiting not far from the plane's parking position for Viktor to get off. The driver glanced one last time at the back of the car. He had prepared everything as requested and arranged for the special equipment that had been ordered.

A bottle of champagne stood ready in a cooler, as well as a 30-year-old Tobermory single malt from the Scottish island of Mull. He had had to get it on the way here in a delicatessen with a whiskey department and had discovered that the bottle cost almost as much as he normally earned in a month. However, his passenger had held out the prospect of a lavish bonus for the extra service and discretion, which he had been only too happy to accept.

The jet door opened and a beefy man in a black suit stepped out. He looked around as if ensuring that the tarmac was safe. It was obvious at first glance that the man was well trained. Surely a professional bodyguard. Then, the bodyguard stepped aside and made way for a second man, who was also dressed in all black. He looked about ten years older than the bodyguard, wirier, but of an almost palpable presence.

The limousine driver got out, walked around the car,

and opened the right rear door. He silently stood next to the car and waited until his passenger approached. He greeted him with a discreet nod but received no response. Then, the driver remained in his position until the man got in and, after a well-measured second of waiting, closed the door behind him.

Meanwhile, the bodyguard went to the passenger door and climbed in. He waited until the driver was also in the car and then turned to him. "I'm going to tell you where you're going. Don't ask any questions and don't talk to anyone about this. Otherwise, I'll be back and it will be uncomfortable."

The driver just nodded and started the limo.

Slowly, the car drove off the airport grounds and turned onto the road heading north.

In the rear, Viktor Nikolaev was satisfied that his instructions had been followed just as he'd ordered. At least that could console him about the fact that he hated the north of Russia. It was terribly cold up here and uncivilized. He thought back with horror to his childhood, which he had spent in one of these bleak, icy concrete cities. But at the same time, he knew that up here, far away from the hustle and bustle of the pulsating metropolises, there were many hidden treasures.

Viktor abandoned champagne and immediately opened the bottle of whiskey. He poured his glass nearly third full, swirled it gently, and held it under his nose. With a deep breath, he took in the complex aromas—woody, peaty, earthy, and floral. This drink was a work of art that had taken 30 years to create, resulting in a symphony in his glass. He resisted the temptation to drink from it.

The limousine drove through the chunky suburbs of

Murmansk and Viktor was grateful that the blackness of night had already settled over the city.

In an hour, they would be in Severomorsk, and the mission would begin as planned—he had no doubt about that. He didn't worry about the fact that Severomorsk, as a so-called closed city, was accessible only to the inhabitants and members of the Russian Northern Fleet. He had his own ship and enough money to gain access anywhere. Boris had already arranged that and made all other preparations for the mission. As usual, the man proved that he had not invested in him for nothing.

Viktor finally took a sip of the whiskey and felt a pleasant burning sensation travel down his throat. So far, everything was going just as he had intended it to. Even the expected bad weather would play to their benefit. Viktor had checked the latest weather report two hours ago. The violent storm front that would pass over northern Norway and the Arctic islands in the next few days was just the right time to strike. Despite it all, he had decided to be at the forefront of what might be the greatest triumph of his career. He believed the greatest treasure imaginable awaited him. To get it, in about an hour, he would climb aboard a submarine he had bought on a whim many years ago—more as a speculative object than something he'd actually planned on using. Luckily for him, after the collapse of the USSR, you could buy just about anything. He had raked in tens of millions from the arms trade. And now the aged diesel submarine from the 877 Paltus series would prove useful. In fact, it was his ace in the hole.

Boris had gone through the navigator's calculations. They would have to leave tonight, which would make it just under 36 hours of submerged travel, and they would arrive at Svalbard right at the height of the storm. The crew there would be completely cut off from supplies at that point and thus correspondingly helpless. He and his men would arrive silently and unseen, complete their mission, and disappear just as discreetly. And no one would find out who was behind it. Viktor was already looking forward to this moment of triumph and to the moment when he would reveal the secret of the treasure. If he was honest, curiosity drove him almost more than the prospect of revenge for the shame he had suffered.

He refilled his glass with whiskey and leaned back on the leather-covered back seat. He wanted to enjoy the comforts once more before getting into that damp, metal coffin.

Station cook, Jörn Svensson, ran the back of his hand over his forehead as sweat drenched his hair. He was dizzy again. He leaned forward and propped himself up on the stainless-steel kitchen counter. Then, he closed his eyes for a moment. The dizziness was gradually improving. If it didn't stop soon, he would have to do something. He had been in the kitchen since just before five in the morning, preparing everything for breakfast, which was stressful enough without the dizziness.

From 6:30 a.m. onward, the hungry mob came into the canteen one by one. In addition to his kitchen duties, he had to make sure that nothing was missing from the buffet, if possible. He had imagined it would be easier to work up here and cook for a few scientists. But he had to realize that taking care of the physical well-being of 26 people around the clock alone required organization, attention to detail, and a lot of discipline.

But things had faltered this morning. He wasn't feeling well and kept noticing that his mind drifted away periodically. At one point, he almost hit the hot plate with the flat of his hand. Unwell was—strictly speaking—an understatement for his condition. Svensson turned the sausages on the large frying surface, then cracked a dozen eggs.

He put the spatula aside and grabbed his forehead. He noticed that it was already wet with sweat again. How could one sweat so terribly in the Arctic?

Anger boiled inside him—anger at this place, at the darkness, and at himself for coming here at all. And he felt anger at the others who never helped and always came to stuff themselves.

"We're out of fried eggs," someone yelled into the kitchen.

"It was that glutton Thoralf!" thought Svensson as he reached for the knife.

Now, he would give him a piece of his mind. Svensson let out a growl and stormed through the kitchen door.

On her way to the cafeteria in the morning, Anika was hit by the smell of fried eggs and sausages. And with the smell came tumultuous sounds, screams, and rumbles. She quickened her pace and ran into the dining room.

In the middle of the room, drilling technician Thoralf Rønne and chef Jörn Svensson circled each other like two animals fighting. Svensson waved a knife and growled incessantly. Thoralf swung a broken chair leg in his right hand. Suddenly, Svensson charged forward, about to stab, but Thoralf fought back. The knife slid along the wood but cut a deep wound in his left forearm. He didn't even seem to notice. Svensson stumbled and went down. Thoralf lunged with the chair leg and was about to hit him, but Svensson had already rolled around and pulled Thoralf's legs away. He stumbled into the buffet and cleared the well-prepared breakfast onto the floor.

For a minute, Anika was as paralyzed by the sight as everyone else. Then, she overcame her rigidity and yelled, "Stop it!" But no one responded. "I said stop! Put down your weapons!" Again, no response.

Svensson waved the knife and let out a scream. Anika ran over to the kitchen door and grabbed the fire extinguisher from the wall. She took the safety off and went straight for the two men. She pulled the trigger as a dense shower of extinguishing powder fogged them both.

The men coughed.

At that moment, Sigurdson rushed in the door. He threw himself on Svensson and overpowered him with well-directed hand grips. He pushed him to the floor and forced him still.

"Will you stop?!" shouted Sigurdson. The knife fell from the cook's hand with a clang. Svensson's tension now eased. He gasped in exhaustion.

Thoralf stood frozen, staring at Sigurdson and Svensson. Then, he put down the leg of the chair and looked around, puzzled. "What the hell happened?" he asked, looking down at his badly bleeding arm.

"Get Matthew!" shouted Sigurdson. "Tell him to bring bandages and some tranquilizers. And the rest of you clear the canteen!"

Meanwhile, Anika ran into the kitchen with the fire extinguisher. Smoke billowed out the door smelling like burnt eggs mixed with the scent of extinguishing agent.

An hour later, Matthew plucked the EEG electrodes from Svensson's head and patted him on the shoulder. "You'll be fine," he comforted, handing the chef a small, plastic box. "Take another pill before you sleep tonight, please, okay?"

Svensson nodded. "What about the food? Who's cooking?"

"Certainly not you. Go to your quarters and get some rest. We'll figure something out." Matthew glanced at Anika who was standing next to him. "If need be, Harry will make meatballs."

"Do we really want to risk another brawl?" asked Svensson, smirking.

"Someone's feeling much better. Now off to your room."

Svensson stood and walked toward the door, where a Sigurdson security guard was already waiting for him. He accompanied the cook toward the exit and back to his rooms.

"So, now tell me, what was going on there?" asked Anika.

"I suspect the same thing that happened with Björn, only different. I have now given the two squabblers a mix of psychotropic drugs that should dampen the delusional seizures. I did an EEG on Björn after giving the drugs, and the spikes we detected yesterday have significantly decreased—almost undetectable. Svensson's EEG looks similar. So does mine, by the way. As a precaution, I have prescribed myself medication to keep a clear head."

"That sounds like a good plan. I hope we have enough medication to go around."

"Actually, I have to ration the dose. We don't have

much. It might last a few days if I manage it well. But if we want to treat the whole crew..." He sighed.

Anika nodded. "And we probably won't get any supplies any time soon. Not in this weather. You can hardly see your hand in front of your face outside in this snowstorm."

"Yes, that worries me, too. But we'll see."

"Did you actually notice that only men have been affected so far? There hasn't been any strange behavior in women yet."

Matthew looked at her, puzzled. "You're right! I hadn't even thought of that. But we can test it right now. Would you volunteer to be a test subject, and have an EEG done?"

"As long as your weird gel doesn't gum up my hair." Anika laughed.

About 20 minutes later, the results were in. Matthew applied his familiar filters and analyzed the wave patterns of the recorded brain waves. "Looks totally normal. No abnormalities like in the men—or they're so faint you can't detect them. I think you're all-clear."

"I don't think I've ever been so happy to be a woman," Anika commented. "But don't get me wrong, I've always been happy to be a woman, but now I am a little more so."

"Well, that also means that if push comes to shove and we run out of medicine, you women will have to hold down the fort here—and lock the men up somewhere where we can't do any harm."

Anika looked at Matthew for a while, wondering if he meant it literally. But she couldn't see the hint of a smile on his face. She finally nodded and stifled a casual reply. "You're serious?"

"Yes, absolutely. I can't stand the thought of going

crazy out of the blue and lashing out at others. We have to stop that from happening. At least until the weather calms down and we can get help," Matthew declared.

"You're right, of course. What does Sigurdson have to say about it?"

"He gritted his teeth as usual and growled something in Norwegian. But I think he accepted that as a stopgap measure. I understand he had a pretty big fight with Harry yesterday. So, they seem to be affected as well. I think they know that."

"We need to keep working on a solution. The answer lies down there, in the artifacts—and, of course, in the ship. If only we could get inside..." She paused, as if a new thought had just occurred to her.

"What is it?"

"If this signal only works on men, maybe women could get down there unscathed?"

"That's a risky theory, though," Matthew agreed. "I've only examined you so far. And besides, it's not for sure that the absence of the spikes in your EEG automatically means that contact with this alien technology can't harm you."

"Yeah, sure. That's true, of course. But sitting around here waiting for either the storm to blow the roof off or someone to come at me with a knife doesn't sound appealing. I like to be in control of things myself."

"I know, but I don't want to rush into anything and then witness the first female berserker being created."

"I guess we'll weigh our options for now."

Matthew nodded and got up to retrieve surgical instruments from the sterilizer. "Speaking of berserkers. Want to assist me?"

"With what?"

"I still have to do an autopsy on the miner. I want to know if this radiation also had physical effects on his brain. This is a once-in-a-lifetime opportunity."

"Sure. I told you, anything is better than waiting for some catastrophe to happen. Even an autopsy."

18

At about 10:30 a.m., Mi sat next to the nearly completed prototype of her signal jammer, which she planned to use to disperse—or at best even neutralize—the harmful radiation from the ship. She took one last look at the design and then adjusted the antenna alignment. The device consisted of a digitally controlled, multispectral signal generator, a powerful transmitter unit, and a whole series of dual antennas capable of radiating a broad frequency spectrum between two kilohertz and five megahertz over several subranges. To Mi's left was a laptop that she had connected via USB to the mobile signal analyzer she used earlier in the cave with the petroglyphs. She checked the amplitudes and frequency ranges of the ship's signal to match the counterpart produced by her jammer to the original from the ship as accurately as possible. For this purpose, she had already started a recording last night.

In the meantime, she collected fourteen hours worth of data, ensuring she had a good picture of the sequence of the transmitted message, or at least of the superficial structure. She knew nothing about what was going on on a deeper level yet. It was all still a mystery. However, she knew with certainty that the content repeated itself with minor variations in the analog portion of the signal, or rather the interference. The second thing she knew was that the signal was still increasing in intensity. The power had increased by 1.63% since last night. Although that wasn't a major jump in intensity, it was still worrisome because it wasn't clear if the increase would continue. And if the signal continued on a linear trajectory, then in two weeks, it would have already increased in strength by half. She couldn't say for sure yet, but initial measurements showed that it was possibly turning into an exponential trend. That, in turn, meant that the signal strength would simply explode at a certain point—with uncertain effects. So, she was aware of the extraordinary importance of constructing an effective countermeasure.

She thought back to the fight that had occurred in the canteen that morning. She was shocked by the furious rage with which the two otherwise very calm men had attacked each other with. Something like that had to be prevented. Under no circumstances did she want to get in the middle of a fight between two colleagues mutated into beasts. She expected that the jammer would likely be the best way to stop that. But Mi was faced with a problem. She could not test her device. Harry and Sigurdson had made it very clear that she was not to use it until she had received clear instructions to do so. And she understood that. But that meant she didn't know if the device even worked as intended in an emergency—a concept she found hard to swallow. She liked to be prepared and had double and triple checked everything for herself before telling others. But she had to adapt. Up here, improvisation was what was needed most of all now. Maybe she could start a simulation? Maybe she could take a Jeep and drive down to the harbor to test the jammer there at a sufficient distance from the ship? She looked at her mobile measuring device. She could use it to check the mode of action and compare whether her jammer was correctly reproducing the frequency spectrum and timing. But she couldn't possibly pull off such an operation alone. The weather was lousy. She would have to ask someone to clear the road with the snowplow first. Or she could take the remaining snowmobile. However, she had no idea whether she could even drive such a vehicle.

A ping from her laptop startled her out of her thoughts. It was a mass email from Matthew, sent with high urgency. She opened it and read. Matthew reported that he had been able to alleviate the symptoms with medication, or possibly even suppress them altogether. Mi relaxed a bit. It bought her more time. But it was certainly not a permanent solution. Who knew if the drugs would still work once the signal was twice as strong.

Mi started another computer-aided diagnosis of the jammer, which was all she could do at the moment. At least she had virtual confirmation that the device was working under laboratory conditions.

Anika pressed a thick gauze bandage in front of her nose, which she had soaked with peppermint oil. Her eyes watered, but that was still better than the stench. She knew now that she couldn't stand the smell of decay setting in and of bones being sawed apart. The mummy they had examined the other day had given off virtually no odor after all these centuries, but the miner's corpse was in the worst condition imaginable—and it was noticeable in the stench. Anika had therefore somewhat withdrawn while Matthew sawed open the skull.

So far, the autopsy had revealed nothing unusual—or rather nothing unexpected. Of course, the man had many wounds from the encounter in the mine. There were lacerations, abrasions, and broken ribs. But none were life-threatening. Everything indicated that he had simply frozen to death on top of the mountain.

Matthew had saved the most exciting part for last: the examination of the brain. He turned off the bone saw and set it aside. "There, the worst is behind us." He carefully removed the skullcap and inspected the brain. "Pass me the large metal bowl, please," he asked Anika. She came closer, picked up the desired bowl from a small trolley and handed it to Matthew.

He made a few cuts with the scalpel and then removed the brain from the skull. He placed the bowl directly under the spotlight and examined the organ.

"An unusual amount of blood," he muttered. "I think he had multiple aneurysms in his brain. The tissue around it looks altered, too."

Anika dared to get closer and took a look. "I've never seen a real brain before. But these dark spots don't look normal, right?"

"No, they're not normal at all." He applied the scalpel and cut out one of the dark areas, which turned out to be a blood-filled cavity. Matthew shook his head. "It looks a little like a patient with Creutzfeldt-Jakob, but again, very different. There's definitely a physical change. And unless the man had a rare brain disease before that, I can't diagnose right now, I think we have to assume that contact with the ship triggered it."

"It probably also means that medication is not a long-term or permanent solution," Anika said.

"It's not. And I don't know if they would have worked on him at all. His transformation was stark. But I also expect that people might react differently. This whole phenomenon would be worth a doctoral thesis on its own.

At least one, if not several. We're just scratching the surface."

"We probably don't have time for more than that, either."

"I'll send an email to the hospital in Oslo and ask if they can do an MRI of Oddevold's head. Maybe you can see changes there, too."

Matthew had insisted that all the male members of the crew be treated with an appropriate dose of psychotropic drugs. Harry himself felt much more balanced again. But he also had to admit that the medication made him a little sleepy at the same time. But that was a side effect that was comparatively easy to bear.

And so, after Matthew declared Chef Svensson unfit for duty for at least 24 hours, Harry took over the lunch shift in the kitchen along with geologist, Linda Janssen. They were late with lunch, although the menu had been reduced to its simplest. They had pasta with tomato sauce and cucumber salad. Harry put two kilos of spaghetti into a huge steel pot and stirred the whole thing with a long, wooden spoon.

Linda stood across from him at the countertop, chopping herbs. Then, she picked up the large, wooden board and walked it over to Harry at the stove. She pushed the herbs with the knife into a bubbling pot of red sauce. The heat dissolved the essential oils and a spicy scent of parsley, basil, rosemary, and sage poured out.

"That smells good," Harry commented. "I don't think we'll get many complaints."

Linda smiled. "No, I don't think so either. But you can't go too wrong with the dish, either."

"How are you actually getting on with your work?

There's been so much going on in the last few days that I haven't had a chance to ask you about it."

"Oh, that's okay. I haven't made any sensational discoveries. I've just been brooding and hypothesizing."

"What kind?"

"Well, I was wondering how a ship got all the way inland here. And especially how it could have ended up in a cave."

"Yeah, that's a huge inconsistency."

"Exactly. That's why I took a closer look at the measurement data from the ice cave. I looked at the peripheral areas to find out how far the cave extends in each direction. The radar and terahertz scans revealed more than I expected."

Harry continued stirring the pot of noodles, listening with genuine interest.

"So, it's most likely that it's not a cave at all. It's just a cave entrance. The ship is lying in front of it in a kind of hollow or on a rock overhang. That's why it's enclosed with ice. Over the decades and centuries, a glacier has formed and pushed over it like a blanket."

Harry stopped stirring. The sauce was already bubbling out of the top of the pot.

"Um...may I?" Linda reached for the stove's control knob and turned off the gas supply.

Harry winced. "Yeah, right. I've been drifting off in my mind. And these pills are making me a little drowsy. But the findings sound plausible. It doesn't explain how the ship got here, of course, but it at least makes things a little less mysterious. And I'm grateful for any clarification."

"Thank you. I think this hollow where the ship is lying might be a former lake or a river. Maybe it came this way.

We can't possibly know what it looked like here 2,000 years ago. The landscape changes with the climate. If my measurements are correct, the ice covering the ship has become very thin. The glacier is disappearing. Maybe in ten or fifteen years, it would have come up on its own." She shrugged. "As I said, most of this is just hypothesizing, but of course, I'll send another detailed report when my kitchen duty is over."

"Thanks. Now we'd better get the food out before people starve." Harry poured out the pasta water and then walked into the dining room with the pot. "Grab some food! he shouted, setting the pot on the buffet table.

It was late afternoon and Matthew started the download again—the third time he had tried to download the data from the Oslo hospital. The storm obviously had a major impact on the satellite connection. Again and again, the internet broke down, and he had to restart the process. He also couldn't explain why the MRI results were 420 megabytes. That was far too large. Or was the size just displayed incorrectly?

Matthew stared at the blue status bar, which kept stalling but finally neared 90% completion. If he had been religious, he would have folded his hands and asked for help. But Internet problems were probably not the domain of supernatural beings, no matter what spiritual direction they came from. A pop-up appeared and announced that the download was successful. Matthew breathed a sigh of relief. Finally! He opened the compressed zip archive and extracted the contents to the server.

He paused. There were the MRI images—but hardly more than 20 megabytes in size. The rest was taken up by a video simply named Patient_A18776.mp4. He opened it. Oddevold was lying on a treatment couch, strapped down by his arms and legs. Looking straight, he spoke incessantly in Old Norse. Matthew didn't understand a word, but it immediately reminded him of the fragments Björn had muttered during his nocturnal seizure. Oddevold seemed almost deeply relaxed. Had they treated him with psychotropic drugs, too? He talked monotonously to himself, as if he were reciting the extensive changes in tax regulations or a similarly dull matter.

Matthew looked at the playing time: 18:47 minutes. This was obviously more than just a few incoherent scraps and phrases, as Björn had mumbled earlier. He had to show this to Anika. If anyone understood what he was saying, it was her.

"What's up?" asked Anika when Matthew knocked on her office door fifteen minutes later.

"Are you busy?"

"I was just going to do some research," she explained.

"Yes, the connection will be gone soon. It took me a few tries to download the data from Oslo. But it may have been worth it."

"In what way? Does the MRI reveal anything?"

"No, it actually looks quite normal. There was a video with it, of Oddevold reciting archaic verses. Maybe the video will help us."

"Where is it?"

"On the server. I'll show you." Matthew walked around the desk to Anika's laptop and opened a file. The computer loaded for a few seconds, then began playing the recording.

Matthew sat down next to Anika and they both

listened to the researcher's words while Anika jotted down notes on a pad. After about five minutes, she paused the video and turned to Matthew. "I understand it rudimentarily, but I need to transcribe it at my leisure. It's very old-fashioned, like the dialect Björn spoke. A lot of it is ambiguous. I can't tell exactly what he means. To better understand it, I have to make comparisons with other language strains."

"But do you understand any of it?"

"I think it's some sort of guide."

"Guide? On what?"

"Well...possibly for the artifacts down there. Or they're clues in the use of this technology."

"That would be incredibly useful," Matthew said.

"Provided I can manage to translate it."

"How long will it take?"

"Definitely a couple of hours, and I'll need access to technical literature and databases. If the internet really breaks down, it's going to be difficult."

19

Sigurdson sat at his computer in his security center, fighting drowsiness. He hated drugs and refused anything that could affect his body—or worse, his mind. At most, he allowed himself a single beer. He knew he was something of a control freak, which was the only reason he had become so good at what he did. A job like his took iron discipline. And it required him to face a number of hardships. Even more, he detested being forced by Matthew to swallow psychotropic drugs.

But on the other hand, he saw what happened to Björn. He saw how two otherwise calm men wanted to massacre each other in the kitchen over fried eggs. And in himself, he felt his emotions threatening to get out of control. The argument with Harry might have escalated if Mi hadn't shown up. So, he determined that enduring the slight drowsiness as a side effect was the better end of the deal and concentrated on the difficult hours ahead.

The requested reinforcements would not be arriving anytime soon. There was no way to fly them in in this weather. And by ship, with the current wind speeds, it would also take longer than the storm would even last. He only hoped that it would not get any worse. They were on their own for now. There was nothing more than his three staff members, the batons, and the four rifles to defend everyone. Still, Sigurdson tried to look on the bright side. If they were cut off from supplies and isolated here, the same was certainly true for their adversaries: the people who poisoned Torger Hansen. Sigurdson desperately wanted to know who was behind it all. But new intelligence was still a long time coming.

Sigurdson lifted a cup from the table and took a large sip of hot coffee. Then, he pulled the keyboard toward him and began to draft a short memo, outlining a contingency plan based on what Matthew had suggested. He would prepare to split into groups in case things got worse. If the storm became more severe, they would have to leave the settlement buildings and seek shelter underground. Sigurdson divided the team into three categories for this purpose. If there was no other way, all the women would seek refuge in the shelter, isolated from the men who, despite medication, were still exposed to the influence of the alien technology. He would send them to the old supply rooms of the Svea I mine where they could hold out for a day or two, although it would be anything but comfortable. The third group consisted of only five people, besides himself, his three security guards, and Matthew, a former U.S. Army staff medic who could handle extreme situations. This third group would stay in the settlement and protect it as long as possible.

Sigurdson still hoped that it would remain only a theoretical plan, a last resort that wouldn't need to be implemented. But after everything that had already gone wrong on this mission, it was rather unlikely that things would play out any easier than expected. It was more likely that the opposite would happen. Sigurdson knew the imponderables were huge, and the weather was probably the least of their worries.

He saved his memo, printed out a few, and copied the contents into a mass email. He looked at the clock. It was just before 6:00 p.m. Most were probably at dinner by now. He planned to go over to the cafeteria, post the printouts on the bulletin board, and instruct everyone to memorize the plan. In case of alarm, anyone could join his group and head to the defined assembly point.

Anika once again skimmed the transcript she had made over the past three and a half hours. She had gone through the video countless times, fast-forwarded and rewound, listened to passages over and over again with her headphones, transcribed them, and checked fragments she couldn't translate against databases of ancient Nordic dialects. Matthew left her alone more than two hours ago. Since then, she sat alone in her office, pottering away. Curiosity had even made her forget the incessant howling of the storm outside. But now it was 9:30 p.m. and she was clearly feeling the hypoglycemia. Due to her fascination with Oddevold's words, she had completely forgotten to eat dinner. Her stomach growled and her concentration weakened. She could no longer ignore it. Anika got up and left her office. She hoped that she would still find a passable snack in the canteen.

She crept through the deserted hallway over to the dining room and stepped through the door. She walked past the empty buffet into the kitchen, grabbed two leftover rolls, packaged salami, and an apple, then returned to the dining room.

"Good evening," a voice suddenly said, and Anika almost dropped her food in shock.

"Herregud! Förbannad!" she cursed in Swedish. She recognized Sigurdson, who was sitting alone in the semi-darkness at one of the back tables drinking a beer.

"I didn't mean to scare you," Sigurdson said calmly, taking a sip.

"You scared me half to death!" replied Anika, walking over to him. "Why don't you turn on a light?"

Sigurdson shrugged his shoulders. "I like it this way."

She eyed him for a moment, then pulled up a chair and sat with him. "Then, you can at least keep me company as compensation."

Sigurdson took another small sip of the beer.

Anika bit into a roll as they sat in silence.

"I'm sure you're a good listener," Anika commented.

The corner of Sigurdson's mouth twitched as if to suppress a smile. "Yes, that's what my job entails. Always listen carefully, take in all the information, but never reveal much about yourself," he explained.

"Sounds lonely."

Sigurdson tilted his head and twisted the corners of his mouth. But he didn't respond to the comment. "And you? Don't you know how to sleep? Why do you steal snacks from the kitchen at night?"

"I was working on a transcript. The clinic in Oslo sent a video recording of Oddevold more or less explaining what the artifacts in the cave are about. It's tedious. I don't understand everything and a lot of it is very convoluted, but I think I'm starting to get an idea of what they're for."

Sigurdson raised his eyebrows and leaned forward, as if to encourage Anika to keep talking.

"Yes, so he speaks of a heritage of the gods and the traditions of the pilgrims. He says it's a riddle that leads to the attainment of wisdom, a puzzle that only the truly virtuous are capable of solving." She shook her head. "It's very flowery language and cryptically worded. I don't know how much can be taken literally. But if I understand it correctly, it's about linking these artifacts to access wisdom."

"What about the ship? Does he explain what it's all about?"

"He speaks of the stranded. Those who were chosen to travel to a new world but found nothing but death. There is also a warning that bold men who are too bold must beware of trying to bring the truth to light without the blessing of the gods."

"And these stranded pilgrims you're talking about, did they create the drawings, too?"

"It seems so."

"Strange. After all, they obviously had access to highly developed technology that could even preserve this knowledge for millennia. Why then did they bother to painstakingly carve it all in stone again?"

"I don't know. It's possible that the pilgrims themselves didn't have that kind of power."

"But who?"

"The gods."

"You mean Odin and Co? The gods my people believed in hundreds of years ago?" Sigurdson put on a skeptical expression.

Anika bit into her apple and didn't answer.

Sigurdson sighed. "Very well, let's throw all reason overboard. We can't reconcile this with what we think we know about history anyway."

Anika chimed in. "Coming up with a theory that considers what we've discovered doesn't have to be unreasonable. We can go off of logic alone and the facts we know. There were obviously people here, and much earlier than was previously thought. And they came on this ship, which houses some kind of technology. What does that tell us?"

"This ship is not from that time?"

"Or it's not of this world."

"Ha, that's a big claim," Sigurdson said. "What was the name of that crazy Dutch guy who's been claiming for decades that Mayan temples are UFO landing sites?"

"Erik van Jänike," Anika said without a hint of mockery in her voice. "Look, I've always thought this paleo-seti thing was a joke, too. But think about it. How might a fairly primitive population at the time have reacted to an advanced race with technology? I would imagine that they thought these beings were wizards or gods. After all, from their point of view, they possessed superhuman powers," Anika explained.

"They thought the technology was magic, okay, that sounds plausible. At least if you go with that theory. But then what happened to the gods?"

Anika nodded slowly. "That's a very good question. If we think that that ship down there bears the name Naglfar—the name of the ship that's supposed to appear at the Twilight of the Gods—then perhaps we could assume that they were destroyed with it. Or that over the centuries, the truth has been transfigured and it was not a warship at all, but something else entirely. Perhaps a lifeboat."

"Doesn't it speak in favor of a warship when you look at the fatal effect it has on humans?"

"I somehow don't think it's intentional. If it is, why would the people in the cave have put themselves in such danger?"

"Were they prisoners, perhaps?"

"Unlikely. It doesn't make sense. The message speaks of pilgrims following the path of the gods. And they did that voluntarily—at least that's what it sounds like. So, I think..." her voice trailed off, as if reconsidering how robust her hypothesis was. "I think the gods may still be in there."

"That a big speculation. But even if they were, they're probably long dead. Or do you think these gods are truly immortal?"

"No. I guess not."

"And the signal?"

"Well...it could be an automated process that emits the signal. Maybe there's a mechanism that waits for a response? A distress signal, maybe. I don't know. Human contact probably woke it up."

"I wish we hadn't done that," Sigurdson muttered, finishing his beer. "Thank you for the stimulating conversation. We should talk things over with Harry tomorrow. But don't get your hopes up that we'll be able to test your theory soon. When the storm passes, we'll evacuate the station. It has become too dangerous." Then, he left the canteen before Anika could even respond.

Anika watched him and tried to figure out what kind of man Sigurdson really was and whether he was serious about wanting to abort the mission. The thought filled her with horror. There was no way she was going to give up. Especially not now, when they were so close to really discovering something—and not just anything, but a life-changing, history-altering discovery. Of course, she saw the dangers; she had experienced them firsthand. But her urge to explore was now fully awakened. From now on, she would use every remaining minute to figure out what was going on here.

20

Last night had been short for Anika. Even before most of the crew had woken up, she had packed up her laptop, the transcript of the video, and a handful of snacks from the office and left for the cave with the petroglyphs.

She knew the content of the video almost by heart, considering she watched it a hundred times yesterday. And now that she was standing in front of the large images from days long past, they suddenly made much more sense. She recognized fragments of what Oddevold had explained. She also recognized the artifacts of which he had spoken in the remains of the destroyed drawing, next to the lock. Those artifacts stood in the burial chamber as if randomly selected yet seemed to have a much greater significance. Anika put on gloves and went into the burial chamber. She carefully took all the artifacts out of the niches and brought them over to the large cave. If this was a puzzle, a riddle, then she should be able to solve it.

She placed all the items on the floor in the middle of the cave and then sat down on a Styrofoam board that she had collected from a storage room. The cave was cold, even through her thick jacket, and it got all the frostier when she wasn't doing any physical activity.

She began to examine the artifacts more closely. However, she was always careful not to touch them with her bare hands in case what had happened to Oddevold might happen to her. She pulled the bulbous vessel toward her that revealed Loki's stone hidden in the wall. Judging by its look look, it would have had to be used to hold some sort of liquid. It was one of the more practical artifacts, as was the knife she had found in the burial chamber. The other artifacts were likely ritual objects or works of art: a statue carved from soft stone, a wooden staff decorated with patterns, an amulet, a shimmering, light pink crystal, and a semicircular object that could best be compared to the hull of a ship or a horse-drawn carriage.

She turned the bowl in her hands and looked at it from all sides. Suddenly, a small engraving caught her eye. It looked like the old Futhark rune for the letter L. Did this L stand for Loki? Was that why the shell had been able to bring the stone out of hiding? She flipped open the laptop and opened a directory of runes with notes on the various meanings they could have according to popular theories. She scrolled through the entries and found the entry for the rune Laguz. This not only represented the sound L, but was also considered the rune of the sea, from which life sprang. "Laguz stands for the unformed life, for still unformed projects," Anika read. This was the kind of information she was looking for. She knew she had to think less analytically and much more symbolically. This was an ancient mystery, something mystical. It could not be solved with the pure teachings of science. Once again, she spun the artifact around and then set it down. So, was this a container for water? For a part of the sea of life, perhaps? Anika made notes on this and turned to the next.

She decided on the knife, the edge of which was decorated with ornaments. She inspected it closely and discovered numerous cross-shaped structures. The knife had the letter X all over it. However, this letter did not exist in the runic series. But there was a very similar looking rune, "Gibo" or "Gebo." The Latin letter G was assigned to this rune. The symbolic interpretation spoke of a gift, which this rune promised. But it was a gift for which something was taken in return. "This rune exhorts to always keep the balance between giving and taking. It holds a gift but expects something in return." Anika read. A knife could give you something, perhaps hunting success? But it could also take life. She made a note of those thoughts.

The semicircular, elongated artifact was made of wood and was partially hollowed out inside. It was likely meant to represent a boat. She also found a rune inside, "Raidho," which had the letter R assigned to it. She skimmed the entry in the directory. "Raidho is considered in places to be the wheel of life. This rune represents our rhythm of life," it said. Anika furrowed her brow. The artifact did not look like a wheel at all. She read on. "Raidho is also mentioned in connection with Odin's chariot and generally stands for travel—both in earthly worlds and other worlds." That already made more sense in this context. Traveling could also be done by boat.

Anika stood and stretched her legs. She walked over to the large mural and looked at the ship for a while. Was that its purpose? A journey to another world? But why hadn't it succeeded? Quite obviously, they were stranded here. Anika felt an urge stronger than before to solve this mystery. She would definitely not let herself be stopped now. There was no time to spare. And so, she turned around again and went back to the artifacts.

She picked up a bronze amulet with engravings, large parts of which were covered with a greenish patina. Hagalaz was emblazoned on the back. This rune stood for the H. In the directory, it was listed as the rune of transformation. "Things end and begin anew. What is destroyed is rebuilt. What dies is born anew."

On a carved wooden staff, among the ornaments, she found the rune "Ehwaz," which corresponded to the letter E. It represented the horse as a sacred animal in Norse beliefs and was therefore related to transportation. But the rune also symbolized partnerships and loyalty to fellow man.

On the shimmering, white-gray crystal, however, she found the rune "Isa," which was assigned to the letter I and ice. "Isa is a rune of silence, clarity, self-control," explained the entry in Anika's database.

The last thing Anika did was pick up the small statue carved out of stone. In principle, it looked like a human being, but the proportions were unbalanced. The figure was tall and thin and had unnaturally long arms and legs. On the back of her head, she also had an engraving: Ansuz—the rune of Odin. The Latin letter A was assigned to her. It was in the fourth place in the older Futhark and was considered a symbol of the great mystery and the so-called link to the gods. Anika also wrote a paragraph about it in her notes and then skimmed over all the entries again. Then, she typed the individual runes into one line each.

    ᚠ - L
    ᚷ - G
    ᚱ - R
    ᚺ - H
    ᛖ - E

ᛁ - I
ᚠ - A

Did the runes spell out a word? She went through the combinations in her head. Nothing jumped out at her. Then, she recalled the words Oddevold had spoken and matched the shapes and spellings she knew with the combination of runes. She murmured the words, "Riddle, gods, journey, chariot, truth, knowledge, heritage, sanctuary..." She faltered. "Holy!" she cried.

This was a sacred mystery after all.

She reassembled the runes. Only this one word came into question for the collection of letters.

ᚺᛗᛁᛚᚠᚷᚱ - Heilagr.

It meant holy or consecrated, possibly also divine. She was suddenly quite sure that this had to be the solution. She arranged the artifacts in the appropriate order next to each other and waited. The silence in the cave was almost as unbearable as her tension. Anika even held her breath. After a while, she realized it and took a gasping exhale and inhale. She had assumed that something had to happen, as it had when she discovered the stone. But nothing happened at all. Was it the wrong word after all? Or had she made a mistake?

A crunching sound jolted Anika out of her thoughts. She turned around and saw Matthew coming through the airlock into the cave.

He was carrying two small boxes in front of him. "I thought you'd be in here!" he said.

Anika looked at him in irritation.

"You didn't go to breakfast. And you weren't at lunch either."

"Lunch? What time is it?"

"12:30."

"That's impossible."

Matthew placed one of the boxes in front of her and opened it. The contents steamed in the cold cave.

"Lunch?" asked Anika.

"The leftovers. Svensson has taken charge of the kitchen again and has been frying steaks—in case there really are only emergency rations over the next few days."

"Smells great. Thanks, Matthew!"

"My pleasure." Matthew reached for the radio he wore on his belt and reported. "I found Anika, she's in the rock cave examining the artifacts." He looked at Anika and took his finger off the radio, "Sigurdson's been looking for you," Matthew shrugged.

Sigurdson's voice croaked from the speaker. "Roger that. Tell her to stand by. Give her the radio when you get back."

"What's wrong?" Anika asked while she took the food out of the box and started to eat.

"Sigurdson is getting everyone ready to activate the contingency plan. You know, the one from the memo."

Anika nodded. "The storm is fierce. It already took me half an hour to get here this morning. Is it worse out there now?"

"Pretty rough. Sigurdson says if we miss the right time, we might not get back into the shelters."

"You seem pretty calm about all this," Anika remarked.

"I used to be a doctor in the army, so you learn how to deal with extreme situations. Besides, you're safe in the mountain. It has withstood wind and weather for thousands of years. Hardly anything can happen to us there. The bigger danger is that we'll run out of medicine."

"I see. And what's in the other box? Dessert?" asked Anika.

"No. The stone you and Mi found. And the implant. We are to store them the box here while everyone is as far away from it as possible. The plan is for the men to go to the old mine. And Sigurdson doesn't want the stone anywhere near there, even if everyone is on medication at the moment."

"May I?" asked Anika, pointing to the box. "I want to look at it again while I have the chance."

Matthew nodded and pushed the box over to her.

Anika took off the lid and immediately heard a strange buzzing sound. "Has it been doing that for a while?"

Matthew looked into the box. "No, that wasn't there until just now." He looked around and pointed to the artifact collection. "What's that?"

"The solution to the riddle Oddevold had spoken of. At least I think so."

"The stone might think so, too," Matthew concluded.

Anika looked back and forth between Loki's stone and the artifacts. Then, she pushed the box a little closer. The buzzing became louder and a little higher in frequency, then lower again. It sounded like a natural resonance, like a kind of wordless chant. The implant, which was next to the stone in a smaller box, also seemed to vibrate.

"Fascinating! They react to each other," she said.

"We'd better stop," Matthew agreed.

Anika looked at him piercingly for a while without speaking. Then, she explained, "I had an interesting but also disconcerting conversation with Sigurdson last night. We were alone in the canteen. He told me very clearly that he was aborting the mission and evacuating everyone as soon as the storm passed. This is my last chance to make a significant discovery. And I sincerely hope that you, of all people, won't try to dissuade me."

Matthew eyed Anika. Her words had sounded more serious than ever before. There was no hint of irony or doubt in them. Her face reflected pure determination.

At that moment, the radio crackled. "Grant, come in. Are you still in the cave? We want to start phase 2," Sigurdson announced.

Anika continued to look Matthew directly in the eye, completely unimpressed by the radio message.

Without averting his eyes, Matthew reached for the radio and raised it in front of his face. "I'm stowing the artifacts now; I'll be right over to the collection point." Matthew put the radio away again. "Alright. I think we have a few minutes left. But please be extremely careful."

Sigurdson paced restlessly up and down the cafeteria. Hadn't he told all the men to get ready at 1:00 p.m.? He puffed, looked around, and counted all those present again. There were still five missing. Damn! Had they not taken his memo seriously? He felt anger boiling up inside him.

At that moment, John McFarland came into the room with a cardboard box and began handing out medications to all the men. "Björn, please take yours right away, the others in two hours at the latest. And please try to stay calm despite the current difficult situation. These are the last of our supplies; we have to divide them well until we get more."

McFarland walked toward Sigurdson and held out a small box with three pills in it. Sigurdson stared at the pills. He was reluctant to take them. But he knew he had to set a good example. And the fact that he had just reacted so irritably again showed that he needed them. McFarland was right. They all needed to stay calm. Especially now. He took the pillbox and put it in his breast pocket. "McFarland is right, we have to stay calm. The storm should be over in about 24 hours, then we can breathe easy."

Harry, Thoralf, and Elvar came into the canteen together with two other employees. "Excuse me, please," Harry said. "We were still storm-proofing the technology, and I just arranged for all data to be backed up to an external disk. I want to take a full backup with me to the mine in case lightning strikes here or everything blows away. But that's going to take a while, so I'll go back later and see what the status is."

Sigurdson nodded. "Alright. We have to divide the supplies now. The bulk will go to the mine with the 13 men, and we'll send some to the bunker with the women. My men and I will keep only the bare essentials here. I'd like to ask everyone to pitch in to make this go as quickly and smoothly as possible."

21

A steel, pitch-black tower thrust itself out of the storm-lashed sea. The sea was rough, even here in the fjord, some distance away. The tower was followed by an equally ominous black hull. Both barely stood out against the gray horizon beyond. It was mid-afternoon, but it might as well have been any other time of day. During the winter months, it didn't matter, especially not in this weather.

Boris Karlov, together with Captain Ali Zakayev, climbed up the tower of the Soviet diesel submarine and took position there. Zakayev took the controls at the small bridge and maneuvered the boat to what appeared to be a makeshift mooring just off Svea. They had decided against going ashore at the much larger Port Amsterdam further south. The jetties there were designed for coal freighters and were much larger and easier to approach. But the journey from there up to Svea would have proved arduous and lengthy in this storm. The jetty here would have to suffice, although mooring was not for the faint of heart.

On the other hand, the settlement was only a few hundred meters away beyond the runway. It could not be seen from here, but it was certainly there. There was no doubt that they had arrived at their destination. Navigation worked without major problems, even in this weather. Karlov didn't mind that they couldn't see the settlement in the driving snow. In fact, it was only an advantage, he thought. After all, it meant that no one over there would see his squad coming either.

Zakayev slowed down and gave orders below for two men to come up to moor the boat. A few seconds later, they climbed down onto the hull and scrambled forward. One of the men jumped over to the jetty. He misjudged, slipped, and almost fell into the sea, but he picked himself up and pulled himself ashore. The second man began to throw him the ropes. With nimble hand movements, the man tied the boat to the jetty.

"Excellent," Karlov said to Zakayev. "You've just earned your bonus." He patted him on the shoulder. "I'm going to get my men. It's show time!"

Anika took Loki's stone from the transport box and held it over the row of artifacts. She tried several positions and registered how the buzzing sound changed as she did so. As she got closer to the bowl with the Laguz rune, the previously wavering tone turned into a stable chord of several notes. It suddenly sounded harmonious and pleasant. She looked over at Matthew briefly, who was undecidedly swaying his head back and forth, as if unsure whether this had been a good idea. Anika ignored it. If you dared nothing, you gained nothing. She placed the stone in the bowl. It fit like a glove. A glow suddenly emanated from the bowl, becoming brighter and brighter, enveloping Anika and Matthew. The glow was pleasant in its own way. It was a warm white that made the cave around them fade away. They felt no fear and felt no urge to run away or call for help, either. They weren't even sure they could have done so if they tried. If they were trapped here in this light, they didn't mind.

The cave was soon gone and there was nothing around Matthew and Anika but a warm, wadded white. Anika tried to speak, but she couldn't. She couldn't communicate—at least not verbally. They looked at each other and sensed that the other felt the same. It seemed like a shared dream or a collective hallucination.

As if from a dense fog, a figure suddenly appeared. It simply stepped out of nowhere and stopped in front of Anika and Matthew. It was a man—a tall, muscular warrior perhaps. His body was wrapped in rough clothes. His long hair fell to his shoulders and his beard was unkempt. He fit the image of a primeval Northlander. Then, a woman joined them. She too appeared rough in the best sense—her long hair braided into pigtails. Her bright, blue eyes shone and a bronze amulet hung around her neck. They stood side by side, just as Anika and Matthew stood side by side. Silently, they lingered. It was as if they were looking at each other through an imaginary mirror across the millennia. No one spoke a word.

The man suddenly stretched out a closed hand, turned it around, and opened his fist. On the flat of his hand was a silver implant, exactly like the one they had operated out of the mummy.

Matthew looked at Anika almost as if to ask, What should we do? They weren't sure if this was reality or a vision. Without really wanting to, Matthew slowly reached out.

The man placed the implant on the back of Matthew's hand. Without pain or uncomfortable pressure, it slid through the skin and traveled underneath to the wrist, exactly where they had found it on the dead in the burial chamber. Matthew felt a tingling sensation, a calming effect, and an increased clarity of mind.

The two figures disappeared, and the white light from

before was now colored, projecting all around them. A scene made of the dancing light took shape: a plain in the north where a battle raged as lightning twitched in the sky and clouds piled up. Away from the carnage, a small group of six women and six men gathered. The two from just now were among them. They led the ten others to a mighty ship that hovered about a meter above the ground. It had no sails, no anchor, and none of the usual superstructure. They climbed in through a hatch in the stern of the ship. It closed. Then, it slid away slowly, floating up into the clouds above the raging battle. The scene faded into a gray mist. The ship rose higher and gained speed. But then it sank. It spun, crashed, braked, and bounced. Anika and Matthew saw nothing but ice deserts, bare rocks, and frozen sea. The ship landed in a dry lake surrounded by snow-capped peaks. Was this Svalbard 2,000 years ago?

The projection changed. They saw the underground caves where the petroglyphs were created as if in fast motion. They saw an excited discussion but could not hear what was being said. They recognized the artifacts that were brought into the cave and watched as a ritual took place. Energetic crackling was felt throughout the cave.

Then, suddenly, the burial chamber was also visible. They witnessed the death of these travelers. As if by magic, they lay in the tomb niches and the secret door closed in on them. The cave with the drawings remained empty.

Now, Anika finally saw the missing drawing that had been destroyed by the blast. It showed exactly what they had just experienced themselves. The bringing together of the artifacts, the solution to the mystery, and the revelation of the history of this place.

In the center of the cave was Loki's stone, which

slowly disappeared after a while, as if it vanished into thin air. Then, everything turned into pure white again. Anika and Matthew suddenly felt the coldness of the cave. It crept back as the vision faded. The two shook off the rigidity and slowly found their way around the cave, into the here and now. They were still kneeling before the artifacts just as before. The buzzing had disappeared and all was silent.

Matthew reached for his wrist; it itched. He felt something under the skin. "This can't be..." he gasped, feeling the lump more closely, which was exactly the shape and size of the implant they had operated out of the corpse.

Anika took his arm and ran her fingers over it. She looked at him, puzzled. "But...how? I thought that was a projection!"

Matthew shook his head. "I have absolutely no idea." He pulled the transport box toward him and looked inside. The implant they had removed from the mummy earlier was still there. "It must be a new one," he concluded. "But how come you didn't get one?"

"You're a man. I believe that even of the mummies, only half wore one. You remember, there were six men and six women."

Matthew nodded. "But why?"

"Maybe as some sort of protection? So, you won't be affected by the technology?"

"Very possible. Then the creators were probably aware of the side effects and tried to mitigate them."

"We need to keep exploring. If this is a way to get to the ship safely, then we should use it."

Matthew shook his head. "We can't go any further now. Sigurdson will go crazy if we don't follow his plan."

Anika looked at the clock. 2:00 p.m. "You go. I'm staying."

"What are you going to do?"

"I'm going to the ship."

"Are you crazy?"

"If I don't do it now, I never will. Sigurdson won't let any more scientists come here, believe me."

"You can't go down there. You don't have an access permit."

"I bet you have one. As a doctor, you must surely have the ability to get in anywhere in case of an emergency. Besides, you're one of Sigurdson's chosen."

Matthew's face stiffened. He didn't say a word.

"Look, I'm not asking you to come with me. It's perfectly fine if you open the floodgate for me."

He tried hard to smile, but failed.

Meanwhile, Sigurdson had moved all the men into the supply rooms of the old coal mine. They were shabby and had not been used for several years. There was still a thick layer of dust in the corners. In their haste, they had only made a makeshift sweep and set up cots. Several gas heaters fought the cold, and outside in the tunnel, a diesel generator rattled away, providing electricity for the lights and a few other smaller electric heaters.

Nevertheless, Sigurdson was satisfied with the improvised shelter. They had brought in enough sleeping bags, blankets, and supplies to get them through the next 24 hours. There were even makeshift toilets, which offered no comfort, but were at least functional.

The men spread out in the large room. Some stood around rather haphazardly, some had gone straight to lie down, and others were reading or watching videos on their smartphones.

Sigurdson once again let his gaze wander over the entire room. The only thing missing was Harry Stadler, who was still copying his data. Sigurdson hated that he wasn't there yet and that he couldn't seal the room as planned. But Stadler had insisted on checking the backup again before taking it to the mine. And Sigurdson couldn't order him not to. First, because it was important to back up the data, and second, despite everything, they were on equal footing. Still, Sigurdson felt growing anger inside him. He was damn well responsible for the security here. And in the current situation, it was irresponsible to let things slide. Time was running out.

Sigurdson walked toward the door, then turned back to the men. He thought he should say a few words in Harry's absence. He cleared his throat. "I know this is far from comfortable, but I think each of you will understand why we are taking these measures. So, all I can say is hang in there. It's only 24 hours."

Björn stepped forward and pointed to three large crates of beer cans. "That could make this go by much faster," he joked.

But Sigurdson did not comment. "Try to lie down and keep calm. When his backup is ready, Harry will join us and lock the door behind him. I'll repeat that it can't be reopened without a key. And we'll keep that with the women in the bunker. I'll take the ladies there now. Then, it's just a matter of holding out until we can safely leave here tomorrow." After these words, he stepped out to the rusty metal door and let it fall, clattering into the lock. It was already 2:10 pm. In five minutes, according to the schedule, all the women should be waiting at the canteen, ready to leave. He hoped that they were more disciplined than his male colleagues.

The exit of the mine was just coming into view when the radio hissed. Deep in the mine, there was no reception, and the old radio repeaters had been impossible to reactivate. Sigurdson ignored it; he already knew the static. But then he stopped abruptly and held the radio to his ear. A croak. Fragments of words. And what was that rattling?

He ran, faster than before, to the exit, then stopped again. Gunshots could clearly be heard from the radio. A shiver ran down his spine. If he wasn't mistaken, they were machine guns!

22

Gunshots shattered the silent anticipation that had spread among the women in the canteen. Even over the howling of the storm, screams echoed. The women looked around in panic. Mi ran to the window. Outside was only swirling white against a night-black backdrop. Harry instinctively reached for the radio, intending to alert Sigurdson. He pressed the talk button. "Sigurdson! Do you hear that? There's shooting out there!" He received no reply, only static.

The door was pushed open, and half a dozen black-clad fighters rushed in, waving rifles. A big, bearded guy yelled in a Russian accent, "Get down! Everybody on the ground or we'll shoot!"

Harry wanted to step forward and address the attacker, but a dull pain in his left arm made him wince and he went down on his knees. He felt dizzy. His heart. "Not now of all times!" he thought. Harry jammed the talk button on the radio and slipped it into his jacket pocket. Then, he curled up on the floor.

The bearded Russian approached him and eyed him. "Who is in charge here? You?"

Harry just groaned and grabbed his chest.

"What's the matter, old man?" growled the Russian.

Mi came rushing over and knelt beside Harry. "He has a heart problem!" she cried.

"I told you to lie down," the Russian roared, banging Mi in the head with the rifle. She went down unconscious.

"I hope I now your full attention! This station is now under our command. Where is everyone else?"

The women huddled on the floor, none daring to say a word.

Harry sat up with difficulty and looked the Russian in the face. "Listen, it's not safe here," he gasped.

"The storm will be over soon. We don't care."

"No, that's not it. It's that ship down there. It's doing..." Harry clutched his chest again and tried to take slow, deep breaths. "Please, I have pills in my office. Let one of the women get them."

"No!" grumbled the Russian. "No one leaves this room until we are sure the entire crew is under control."

"The men are in the mine. They're not a danger, but the ship is sending out something that can drive you crazy," Harry explained with difficulty.

"Do you take us for a bunch of fools?" Then, he turned to one of the black-uniformed soldiers behind him. "Take the snowplow and get Nikolayev. Let him decide what we're going to do with this one."

The soldier nodded and walked out with brisk steps.

Sigurdson froze at the mine exit, listening to the radio transmission. All he could hear was hissing, wheezing, and distant muttering.

That was a nightmare. Apparently, the guys who had poisoned Torger Hansen had taken over the base with brutal force. What was he supposed to do? Get the men and attack? Hopeless. They had machine guns. What could he and a few scientists do with bare fists against heavily armed soldiers? His own men were probably already dead. How could he prevent more casualties? What were these guys even doing here?

Sigurdson knew there was only one logical answer: the ship. And to all appearances, they knew of no scruples that would stand in their way.

Sigurdson turned around and ran to the storage room just beyond the mine entrance. He had made a very useful discovery during the last inspection. He yanked open the door and ran inside. From a tin cabinet on the far wall, he took several packets of explosives, detonators, and cables. He put everything in an old backpack lying around and sprinted back to the exit. If his plan was to succeed, he had to hurry.

Matthew held his access card up to the reader next to the airlock and a green light followed by a soft beep signaled that access was granted. He pulled the heavy steel door open a crack and paused. Without taking his hand off the handle, he looked back at Anika. He said nothing, but she noted the reluctance in his gaze.

"It's the right thing to do," she said tersely. "We're researchers."

Before Matthew could answer, the radio cracked, and the rattle of machine guns came out. Then, a panicked radio call from Harry came through, followed by screams. It took Matthew and Anika a moment to realize what was happening. Then, Matthew broke free of his stupor. "Get inside! Make it quick."

Anika didn't move. "No, we have to help them!" she said firmly. "Those were machine guns."

"Yes, they were machine guns, damn it. What are you going to do? Throw your notebook at them? Or the artifacts?"

Anika ran to the center of the cave, packed all the

artifacts and Loki's stone into the transport box, and returned to Matthew. From the radio, they heard the attackers' instructions and Harry's gasps.

Anika stared at Matthew. Her expression was tortured, as if she was fighting an inner battle.

"We can't help them," Matthew said calmly. "Not like this. But we can move this to safety." He pointed to the box.

Anika nodded.

"Let's go. We don't have time to waste." Matthew gently maneuvered Anika through the airlock and followed behind her. He closed the door, and they were alone in the narrow tunnel, at the end of which no one had been since the accident with the miner. In front of them lay the great secret and behind them lurked death.

Viktor Nikolaev strode into the canteen like a king entering his audience chamber with his waiting subjects. He settled down in a chair next to Harry and eyed the barely conscious explorer. "Expeditions like this can be quite exhausting, can't they?" he asked in a sarcastic tone. "But be glad you've got the stress behind you now. We'll take it from here. Just sit back and relax as it all unfolds before you."

Harry gasped and tried to raise his hand.

"Well, I think you've earned your retirement." Nikolayev looked around the canteen. "Quite a surplus of women. Aren't there any brave men here?"

Boris Karlov stepped next to Nikolayev. "They should be in the mine, for security reasons," he said.

"Alright. How about the ladies bring us up to speed? And where is this Sigurdson? I only counted three guards outside."

None of the women answered.

"I have already sent two people out to look for him," Karlov explained.

"Tie them all up, then send the rest of the men, too. I want everyone brought in. Then, go through the crew list. I don't want any surprises." Nikolaev leaned down to Harry. "And before you retire, I need two things. First, I want to know where you have my gold. And second, you'll tell me everything I want to know about that ship down there."

Harry reared back. "Leave it alone!" he gasped, then slumped. The radio slipped out of his jacket pocket.

Nikolaev picked it up and handed it to Boris. "Look at that. A rat."

Sigurdson drove the Landrover as slowly and inconspicuously as possible along the snowy path from the old mine entrance toward the settlement. He even drove without lights so that he would not attract attention in case the attackers were out here. It was a difficult task in the driving snow, but soon, his eyes got used to the dim light. Surprisingly, he could see almost better than with headlights, which before had made the glaring snowflakes shine. But that was the only positive thing about the situation. The storm was shaking the car and Sigurdson was sure that it would soon reach its peak. He headed for the entrance to the Svea II mine, still listening to the radio message. Now, the voices were clearer. The content of the message, however, did not please Sigurdson at all. A cold, sober voice came from the loudspeaker. His instincts told him this was someone who would walk over corpses. This man was also most likely Russian, but his accent was barely audible, and he spoke in a distinguished and considered manner. This was no mercenary, and so, this had to be the one calling the shots. What if this madman and his mercenaries got to the ship and were exposed to his influence? That would be a disaster. Sigurdson gingerly stepped on the brakes and brought the car to a halt in front of the entrance to Svea II. It was clear to him what had to be done. He would have to destroy the ship down there before it fell into the wrong hands. Maybe they should have done it much earlier.

The radio message ended with a crackle. After a few seconds, the grumbling voice with the strong Russian accent he had heard at the beginning answered again. "To all those still out there. Make your way to the canteen and you won't be harmed. Do not refuse. If my men find you, it won't be good for you."

Sigurdson shook himself. "Bastard," he screeched, banging on the steering wheel. But he didn't answer the radio. As much as he would have liked to tell the guy directly what he thought about him, it was tactically wiser to maintain radio silence in any case. He had to keep the guys guessing about how many more men were unaccounted for. Sigurdson thought about Matthew and Anika.

Shit!

Hopefully, they also kept radio silence and did not run straight to their doom. The mercenaries had no way of knowing where they were. Sigurdson grabbed his backpack and jumped out of the Jeep. Through the storm, he ran toward the mine entrance. There, he held his access card up to the reader and the airlock opened. He slipped through. The wind tore at the door, making it all the more difficult to close. But he succeeded. He locked it manually from inside but knew that wouldn't do much good if pressed. Those who had machine guns surely had provisions for such cases.

But they hadn't been able to count on everything. For example, he was quite sure that the guys wouldn't manage to clear away tons of rock in a hurry and that's exactly what he planned to put in their way. He ran through the tunnel into the interior of the mine and toward the cave with the petroglyphs.

"Grant!" he roared.

No one was to be seen. He ran to the burial chamber and stuck his head inside. "Anika?" There was no one there, either. "Damn it!" he yelled. Had they followed the radio message after all? He hoped they hadn't been that stupid. Then, he remembered his task. He went to the airlock that led toward the ship and unlocked it. He crawled inside and closed the door again. Sigurdson swallowed the last pill that was given to him earlier. Then, on the inside, he placed two explosive charges on the ceiling about ten feet apart and inserted two detonators into the charges. He set the timer to two minutes and started the countdown. Then, he crawled as fast as he could toward the ship. He was about to find out how well the drugs really worked—if they worked at all.

Anika and Matthew crawled through the narrowing tunnel. Anika saw a faint light around the next bend. "It must be down there," she said. "It's probably the headlights from the cave."

"Be careful I think it's going steeply downhill."

They crawled around the bend. "There it is. I see the drop-off device for the robot."

"Well, we'd best lower ourselves down the rope," Matthew suggested.

Anika inspected the hooks and ropes, then took one of the wide risers and put it around her hips like a belt. She latched the hook and swung her legs over the opening. „Lower me."

Matthew operated the manual controls and the winch started whirring.

Anika slipped through the hole. She quickly took the transport box from the edge as the winch slowly lowered her down.

Meanwhile, Matthew grabbed a second harness and tied it around himself. "I hope this goes well," he muttered.

After about a minute, they both arrived at the bottom and were amazed at how large the cave had become. The radiant heaters had cleared ice. The melted water stood a few centimeters high on the floor.

"Now what?" asked Matthew, looking around the cave indecisively.

23

Dried blood was stuck to Mi's forehead. But she didn't let any pain show. She knew she would get back at that bastard—someday, when the opportunity presented itself. But for now, she would play along and pretend to follow orders. Maybe there would be an opportunity to sabotage the technology or secretly call for help.

Mi led the two men, whom she identified as Karlov and Nikolayev, toward the control room. "Here we are," she said, "we need the map now."

Karlov stepped forward and opened the door with the access card he had taken from the dead Harry Stadler.

"Everything has been shut down because of the storm. I have to reboot the systems first," Mi explained as she walked in and sat down at one of the computers. She began the startup procedure and initiated a covert satellite scan.

Viktor Nikolaev took a seat in the second row and Boris Karlov took position at the door.

Nikolayev pulled a cigar out of the inside pocket of his jacket and clipped the ends with a small pair of silver pliers. Then, he began to light the cigar, puffing the smoke into the room without regard for the delicate technology.

Mi twisted one corner of her mouth. This guy was a creep. She would love to kick the heel of his boot into his face. She had to smile at the idea.

"What are you grinning at!" Karlov yelled.

Mi winced. "Nothing, I'm just glad everything is still working. We had some tech failures when the storm hit."

Karlov eyed her suspiciously. "Don't try any dirty tricks, or I'll sink you in the Arctic Ocean. Got it?"

"I-I'm just doing my job." she stuttered.

"Let her do what she needs to do. She will cooperate," Nikolaev said. "Right?" he turned to Mi.

Silently, she entered more commands into the computer's terminal window. She quickly realized that the satellite connection was dead. Either the storm had cut it off completely or the attackers had disabled the dishes. Mi gulped. This was bad. Plan A would not succeed.

Images from the cave and the mine tunnels now appeared on the monitors. The transmission from the tunnel area, where they had installed the winch for the robot, was completely unusable, as the images were cracked and blurred. The robot in the cave transmitted a better—but somewhat disturbed—image of the ship.

"There, that's it. That's where I want to go," said Nikolaev.

"Why is the picture so unclear? Is it because of the storm?" Karlov prompted.

Mi made a few entries on the keyboard. "No, I don't think so. That ship down there is sending out a signal. Harry had tried to explain it to you. It's affecting people. And our technology, too. The closer you get, the more danger you'll be in."

"Really original. But you'll have to come up with something better to keep us away," Karlov said.

At that moment, they felt a vibration from the ground. The images shook as the camera on the winch shut off completely.

"What the hell was that!" shouted Nikolaev.

"An explosion," Karlov answered. "Someone blew

something up down there, by the looks of it. It was probably the access tunnel."

"Go check, damn it," Nikolayev blubbered. "What the hell am I paying you for?"

Karlov nodded briskly and ran out of the room.

Looking for another passage that might lead out of the cave, Matthew scanned the bare rock walls.

Anika put a hand on his shoulder. "Come on, we knew there were no other openings here. We've got to get inside the ship and somehow shut off that signal before it makes those guys up there even crazier than they already are. They've got hostages."

Matthew nodded. "I know. But how are we going to get into this thing?"

Before Anika could say anything, they felt a vibration and heard a loud bang. Dust trickled out of the rock opening above them.

"Shit, that was really close! Did they blow open the airlock?" Anika asked, aghast.

"I don't know. Go to the back. Hide somewhere on the ship."

Anika ran off in the direction of the hull.

Sigurdson was caught in the blast wave of the explosion and went down, belly first. He gasped from the pressure that was making his ears ache. But that wasn't the worst of it. With each meter he crawled further into the shaft, his headache increased in intensity. He felt like his temples were going to burst. This was the end for him. Would he make it to the ship to place the final charges?

He had hoped that blowing up the tunnel would buy

him enough time, but he hadn't counted on his body letting him down. It was that damn signal from the ship. He had to turn it off before he lost his mind.

He continued to crawl through pain. Finally, the winch came into view. Sigurdson heaved his legs over the edge and clutched the rope as tightly as he could. He slid down, unable to hold on, and finally fell more than he slid along the rope. He hit the ground, nearly passing out, overcome by the throbbing pain in his head. Another stab in his temples. He screamed and threw up his hands. Then, he caught sight of a figure.

"It's Sigurdson," Matthew yelled. He ran over to him and knelt beside him. "He's in a lot of pain!"

Anika came running and looked up at the hole. "Did he blow up the entrance?"

"I don't know. We have to help him. I think the signal is killing him."

Anika remembered Matthew's descriptions of the burst vessels in the miner's brain. She didn't think twice, jumped to the transport box, and ripped open the lid. She took out the box with the implant and held it out to Matthew.

He stared at it for a second, as if unsure what to do with it. Then, he reached out and opened the can. "We don't have a choice. If we wait any longer, he'll be dead. Let's hope it still works."

Sigurdson only whimpered and held his head as if to prevent it from bursting.

Matthew took Sigurdson's right wrist and turned it over. The implant landed on Sigurdson's arm and slid under the skin almost immediately.

After an anxious second of waiting, Sigurdson finally

relaxed. His panicked whimpering turned into a deep breath of relief. His eyes opened and he looked around cautiously. "I...I thought I was going to die," he said incredulously. "But now I feel so light."

"Lie still for now," Matthew advised, feeling Sigurdson's pulse.

Sigurdson shook his head. "We don't have time to rest. Russian mercenaries have invaded up there. And they're heading for that ship. We have to destroy it."

"Destroy?" Anika blurted out. "We don't even know if we can do that. Apart from that..."

"I don't see any other way," Sigurdson interrupted her and stood. He walked over to the robot and yanked out the camera's cables. "I'm sure they have access to the technology by now," he explained.

"Slow down," Anika interjected. "There's another way. We go into the ship and shut off the signal. Then, we hold out until reinforcements arrive."

Sigurdson tilted his head. "This technology is malicious. We have to destroy it. If it falls into the wrong hands, it would be a disaster."

"It's not malicious," Matthew said, raising his arm. He pointed to the lump on his wrist. Then, he grabbed Sigurdson's hand and turned it over. He held their arms side by side. "The alien technology is saving our lives right now. So, it's not inherently bad. I just think it's incompatible with something and causing fatal side effects."

"But that doesn't mean it isn't dangerous," Sigurdson insisted.

"Right," Anika agreed. "That's why we go in and shut it down. We have the key." She pointed to the transport box.

"There's a hatch at the back of the ship. We'll go in through that." She didn't wait for a response from Sigurdson, picked up the box, and headed toward the ship. Then, she turned again. "If my plan doesn't work, you can always blow it up from the inside. That's probably more effective anyway, isn't it?"

"There's something wrong," Elvar said sullenly. "Harry should have been here by now! Where is he?" For fifteen minutes, Hauge had been pacing back and forth in the old mine's supply room. He grew more nervous and irritable by the minute. "And what about that damn radio?" he snapped at Björn, who was sitting unconcerned at his side.

He looked up and fumbled the device out of his pocket. "It won't work anyway. We don't have reception this deep in here," he replied. He turned it on, but nothing came out of the speaker but crackling and static.

Hauge groaned. "We should bloody hell go and see!"

Björn shook his head. "No, we should stay here and wait. Just like Sigurdson said."

"Sigurdson!" echoed Hauge. "He's got a lot to say, of course. It's not like he's locked up in this hole here."

"Sit down, please," John McFarland said, putting a hand on Hauge's shoulder.

"Don't talk to me in that psychologist tone."

McFarland took a step back. "I just want to help. Do you want to get something to eat, maybe?"

"I don't want to eat; I want to know what's going on out there! I'm going to go out and see." Hauge walked over to Björn, took the radio from his hand, and then turned toward the door.

Thoralf Rønne and Peter Eriksson followed him.

"What are you guys doing?" asked McFarland.

"We're going with him. There's no way he should go out alone," Eriksson said. "And we also want to know what's going on. Harry really should have been here by now. And if something had come up, Sigurdson would have informed us. We all know how much importance he places on his plans."

"The storm is raging outside," McFarland protested.

"We'll just go as far as the mine entrance for now. Maybe we can get a connection there," Rønne explained, opening the steel door that led to the tunnel. He looked straight into the muzzle of a machine gun.

"Here are the guys we're looking for," said a black-clad soldier with a Russian accent. "Come along!"

Hauge sprang forward, grabbed the rifle, and tried to snatch it from the soldier. The soldier staggered but did not let go. A second soldier came from behind and brutally pushed Hauge to the ground. The first soldier, without a moment of hesitation, pulled the trigger. A deafening sound echoed off the mine walls. A hail of bullets riddled Hauge. He was killed instantly.

After a few seconds of silence, the soldier turned to the men in the supply room. "Anyone else want to play hero?"

Nobody moved. Some demonstratively took a step back.

"Good! Now come along, all of you. And don't do anything stupid—we have 300 rounds of ammunition with us."

Boris Karlov felt anger rising in him. What was this snob Nikolaev thinking, ordering him around like that? Yes, he had money like hay, but that didn't give him the right to charge at him like that, especially not in front of this cheeky bitch! Karlov shook himself. Why was he suddenly so frustrated?

He trudged on through the corridors of Svea II and approached a lock in the wall. This had to be it. He held Harry Stadler's access card up to the reader and was let in. Inside the cave, individual rocks lay about and dust hung in the air. A meter-long jagged crack ran through the large rock drawing on the wall. The detonation must have been violent. In one corner, he spotted an opening. He walked over and peered inside. It was a burial chamber with several bodies. Karlov moved to the left and looked around. On the opposite side, he found the remains of another completely demolished airlock. It was wedged between rocks. This must have been the entrance to the ship. He continued to look around. There was no other way. Karlov reached for his headset and established a radio connection. "Karlov here. The entrance is buried. There's no way through!"

"Damn!" roared Nikolayev. "Your incompetence is unbearable."

Karlov's face froze into a mask. His knuckles turned white as he squeezed the barrel of his rifle with his hands. He turned and stormed back through the tunnels.

But with every meter he moved away, the feeling of unbridled anger grew weaker. By the time he had fought his way through the storm to the canteen, he almost couldn't say what had upset him so much. Was there something to the story about those ominous signals from the ship after all?

He stepped through the door and went into the dining room where all the women and men were now sitting tied up. "Status?" he asked.

A soldier stepped forward. "We have all but three men. One attacked us in the mine and was eliminated, two are fugitives. According to the list, it must be security chief Øystein Sigurdson and station doctor Matthew Grant. Also missing is a woman, archaeologist Anika Wahlgren."

"You searched everywhere?"

"Two men are still out on the site checking the last living quarters. There are some abandoned buildings where they could be hiding."

Boris Karlov nodded. "Carry on," he ordered. Then, he walked over to the bound crew members. "Which one of you knows about mining technology?" he asked.

Thoralf Rønne and Björn Lange came forward by raising their joined hands.

"Alright, come with me!" ordered Karlov as he turned around. He murmured to one of the mercenaries as he passed. "You, guard them!"

Karlov went ahead to the technical control center and opened the door.

Nikolaev stared at him with a grim expression. His cigar had burned down to a stub. He demonstratively stubbed it out on the table and flicked it away. "Well?"

"Just about everyone is in the canteen. The last fugitives are being tracked down now. My men suspect they are in the abandoned shelters."

"Bullshit! They're down there." Nikolayev pointed at the screen, which had long since shown nothing but flickering. "They're doing who knows what down there. They're messing with us. Do you like being fucked with?"

Karlov did not answer but dragged Rønne and Lange into the room. "These two claim to know about mining technology."

Nikolayev stood and stepped forward. He eyed the two with an ice-cold stare. "Are there any more explosives?"

Rønne shook his head. "No, not that I know of. Sigurdson must have taken the last scraps. But there's drilling technology. We can dig our way down."

"Then do it!" said Nikolaev. "You have two hours. After that, I'll have one of the women shot every ten minutes. How does that sound?"

"Terrible," Björn responded. "Listen, I'm sure it won't get to that."

Karlov poked him in the back with the rifle. Björn doubled over.

A smirk appeared on Nikolayev's face. "Better get started then. Time is running out." Then, he walked past the men into the hallway. "I'm going to take a look around this old rascal's office. And take the Chinese woman to the others. I don't trust her."

Anika tugged one of the heaters forward toward the ship. "The stern must be here on the right. There's not much missing and we can get to it. Let's focus the radiators here," she said. She glanced at Matthew. "You remember that vision, don't you? The hatch at the stern? I'll bet we can open it with that rock."

Sigurdson shook his head. "She's betting! She's guessing! That's exactly what we need," he muttered, pulling the second heater closer. "Look, we've got to hurry. Things could escalate up there at any moment. We have to put a stop to this."

"We will," Matthew said firmly. "I'm just wondering what we're going to do once we shut down the signal. How are we going to get out of here?"

"Maybe there's a way. Linda Janssen sent around a report," Sigurdson suggested. "The geological evidence suggests there's no rock above us at all, just glaciers. Maybe we'll get lucky and find crevasses to climb out through."

"There's certainly no rock," Anika said. "We saw it in the vision. The ship landed in some kind of depression with a cave entrance at the edge. Over time, a glacier must have pushed over the rock overhang."

"That's consistent with Linda's report," Sigurdson said. "But she also writes that the ice sheet has become quite thin due to climate change. We may be able to break through."

Meanwhile, Matthew explored the exterior of the ship. He stroked his fingers over the hull and felt it. It felt like the tongue of an animal, rough and elastic. The material yielded to pressure, like a well-done steak, only this one had been coated with sandpaper. He also thought he could feel a very faint vibration underneath. But he wasn't sure if it was actually coming from the ship. Then, he turned back to the others. "We should take one thing at a time," he finally said. "Right now, we have to get inside this thing first . There's no way around it."

Boris Karlov pushed Mi into the dining room and pointed to the back corner. "Go join the other women." Turning to one of the guards, he said, "Tie them up and then check the supplies in the kitchen. I'm getting hungry!" With those words, he disappeared from the room.

Mi sat down cross-legged between geologist Linda Janssen and data analyst Dorothea Berg. One of the soldiers tied her hands together with thick cable ties that cut painfully into her skin. When he had moved away, Mi murmured to the other women, "Sigurdson has blown the entrance to the ship. They can't get any further. I don't know if that was wise, though. They're threatening to shoot us one by one if Thoralf and Björn don't clear the way."

Linda heaved a startled sigh.

"Shut up back there!" one of the soldiers bellowed grimly.

The women fell silent.

Mi looked around. All the men in the room seemed irritable, some restless. In her mind, the scenes from the other day, when Svensson and Rønne fought a brutal fight in this very room, were playing again. Perhaps it was a good thing that all the men were tied to chairs. For the moment, the drugs seemed to still be working to some extent. She was more worried about the guys with the guns. They had only been here a short time, but even they were already showing signs of agitation. They were certainly not immune to the effects of radiation from the ship. Mi thought hard about how to take advantage of that. Could they be played against each other?

Viktor Nikolaev inspected Harry Stadler's office. Why had this man dragged so much useless stuff all the way up here? This was not so much an office, but more a cross between a museum and an antiquarian bookshop. On the shelves along the wall and on the desk were exhibits from all over the world—probably finds from excavations: clay jars, rusty arrowheads, and carvings. Between them were thick leather-bound books, original manuscripts, and stained scrolls. The room, not even ten square meters in size, was full. For Viktor, it was all silly junk that had no value. The stuff wasn't even representative. Viktor was not interested in the history of any of the vanished peoples. He was interested in numbers and presentable achievements. On the latter point, however, he could understand what had moved the guy to collect this stuff. He thought they might have been trophies for Harry, and if they were, they weren't all that great.

Viktor sat down at the desk. Where the hell was his gold? If the miner's report was true, it had to be somewhere here. But where had they hidden it? Or had those damned Norwegians got hold of it? Had they taken it down there to the ship? It may have been worth just under a million, but it was his million.

Viktor felt a burning hatred rising again, creeping up his throat like a nasty heartburn. He had been wrestling with the anger even before he left Russia, but since he had been here, it had increased at least tenfold. Something about this place made him furious.

Viktor pulled another cigar out of his box and began to light it. If he kept smoking like this, the cigars would only last him two days. He took a deep drag and felt the smoke calm him down.

As soon as Karlov had rounded up the last of the fugitive men, he would send search parties into the mine tunnels and storerooms. The gold was surely still here somewhere.

The ice retreated further and further. Meanwhile, a gap had appeared at the stern of the ship, wide enough for a person to squeeze through sideways. Anika had the most petite stature and was the first to go. To her surprise, there was a cavity under the overhanging stern of the ship where no ice had penetrated. It was dim in there because little light leaked through the gap and she had no flashlight handy, making it difficult to look for an opening mechanism—a lever, a knob, or anything of the sort. Or maybe there was no such thing. She turned and crawled back to the crack. "Push the box through for me," she asked Matthew.

He tried, but the container was a few inches too wide. "Won't fit. I'm looking for tools. Maybe we can chisel away some ice."

"Yes, or just open the box and I'll take the stone out. I want to try if it really works as a key."

Matthew flipped open the latches on the container and tilted the box so that Anika could grab the stone with her hand through the gap. She didn't hesitate for a second. She did not think about whether it might be dangerous to touch the stone with her bare hands. She had long since trusted that the builders of the ship, the creators of the stone, would have warned her in the vision or, like Matthew, provided her with protection if she needed it.

She retreated into the cavity at the stern and held up the stone. All at once, a humming sound came from the ship.

"Is something happening?" shouted Sigurdson through the crack.

"Yes, it sounds like something's happening."

Then, there was a short hiss and a creak. Part of the hull in front of Anika folded inward. The opening was so large that a person could very comfortably walk upright into it.

"The hatch is open!" shouted Anika outside.

Meanwhile, Matthew was chipping away pieces of the ice with an iron bar. "I think we can fit through now."

Anika stepped halfway into the opening in case it tried to close again.

Matthew pushed the box with the artifacts through the gap, and the two men squeezed through one after the other. Anika leaned out of the ship's hatch and pulled Matthew through with one hand. Then, they were all in the hollow space behind the ship. "We made it," Matthew said.

"Let's go inside!" commanded Anika, grabbing the box and heading in the ship. It was as dim as the cavity under the ice.

"This better be a good idea," Sigurdson grumbled, following after her.

"We don't have a better one," Matthew said, going in last. The hatch closed behind them with a soft hiss.

Thoralf Rønne eased the heavy mine drill toward the wall in the rock cave. He nodded to Björn, who stood at the controls and started the drilling process. The large plate-like drill head started moving. It had taken them a good half hour to get the device here from the depot. Now, it stood in the cave like a foreign body—a smaller edition of tunnel boring machines, like those used in the construction of road tunnels. It was equipped at the front with a large rotating disc that gnawed away at the stone so that the device could mill a passage of about 1.20 meters in diameter.

Thoralf was sweating. He was not only more than warm from the work. He felt that the medication was slowly wearing off and his restlessness was growing. And the fact that soldiers were standing behind them, threatening them with weapons, did nothing to calm him down either. He made an effort to take a few deep breaths in and out, just as

McFarland had shown them. But it did little to reassure him. They hadn't told the guys that the drill usually only managed a foot an hour, and they couldn't tell how much boulder lay ahead. The old rock passage might well be buried along its entire length, or at least in large sections. Whether the drill would even work reliably with the loose rock was the next question. But they didn't want to bring that up to the ruthless fellows with the machine guns. There was still an hour and 15 minutes until this psychopath's ultimatum expired. Thoralf hoped that he would eventually realize that they simply needed more time and that it was therefore pointless to shoot anyone. But he didn't buy into that hope.

He looked again at Björn, who was monitoring the speed and forward motion. The usually jovial German also looked tense and anxious. They were both very close to the ship and the harmful signal source, protected only by the residual effect of the drugs. Thoralf cast a furtive glance at the two grim-faced soldiers standing two meters behind them, one with his rifle ready. The other, however, seemed distracted. He jerked his head every now and then or shook it briefly. Did he already feel the radiation? If so, things could soon get ugly.

Thoralf turned back toward the drilling machine. The milling process progressed fairly quickly, presumably because the stone was already loosened and no longer a solid wall. Nevertheless, smaller chunks kept getting caught and causing unpleasant scratching noises and rumbling in the machine.

"That growling!" suddenly shouted one of the soldiers from behind. "My head is going to burst."

Thoralf turned around very gently.

The man covered his ears.

"Drill faster, you idiots!" he ordered.

The other soldier was now talking to his colleague. Thoralf could tell that it was Russian. He had learned the basics of the language at school but didn't understand a word over the noise.

Björn turned around and reached into his jacket pocket.

"What are you doing?" shouted Thoralf.

Björn raised his hand and waved at the soldiers. He had a small box in his hand.

The man with the rifle stepped closer and looked at it. "What is this? Are you trying to poison us?"

"No, look at the package. These are painkillers," Björn explained.

The soldier took it from his hand and stepped back again.

"That thing down there is dangerous. It can drive you crazy," Björn explained.

"I'm not insane. I have a headache!" the second soldier growled.

"Take them. Maybe they'll help. That radiation affects the brain. I'm not lying. It made me run out into the ice in the middle of the night—barefoot!"

"That's enough!" the first soldier shouted. "Keep drilling." Then, he passed the pack of painkillers to his colleague and said something in Russian.

The second man took the package and tore it open. He squeezed two pills out of the blister and swallowed them.

Björn nodded to him and turned back to the drill controls.

Thoralf put a hand on his shoulder. "Well done," he

murmured. "Now, let's hope this works. I don't want to get caught in a hail of bullets."

24

Boris Karlov used Harry Stadler's RFID card to open access to the site's security center. He thought he could use the technology there to his advantage. Or maybe there were records of recent developments that would shed more light on the situation. He wasn't particularly comfortable with it all. It wasn't that he wasn't used to extreme situations or that unforeseen changes of plans were something exotic to him. But his abrupt emotional outburst at the mine worried him. It was completely out of character. He always aimed to complete a mission as soberly, precisely, and flawlessly as possible. There was no room for emotion. And he had noticed that Nikolayev was even more affected. So, if there was indeed any truth in the scientists' talk about the harmful influence of this place, it could be a hard-to-assess threat to the mission objective.

Karlov sat down at the computer and tapped a key on the keyboard. The monitors came to life, showing a blue-greenish background with a pop-up window in the middle. The computer demanded a password.

At that moment, a knock came at the door. Karlov went over to open it. Outside stood Vitaly Smolski, number two in the troupe.

"What is it?" he asked.

"That annoying Asian woman. She wants to talk to you. I told her to shut her mouth, but she won't listen. She says she has important info. She might even know where the gold is. I think she's lying. Do you want me to shut her up?"

Karlov thought for a moment. Then, he answered, "No, she can still be useful. I'll listen to what she has to say. Bring her here. I also want her to help me with the system. It's locked. I bet she knows the password."

Smolski nodded and turned back.

Karlov left the door open and sat down in one of the swivel chairs. He rummaged through a bag of dried bison meat that he had tucked in breast pocket, tore open the package, and began chewing.

Less than three minutes later, Smolski shoved Mi through the door. "Get in there, and don't make trouble," he ordered. "You want me to stay here and guard her?"

"I can handle her," Karlov said, rolling his chair aside to make room at the PC. "Password!" he demanded sternly.

Mi looked at him challengingly.

Amused, Karlov raised his eyebrows. "What do you think this is, a game? You wanted to talk to me, so talk!"

Mi silently sat down at the computer and typed in the password.

"Good girl," Karlov praised.

She turned and looked Karlov straight in the eye. "You are trying really hard to appear like a brutal thug. But I can tell you're not stupid," said Mi.

"Oh, thank you very much. And I realize that behind your petite façade lurks a hardened bitch."

"Alright. Let me show you something, if I may. Because I don't suppose your friend Viktor told you what you're getting into here."

"I'm sure I got all the information I need."

"Then you've seen the video of the berserker, I take it?"

"Berserker?" Karlov repeated.

Mi typed in a few commands. "Don't worry, I'm not doing anything. The satellite link is gone anyway, I checked earlier."

Slowly Karlov nodded. "Because of me. Show me the damn video!"

Mi opened a video player and slid the window onto the big screen. "This is the recording of the mine workers from the day the rock cave was discovered—and the ship. I suppose I'm not giving anything new away when I say that both of them are no longer alive. Six other men are also dead." She pressed play.

Karlov watched the entire video without the slightest emotion showing on his face. After the recording ended, he took another piece of bison meat from the bag and put it in his mouth. Then, he repacked it. "I've seen worse," he said calmly.

"I don't doubt it," said Mi. "But still, you have to realize that the danger lurking down there is unpredictable. We've had more incidents lately: irritability, migraines, sleepwalking, the cook even tried to stab a technician. This ship emits something that makes men go crazy."

Karlov shook his head. "My men are disciplined; they are used to rough operating conditions. Your scientists are just unstable."

"You know that this is nonsense. Is Nikolaev always like this? He's going to turn into a psychopath."

Karlov groaned in annoyance. "Viktor may seem a bit overwrought, but you don't have to worry about that. My men and I have everything under control, you can..."

A crackle from his radio headset interrupted him mid-sentence.

Ten minutes later, Karlov stormed into the cave with the petroglyphs with station psychologist, John McFarland, in tow. "What the hell is going on here?" he yelled.

Thoralf, Björn, and one of the mercenaries were standing next to the tunnel boring machine that had been switched off. The mercenary pointed in the direction of the burial chamber. "Dimitri!" he said curtly.

Agonized screams and muffled thumps came from the chamber.

Karlov nudged McFarland over to Björn and Thoralf. "Guard!" he growled at the soldier, who immediately tightened up and pointed his rifle at the three men.

Karlov walked over to the burial chamber and looked inside. Bullets whizzed through the entrance. He was just able to get his head out of the line of fire. "Shit, damn it! Dimitri, what are you doing?" Karlov felt hatred rising inside him. What was this guy thinking?

Again, he heard thumping. Karlov peaked around the corner. Just then, Dimitri hit his head against the rock wall, his face completely covered in blood. On his forehead, he had a thick laceration.

Karlov's anger was mixed with dismay. "Cut the crap!" he roared.

Another shot rang out—only one this time. Karlov instinctively took cover. Then, there was silence. No more thumping. No more wild gasps. No shots were heard either.

Cautiously, Karlov stood and looked into the chamber. Dimitri had shot his head off with the rifle. The burial chamber was drowning in blood.

Karlov walked over to the others. He stood in front of McFarland and glared at him. "What kind of psycho shit is that? Is that really coming from the ship?"

McFarland nodded. "We're way too close. We need to get away from here. You feel it too, don't you?"

Karlov uttered a growl.

"How are you not affected?"

"We are affected. But we have taken medication that dampens the impact," explained the psychologist.

"Give it to me!" roared Karlov.

"I can't, they're all we have..."

Karlov sped forward, grabbed McFarland by the neck, and squeezed.

The psychologist threw up his hands, wanting to free himself from the grip. But Karlov was too strong.

"Give me what I want!" he yelled at him.

In the background, Thoralf and Björn took a step forward, as if they wanted to rush to McFarland's aid. But the soldier stepped between them and put the barrel of his rifle to Thoralf's head. "Nice and easy!" he said.

Karlov didn't notice what was going on. The hatred threatened to overtake him.

McFarland emitted a hoarse gasp. "Please!"

It only made Karlov angrier. That wretched maggot—he would crush them. These weaklings had it coming to them. He squeezed even harder, feeling something crack under his grip, then abruptly give way. McFarland's body went limp. Breathing heavily, Karlov stood there and only let go after what felt like an eternity.

McFarland slumped to the ground, his head hitting the rocky floor.

"Keep going!" Karlov yelled at the others and stormed out to the airlock.

After the ship's tailgate closed, it was so gloomy inside for a moment that Anika, Matthew, and Sigurdson could barely see their hands help up before their eyes. Then, it gradually became brighter. At first, they didn't know where the light was coming from because it was everywhere. But then, they realized that it must be coming from the materials of the ship itself. Matthew stopped and felt the surface. The walls, ceiling, and floor seemed like a finer variation of the rough outer skin. The only difference was that the material seemed to glow from within. "This is actually a spaceship," he breathed.

After just under a minute, the light was at a pleasantly bright level, almost like the morning sunlight—warm, but not so harsh, but as if filtered through absorbent cotton.

"Remember that white light in the vision?" asked Matthew.

Anika nodded. "Yes, this is almost the same. Only this time, it's real. We can move freely and talk to each other."

"That vision you experienced..." started Sigurdson. "Was there anything in it that I should know about?"

"No, not really. It was more of a historical record. It showed the departure of the ship from a war and the emergency landing here," Anika explained. "Well, I suspect it was an emergency landing. I don't think they would have come here voluntarily."

"I see, but it didn't happen to contain the information about where we need to go in this thing? Or where we can find the shut-off button for the signal?"

Anika shook her head. "No, we haven't seen anything from inside at all. But I assume there must be some kind of command bridge here."

"Then we should hurry up and find them before chaos

breaks out up there," Sigurdson said and continued through the corridor into the interior. Anika and Matthew followed him.

With each step they took, the illuminated area around them adjusted as the walls in front of them brightened, and the area they left behind dimmed back down.

"The ship is responding to us. It senses someone is here and is starting up its systems," Matthew noted. "I felt like I could sense a vibration earlier. And now I'm noticing it even more clearly below us."

Sigurdson nodded. "Yeah, I can feel it, too. It's ramping up. I just don't know if that's good or bad."

The corridor they came through ended in a circular room about six meters in diameter, with corridors branching off in three other directions.

"Where to now?" asked Matthew.

Anika shrugged, then turned once in a circle to examine her surroundings. "Well, it would help if they had the signs pointing toward the bridge."

As soon as she said that, the lights came on in the hallway to their right.

"That works," she said, and started to walk off.

Sigurdson held her by the arm. "Careful. I have a funny feeling we're not alone."

Anika and Matthew stared at him in disbelief.

"Excuse me?" said Matthew. "Who would possibly be here after 2,000 years!"

Sigurdson tilted his head. "I know it sounds absurd. It's also just a hunch, an instinct. But I've almost always been able to rely on it."

"We still can't stop here, can we?" asked Anika. After a second of silence, she strode ahead toward the lit hallway.

Viktor Nikolaev waved his pistol around the canteen. "Go find my damn gold!" he yelled at one of the mercenaries. "And give those drill guys a run for their money. I'm gonna shoot somebody in ten minutes." He spun around and took aim at individuals in the crowd one by one. Some instinctively ducked away while others simply closed their eyes. The mercenaries at the edge of the room cast skeptical glances at each other.

Boris Karlov came running into the canteen and stopped abruptly. He surveyed the situation, then addressed Nikolaev. "A word, Viktor?" he asked, nodding toward the door. "We need to discuss a few things."

Nikolaev narrowed his eyes and fixated on him. One corner of his mouth twitched. He didn't answer, and instead just pocketed his gun and followed Karlov out.

They went through the hallway to the attached container area where the security center was located. Karlov opened the door and invited Nikolaev inside. Then, he closed the door and locked it from the inside.

"We need to seriously consider aborting the mission. We're starting to lose our minds," he noted.

His boss stared at him as if he were insane. "You're really out of your mind. Do you think I'd give up so close to the finish line?" he hissed.

"Viktor, I can feel it. I just strangled the psychologist over at the mine. I didn't even want to do that. I watched my hand crush his neck like I was in a movie and I didn't feel any better until I moved farther away from that ship down there."

Viktor looked at him pityingly. "I thought you were tougher than this. Who cares about this psychologist? We don't need him!"

"It's not about the psychologist. It's about what's happening to me—and to you." He paused for a moment and pointed to the monitor behind him. "Did you see the video of the miner who went nuts?"

Viktor remained silent.

"Don't you notice this restlessness and aggression? It's not just an isolated incident. Dimitri just blew his head off over there after banging it against the wall repeatedly. They weren't lying. There's something that's driving us crazy."

"Gossip," Viktor said succinctly. "So what if it is? We just have to hurry."

"Don't you understand? The closer you get to that damn thing, the worse it gets! What are you going to do when they clear the tunnel? Walk down there? How far are you going to get before you crack your own skull?"

Viktor took another cigar out of his pocket and lit it leisurely. "It's a question of mental strength."

Karlov shook his head. "Dimitri was in a special unit for over ten years. If anyone had discipline and mental strength, it was him."

Viktor tilted his head. "Okay, let's say we really can't get to that ship. Then I want my gold at least. Surely you remember our deal. A fair share for everyone. No gold, no shares. So, let's not waste our time arguing."

"I can't send anyone else out to look for it. The storm is too violent."

"Excuses! All I ever hear is excuses. I hired you and your squad because I thought you guys were getting things done quickly and efficiently. Instead, here I am being put off and stalled."

Karlov clenched his right hand into a fist and

unconsciously raised it a little. When he noticed it, he lowered it again. Then, he turned around and walked out of the room without a word.

"Go find my gold!" shouted Viktor after him as he slid his chair forward to the computer and began rummaging through the files on the station server.

25

Anika, Matthew, and Sigurdson found a door at the end of the second corridor. As they approached, it slid open silently, revealing access to a cubicle.

Anika stuck her head inside and looked around. There were no buttons, displays, or other controls. "This could be some kind of elevator," she said, and went inside. After Matthew and Sigurdson followed her, the door slid shut and the car started moving almost imperceptibly. After a few seconds, the door opened again and they saw a spacious room outside, but it was still mostly enveloped in darkness.

They stepped out of the booth as the light in the room gradually became a little brighter. It was not as bright as it was in the corridors of the other floor, but at least the light was strong enough for them to recognize that the room had some sort of special meaning, which was still a mystery to them. In the middle of it were several large apparatuses with glazed tops. They walked up to them and realized that they resembled small, enclosed chambers with a reclining area inside. Each chamber was about the size of a car and they were all empty. Only one of the glass panes was milky opaque from the inside, so that the interior could not be seen.

"Is there something in there?" asked Sigurdson incredulously.

At that moment, the stone that had Loki's name in it began to hum again in Anika's hand.

"I guess that's a yes," she said, stepping even closer.

The buzzing grew more intense. More sounds from the ship's systems mingled with it: whirring, a slight drone, and a short thump every now and then. The chamber in front of them began to glow with a bluish light from within, then fine drops appeared on the inside of the milky pane.

"There must be someone inside. And ship is waking him up," Anika said absent-mindedly. She was fascinated by the sight and felt overwhelmed. Her heart was beating up to her throat; the hairs on the back of her neck were standing. "This is unbelievable!" she said.

Then, with a hiss, the window slid open. A body lay inside. It had a head with large, dark eyes, which were directed rigidly upwards. No eyelids were discernible. The creature had a flat nose and a small mouth, but to all appearances, no ears nor hair. Its skin was whitish and almost transparent, like thin parchment. Beneath it lay magenta tissue and strands of muscle. The creature had two arms and legs that were unnaturally long and thin. They hung from an equally thin body.

"Is it still alive?" asked Sigurdson.

Matthew stepped forward and examined the body. He looked for signs of life. Suddenly, the creature took a deep breath and stirred. It turned its head slightly and looked directly at Matthew. Then, it looked at Anika, who was holding the stone in her hands. Now, it emitted a dissonant chord. The creature bent over, inhaled and exhaled a few times, and then very slowly climbed out of the chamber. It straightened to its full height and stretched. It was tall—certainly at least 2 meters. Then, it walked with spindly steps towards Anika and pointed with an outstretched hand to the stone.

"We found it," Anika said. "In the cave over there."

No answer.

"I...do you want it back?" She held out the stone, offering it to him.

The creature took it with its delicate fingers and walked with it to a pentagonal construct about waist high in the back of the room. It was flat on top and had numerous depressions, each with a faint glow of light coming from it. Each depression had its own unique hue—some yellow-orange, some turquoise, and others magenta or deep purple.

The hum of the stone changed as they approached. The chord harmonized as the stone was placed in a precisely cut depression, then fell silent. No light shone from its hollow.

"Can it speak?" asked Sigurdson.

"I don't know," Anika replied. "And even if it did, what language would that be?"

The creature came back and stood in front of the two men. It stretched out its right arm and pointed at Matthew's hand. He lifted it. The creature grabbed it and turned his wrist so that it could feel the implant. Then, it turned to Sigurdson and did the same.

The creature pointed at its mouth, then at its forehead.

"What does that mean? Is it saying hello? Or is telling us it's crazy?" Matthew asked.

Meanwhile, the creature went to another apparatus and wiped its hand across a shiny surface. After a short moment, a small flap opened. It removed something and approached Anika again. The stranger held out a flat, silver object that looked like a brightly polished coin in Anika's direction. He tapped his temple and then pointed at Anika.

"You want me to stick this on my head?" she asked.

"Wait, is that a good idea?" interjected Sigurdson, taking a step forward.

The creature looked at him silently and raised its hand in a placating manner.

Then, it took the small, silver disc and brought it to Anika's temple.

Immediately, she felt like she was choking, then, she felt a slight tingling sensation.

A soft voice echoed through her head. "Can you understand me now?" she asked.

"Yes!" thought Anika.

"Very good," said the voice. "I am Loki. I thank you for reawakening me."

"Loki…I have so many questions!"

"So do I."

"What about them?" She pointed to Matthew and Sigurdson. "Can they hear you, too?"

Loki looked at the men as if he didn't know what to answer. Then, Anika heard the soft voice again. "It would be dangerous. They are only protected by the inhibitors."

"The implants?"

"Yes, they prevent our technology from affecting them. It is incompatible with human males."

Anika nodded. Then, she turned to Matthew and Sigurdson. "I can talk to him. It works telepathically. I think. He says you're protected by the implants, but you can't hear him because of it."

Matthew turned to the creature and put his hand on his chest. "It's alright," he said.

Sigurdson shook his head. "Okay, then please ask him how we can shut off that signal. He needs to know that there are other people in danger up there."

Anika nodded. "We're here because we need to ask you to shut down your systems. The signal from the ship is driving our people crazy."

"I can't," Loki explained. "It's complicated. Our technology is based on a telepathic interface between us as fully organic life forms and the partially organic ship. I can't turn off the interface. That's why I tried to mitigate the effects with the inhibitors. And that's why we ultimately wanted to leave this world again. But we failed."

Anika was about to ask what had happened when Sigurdson intervened. "What is it? What's he saying? Is he shutting it down?"

"He can't. He says it's a side effect of the ship's elemental systems that can't be deactivated."

Sigurdson threw his hands up in the air. "Nice!" he shouted. "What do we do now?"

Anika turned to Loki again. "You have to help us. What can we do?"

"Get away from here," Loki thought.

"We can't! The access is buried. Besides, our people are being held hostage upstairs. They will die if we do nothing."

Silence spread—both in the room and in Anika's mind. It seemed to her that Loki was concentrating entirely on thinking.

"What's he doing?" asked Matthew. "Did you tell him our people are in danger?"

"Yes, of course I did. I don't know what he's doing now."

Boris Karlov had called all his men together in the kitchen at 7:00 pm. Only Yuri Tatchenko, who had earlier escorted

Björn and Thoralf back from the mine, had stayed behind as a guard in the dining room of the canteen. He kept an eye on the bound men and women while Karlov held the briefing next door. He had deliberately not asked Viktor Nikolaev to come, and he was glad that he had not shown up of his own accord.

"I want a comprehensive status report from everyone. Then, we'll plan how to proceed. I will report on the status at the mine," Karlov declared, then pointed at Vitaly Smolski. "You start. Have you tracked down the rest of the employees?"

Smolski shook his head. "No, we searched almost the entire compound and all the buildings. There was no trace of them. We're no longer concerned whether they're still hiding somewhere. The storm has gotten so bad in the last hour that it's hard to venture outside without a vehicle. And even that is dangerous."

Karlov nodded. "I think all three are at the ship anyway. And that probably means we won't have to worry about them soon. If they haven't already killed each other, that is. After what happened in the mine, I think that is a realistic assessment. As I told some earlier, Dimitri attacked me and Tatchenko. He also strangled one of the scientists and eventually shot himself in the head."

Karlov looked around at the ranks of his men. He saw signs of restlessness in some, but most still seemed to have a good grip on themselves. Above all, it was important to him that no one questioned his lie. He had deliberately not mentioned that he had killed the psychologist himself in a delusion. He did not want to show any weakness in front of his subordinates, did not want to admit that he had succumbed to this mysterious influence. He had made it more than clear to Tatchenko that he had to keep his mouth shut.

"Be that as it may," Karlov continued. "I want you to keep a cool head. No one goes to the mine anymore. Eat dinner, lie down, and divide your shifts for the night watch. We hope the storm will let up tomorrow morning, then we'll look for the gold and get out of here. And then I don't really care whether Viktor comes with us or not. I don't give a damn about that ship down there either. Everyone will get their fair share."

Nods of approval signaled that his men were on board with his plan. Only Fyodor Kozlov slowly raised his arm.

"What is it?" asked Karlov.

"Just one question: What do we do if one of us goes crazy tonight?" he wanted to know.

" Hopefully it won't come to that. If we're quick, we can complete our mission and get out of here before any of us are severely affected."

"Now, please ask him if there are any weapons on board," Sigurdson asked.

Anika looked at him in irritation. "Weapons?"

"Yeah, anything we can use against that mercenary squad."

Anika sighed. Then, she turned to Loki. "Pardon the direct question, but is this ship armed? I mean, is there any way we can defend ourselves against the attackers?"

"This is a research vessel. We have nothing on board that comes close to your idea of a weapon. There are only defensive systems to protect us from cosmic rays and such. I have already said that you must leave. Either you move away from the ship or I will move our ship away from here."

"Are there any more of your kind here? The other chambers all look empty."

Loki pointed to the apparatus in which he had placed the rune stone. "I am not alone at all. My brothers are with me. Their souls are preserved in the stones. My task was to bring them home."

"Your home must be far away. What caused your return to fail?"

"The ship got damaged. I had to land here. I and the twelve chosen representatives of your people. It is a tragedy. I didn't repair the ship in time."

"It's fixed?"

"Yes, only it took years. I had to regenerate it, which was very lengthy in this climate. And by the time I completed the process, the ice cover was so thick that we were stuck. I put myself in stasis and waited for the ice to melt and for my distress signal to be picked up. I had hoped that the others would detect our tracks. But it didn't work. You are the first to make it here. And even that took millennia—if I analyzed the data correctly."

"More than 2,000 years, yes," Anika confirmed.

"It is sad. Now I have reached the end of my life. I can't put myself in stasis again. At most, I have enough time left to transfer my spirit into the last stone."

"Wait a minute. You said the ship was fixed. Why don't you launch it? The ice layer has gotten pretty thin."

"Not thin enough," Loki explained.

Anika settled down cross-legged and sighed.

Sigurdson and Matthew leaned down to her. "What is it now? Do they have weapons?" asked Sigurdson.

During the telepathic conversation, Anika had almost forgotten that the others didn't notice anything. She shook her head. "He says it's a research ship and therefore unarmed. He understands it causes problems and he would fly it away, but the ice is stopping him."

"Then we'll blow it up," Sigurdson said grimly.

"That's it!" exclaimed Matthew suddenly.

"You agree with him? Are you out of your mind?" Anika shot back.

"No, no," Matthew fought back. "I don't want to blow up the ship. I want to blow up the ice!"

Sigurdson looked at him scrutinizingly. Then, he nodded. "Could work. But we really have to hurry. We're wasting too much time. I hate that we can't do anything to help the others up there."

Anika turned back to Loki. "We want to blast the ice. How long will it take you to get the ship ready to go?"

"Not very long. But I have to transfer into the stone first and activate the automatic controls. You'll have to help me. And then get off the ship before the ship takes off."

"Where are we supposed to go? The entrance to the cave is buried."

"There is a second tunnel that leads to the burial chamber. I have sealed it. But with the artifacts, you can open it. It starts at the front of the ship. There is also a hatch there."

"I'll help you get into the stone," Anika said, then turned to Sigurdson. "He says it won't take long. But we have to get off the ship before he initiates the launch procedure. There's a tunnel into the burial chamber we can take."

"I'm leaving," Sigurdson said, trying to turn around.

"Wait a minute. What are you going to do? Knock these guys out?"

"I'll figure it out."

Loki suddenly raised a hand and pointed at Sigurdson.

"What does he want?" Sigurdson asked.

Anika heard Loki's voice in her mind again. "He wants to give you something," she said.

Loki went to the box with the artifacts and took out the small statue. He stroked it with his hand and then turned it over. Out of its mouth tumbled a dozen of the silver implants. He went back to Sigurdson and handed them to him.

Anika translated Loki's words. "These are the last ones. You're supposed to hand them out to the men so they're protected when the ship launches. He says there will be signal spikes, which should be extremely unpleasant if you're not wearing an inhibitor."

Sigurdson picked up his backpack, removed the explosives, and put the implants and artifacts in it in exchange. "Thank you," he said to Loki and nodded. Then, he looked at Matthew and Anika. "We'll split up. Everyone has their task, and the success of the whole thing depends on everyone equally. But we finally have a real chance. And I've got a score to settle with those Russian bastards up there." He pressed the explosives and a timer into Matthew's hand. "It's self-explanatory. Type in the time here, start it, and then run!" He looked over at Anika. "Please don't waste any time."

Meanwhile, Loki activated a projection screen that displayed a schematic map of the ship. The way to the bow hatch was marked. The artifact appeared next to it. It was the bronze-colored amulet with the engravings and the Hagalaz rune on the back. He pointed to it.

"He says that the ship will take you there and you

should use this artifact. He wishes you luck," Anika explained.

"Thank you." Sigurdson turned and ran off.

26

After a few hours of rummaging through the mission logs and scientific data, Viktor Nikolaev left the security center with a new goal. By now, it was 9:00 p.m. and most of the mercenaries and hostages were trying to get some rest. It certainly wasn't easy with the storm shaking the buildings so loudly.

Nikolaev stepped into the canteen and looked around. Many of the men seemed to be in a fitful doze as some tugged at their shackles. Two of Karlov's mercenaries sat on the sidelines drinking beer. He disapproved but didn't want to dwell on it now. He spotted Mi curled up under a table in the back of the dining hall. He strode across the cafeteria and kicked the table with his foot. "Come along!" he growled.

Mi startled and turned around, "Where to?"

"Come with me, I said," Viktor repeated without answering the question.

She awkwardly crawled out from under the table and stood. Viktor nudged her toward the exit. "Come on. I have a few questions."

He led them to Sigurdson's security center. Several photos of the artifacts were open on the large screen.

"What are these things?" asked Nikolaev.

"Artifacts," said Mi. "We found them in the cave with the drawings."

Nikolaev pointed to a picture of the stone of Loki. "I want that one!" Greed shone from his gaze. "Give it to me."

"I don't have it. All the artifacts were returned to the rock cave," Mi explained.

"You're lying!" he snapped. He got up close to her face and sniffed her. "You know, I can smell it."

Disgusted, Mi turned her head away.

"What's the matter? Am I not your type?" He put on a grin. "I should probably mention that I've always had a soft spot for submissive Asian girls."

She had to muster all her control not to spit in his face. But she knew that would have been her death sentence. "I...I know where the things are," she finally said. "They're hidden in the burial chamber. There's a mechanism. I can take you there and get the stone out."

Nikolaev looked at her mildly. "Very nice," he purred.

"But I need an apparatus from my lab."

Nikolayev's brow furrowed. "Alright, but don't try to trick me." He took his silver pistol out of his pocket and ran it across Mi's forehead, then along her temple, down her cheek, to her neck, and then into her cleavage.

"We have to go," Mi said, "The storm!"

Nikolaev took the pistol from her chest and pointed it at the door. "Let's go then!"

As it had before when he made his way to Loki's stasis chamber, the ship now directed Sigurdson to the hatch by turning on lights in the areas where he needed to go next. He wondered how big this ship was and how tall the crew must have been. But he didn't have much time for reflection. He knew that he had to concentrate on his task now. And he hated that he had no plan and no time for preparation. He hated that he was stumbling head-first into a dangerous operation. But he also knew there was no other solution. And despite everything, he alone bore the responsibility for the safety of the people up there. It was a heavy burden given the circumstances, but it didn't frighten him. It was too late to worry about it anyway. He was going to kick this guy's ass, even if it killed him. At least he'd take as many of them with him as he could.

Sigurdson approached the bow hatch that had been marked on the plan. He stood in front of it and waited. It took less than two seconds for it to swing open inward with a hiss. He looked out into the gloom as the cold crept into the ship. Sigurdson rummaged through his backpack to take out the artifact that would open the hidden tunnel for him. Then, he stepped out of the hatch. Apparently, there was a small cavity in the ice here, too, where one could even stand upright. From the bow of the ship, a kind of tunnel in the ice led to the rock wall behind. It was hardly more than five or six meters away. Sigurdson left the ship behind him, and the hatch began to close. There was no turning back.

Sigurdson found himself in almost complete darkness. Only a very faint glow came through the ice. He guessed it must be the headlights in the cave. His eyes became accustomed to the black backdrop before him and he moved closer to the rock. There was no passage to be seen, nor any door. He only found a sign about twenty centimeters high, carved into the stone at eye level. That had to be it. He recognized the rune from the projection Loki showed him: Hagalaz, an H with a diagonal cross stroke. But this rune was misaligned. It lay across, twisted 90 degrees clockwise. Sigurdson felt the indentations in the rock. He felt no handle, lever, or other opening mechanism. Finally, he picked up the amulet. On the artifact, the rune was correctly aligned. When he held the amulet aloft in front of him, something happened. A hidden mechanism was set in motion. With a quiet crunch, the rune slid outward. The depressions became a raised structure. Sigurdson was amazed. Then, he turned the rune counterclockwise to match its position on the amulet. With a soft crack, it snapped into place. Then, a previously invisible rock door slid aside. Behind it lay a dark, bare rock shaft. Sigurdson packed up the amulet, put his backpack on, and quickly disappeared into the tunnel, feeling his way forward along the walls.

Matthew and Anika followed Loki to the apparatus with the rune stones. He was making preparations to transfer himself into the last remaining stone.

"Can we help?" asked Anika.

"Yes, in fact, you have to. Someone needs to supervise the process until the end and then seal the stone. But before I initiate the process, I will program the ship's startup sequence. And once it's running, I can't stop it. Your friend will have to go up first and clear us of the ice. I've scanned the ice cover. There are some crevasses. He'll have to break them open. The ship will do the rest when we launch. I'll show him the way."

Anika turned to Matthew. "He says you are to place the charges in the crevasses of the glacier and detonate them. He'll guide you to the top."

"Do you want me to do that now?" asked Matthew.

In response, a projection appeared again, marking the way to the upper decks, and from there, the way to the ideal detonation point. Loki raised his hand and pointed to a specific spot with his delicate fingers and looked at Matthew with his black, infinitely deep eyes.

Matthew nodded. Then, he looked to Anika. "You're going to be okay here? Meet me at the bow hatch later?"

"Yes, I'll get there as soon as the process here is complete."

"Oh man, wish us luck, Loki," he said shaking his head, then ran out of the room.

Anika watched him for a while and suddenly felt a sense of loneliness that she had never known before. She fervently hoped that nothing would happen to Matthew and that they would both make it out of the ship in one piece.

She heard Loki's voice in her head again. "We will succeed," he assured her.

"I hope so."

"Your people have evolved amazingly since I last communicated with representatives of your species," Loki informed her.

"Well, a lot can happen in 2,000 years. And I must confess that I would like to know what has changed. We know little about that period in the Nordic countries. That's my job, you know. To research history. Maybe you can tell me more? When does an archaeologist get a chance to talk to a contemporary witness?"

Loki looked at her for a while. Then, he replied, "We don't have very much time, but I'll try to answer your questions while the trials are starting."

"Alright, what is this ship used for? Our sagas and legends are very vague. But it's generally described as a bearer of doom—a ship that goes to war."

"I already said it was a research vessel. Now it is a lifeboat. Its purpose was to bring us to this world to study your people. We wanted to bring you closer to civilization.

We were looking for ways to nurture you and to guide your development. Not everything went according to plan. The people reacted rather irrationally. We didn't understand why for a long time. Until we adapted the concept of gods. Such a concept was absolutely alien to us, but we eventually grasped the logic and used it for our purpose. Still, it was clear that our appearance here caused confusion. And the side effects of our technology could no longer be denied. In the process, we wanted to transform your world for the better. But our efforts often ended in war. After completing the mission, it was supposed to be my job to fly everyone back to our world. And the return, as you have seen, failed. I hope that now I can finally complete my task."

"That's unbelievable. But why the northern peoples? Other civilizations were much more advanced. Why didn't you try your luck there?"

"Oh, we did. We're not the only ship. There have been others here before us, on other continents, with other people. And the fruits of their labor have been amazing."

"This explains the great progress of ancient, advanced civilizations. But they all decayed or disappeared at some point."

"Yes, your people have an irritating tendency to self-destruct. Representatives of our people have been here for a total of 217 of your years and have witnessed much. Some from a distance, and some from tragically up close."

"We still haven't overcome that destructive tendency, there's no denying that. But we are much further along now than we were then. If only people knew they were not alone in the universe, maybe they would have a goal, a reason to overcome their problems?"

"That may be, but I don't know how realistic it is. I only have time left to complete my task; I can do nothing for your people. We are very long-lived—more than 300 of your years. But at some point, our end crept up on us. That is why we have developed the stones. Our memories and our essence live on in them."

"Your technology is fascinating. But it's also dangerous for us. Why is it only the men who react so strongly to it?"

"That's an important question, but I don't have a good answer for you. Our technology affects everyone a little differently. Some react very little to it, while others have severe reactions. But it always brings out the bad side in any men, repressing animal-like urges. I have not had the opportunity to research extensively why only men are affected. It must be due to genes or the way their brains are constructed. You have to know that these signals are for communication. It is the way we pass on our knowledge and control our technology. You are also, in principle, capable of understanding this communication, even without this tool." He pointed to the coin-sized silver device at Anika's temple. "With sufficient discipline and training, you could hear and respond to me without the amplifier."

"I wish I could learn how to do that," Anika responded, fascinated.

"But we don't have the time for that either. It's the same today as it was then. I was glad to have found a way to suppress the side effects. Of course, this is only a stopgap measure. But it allowed us to take both sexes of your species with us on the journey."

"The dead in the burial chamber?"

"We were already trying to build a bridge between this

world and our homeland. That is why twelve of you were on board this ship as ambassadors. They were the wisest and most learned among you. They were explorer spirits, like us, but it ended tragically."

"What happened?"

"I would like to explain everything to you, but I must complete my task now. I have spent far too long in the stasis chamber and will soon die. I can feel it. I must go to the runestone to preserve my knowledge. I am now programming the ship for automatic homecoming. Then, you must start the process."

"I still have so many questions," Anika said.

"I know. But there is no other way. Take the artifacts if you can. They contain the collected records of the pilgrims who wanted to travel with us. Their knowledge is encoded organically. You are smart; you will decode them."

With that, Loki fell silent and concentrated on communicating with the ship. Anika stood there and looked at the strange being that seemed so unreal and yet so real at the same time.

27

Viktor Nikolayev managed to keep the Jeep on course with difficulty as he maneuvered through the snowdrifts, some of which were several meters high. If the car hadn't had the clearing attachment at the front and the four-wheel drive including snow chains, they would have gotten stuck shortly after the canteen. But Nikolayev apparently did not even register it. He stared doggedly through the window, as if he wanted to melt the thick snowflakes dancing around them with his gaze.

Mi sat in the back seat, tied to the headrest with cable ties, watching him. He seemed downright obsessed. And with each meter they approached the mine, he grew grimmer. Mi glanced at the signal jammer resting on her lap. If her plan worked, hopefully the device would finish him off. It all depended on whether she had programmed it correctly.

Nikolaev parked the car as close as possible to the entrance to the mine and then bent over backwards. He had his pistol in his right hand and a knife in his left. He stretched out his left to cut Mi loose, giving her an indefinable look that expressed both desire and disgust.

Mi could smell his breath: a mixture of cigars, expensive whiskey, and heartburn. She pressed her head against the headrest and hoped he wouldn't come any closer.

Viktor cut the last cable tie, pulled back, pried open the Jeep's driver door against the wind, and then came to the back door. He silently dragged Mi out of the car, and they rushed over toward the airlock. She let them pass.

Inside, it was surprisingly quiet. Almost nothing could be heard of the raging storm. After a few minutes, they reached the cave with the petroglyphs. The airlock was open. Mi stopped at the entrance and felt her goosebumps rise. Everything was still as chaotic as the mercenaries had left it.

The drill had eaten into the wall a good three feet. Pieces of loose debris lay along the sides of the borehole and behind the massive device. Next to the front airlock, she saw John McFarland's lifeless body lying in a strangely contorted position. Mi felt a thick lump in her throat. She looked backward to the entrance of the burial chamber. There, she could see large splashes of blood on the wall.

Nikolaev pushed her further into the cave, waving his hands in the air. "Come on now! Where's the stone?" he said in an alienatingly shrill voice.

Mi placed her device in the center of the cave and initialized the signal generator. As she regulated the output and set it to the highest setting, she hoped the thing would make his brain boil.

Nikolayev paced up and down in the cave. "What is it?" he growled again.

Mi checked the displays. It didn't work. She got up and went to the petroglyph where they had discovered the secret mechanism that opened the burial chamber. What was she supposed to do now? Could she trick him and run away? Maybe she could lure him into the burial chamber and lock him in?

"I...they're in there," Mi stammered, pointing to the burial chamber.

Nikolaev stepped forward and peered into the chamber. "There is nothing there! Only corpses!"

"Yes, they have to be there," Mi lied, knowing she had to put all her eggs in one basket now.

Nikolaev took another step closer to the entrance of the burial chamber and looked inside.

Mi sprang forward and threw herself against Nikolayev, pushing him into the chamber where the dead mercenary still lay. She turned back with a speed she didn't know she was capable of and pressed the button that was supposed to lock the chamber.

Nothing happened.

She pounded on the stone, but it did not move. The door to the burial chamber remained open.

She looked at the thick crack that went through the wall. The mechanism must have been damaged. She turned and ran. But she didn't get further than the center of the cave.

With a furious cry, Nikolaev rushed out of the chamber and grabbed her. "You miserable bitch! I'll teach you a lesson!" He wrestled her down and dragged her along the floor. He shook his pants and tried to undo his belt while pushing Mi to the floor. His whole body pulsed with lust and rage, so he didn't notice the grinding sound coming from the burial chamber.

Sigurdson blinked to adjust his eyes to the light. He looked around. He had indeed landed in the burial chamber. It was smeared all over with blood. In front of him lay a dead man without the back of his head and his rifle resting on his lap. Then, he heard screams echoing through the cave. Sigurdson crawled out of the opening at the far end and pulled the rifle toward him, then crawled forward and peered out. He saw two bodies wrestling on the ground, half obscured by a large shipping crate. A man was bending over a woman. "What the hell?" he groaned. Then, he aimed his gun and fired. He hit only the man's leg. An angry yelp was heard, and the man jumped behind the crate. Sigurdson fired again. The bullet slammed into the side wall of the crate. Then, the man behind it fired twice, narrowly missing him. Sigurdson hastily took cover.

"Come out, you pig!" Sigurdson heard the guy yell. His voice sounded high-pitched and hysterical. Again, the man fired. Sigurdson thought feverishly about how to take him by surprise.

Mi took advantage of the distraction and crawled for cover behind the mine drill. Was she supposed to escape? Who was there in the burial chamber? The mercenary could not possibly have risen. Again, she heard gunshots and knew she needed to act while she still had the opportunity. Her eyes fell on a large wrench used to assemble the drill bits. It was almost as big as a baseball bat and certainly five times as heavy. She picked it up as silently as possible and crept out from behind the drill.

Nikolaev lurked behind the box, trying to find a better shooting position towards the burial chamber. Mi gritted her teeth and raised the wrench high above her head.

Viktor saw her shadow on the floor and wheeled around, but it was too late.

Mi let the wrench whiz down and hit him head-on. There was a dull cracking sound and Viktor's eyes twitched in two different directions at once. Then, his body went limp. Mi raised the wrench a second time and let it come down even hard. Then a third time. As if in a frenzy, she kept hitting him until his skull was crushed into an unrecognizable red mass.

Suddenly, Sigurdson stood in front of her and looked at her with a mixture of admiration and horror. He did not say a word, but only nodded. Mi slowly became aware of what had happened. She gasped and felt an attack of dizziness. Clanking, the wrench fell to the floor and remained beside Viktor's body. She looked down. "One less pig," she said coolly.

"I have everything ready," Loki reported. "See that console over there?"

Anika looked at a flat terminal on which a kind of screen had come to life. Next to it was a silver area the size of a paperback book, reminiscent of an oversized touchpad. "Yes, I see it. Do you want me to use it to control the ship?"

"No, you don't need to do anything other than launch it. I've programmed the ship to automatically execute the launch procedure and set the right course to return. You just put your hand on it and think about going home."

"That simple?"

"Yes, that simple. Our technology is aimed at overcoming barriers and supplementing organic living beings with technology. And that is what we need to do next. I will go to the stasis chamber and start the transfer process into my soul stone. I need you to monitor it. When it is completed, you will know. My body will then be dead, but my spirit will live on. Once that is done, start the ship and leave immediately. You will have only a few minutes, so do not hesitate."

Anika walked over to the apparatus where Loki's stone was joined by a dozen or so others. "Are these your companions?"

"My brothers and sisters. We have only one race. There lie the preserved souls of Odin, Freya, Thor, Heimdall, and all the others who once came here with me."

"It's crazy. I know all these names. They are mythological figures. Gods from ancient legends and lore. I've studied these stories and often wondered how they might have originated. Now I stand here and recognize the origin, but it is so incredible. No one will believe me."

"Faith is a strange concept. We never really understood it. It did, however, provide us with some access to your people. But it ended up being very dangerous, and I think we probably shouldn't have used it for our own purposes. Rather, stick to what you know—to what you can prove. You have great potential, but you must overcome your unreasonableness, your irrationality, and your destructive tendencies. Perhaps one day we will return and make new plans for friendship between our peoples. That is, if my world still exists. So much time has passed."

"I would like to be part of it. I would like to see it, your world. But my lifetime is limited."

Loki was silent for a while. "I can't take you with me. We're out of supplies and hopefully the energy is just enough for the flight back. Besides, I don't know what it's like back home. You'd be on your own for the whole trip."

"I understand that it can't be done. I may not be ready to leave this world behind either. We should take you home now. You need to return so your mission can still be a success."

"Yes, you're right. It's time." Loki strode to the stasis chamber and lay down inside. "I'm going to explain what you have to do. We only have one shot at this, so please listen to me carefully."

28

Linda Janssen tried to distract herself and calm down somehow. Sleep was out of the question in this madhouse of a canteen. But she at least wanted to prevent herself from having a panic attack or a hysterical fit. Outside, the wind howled and inside, the men rattled their shackles and muttered restlessly to themselves. Some were spouting ancient gibberish that she couldn't understand while others grunted like animals.

Linda wanted to think of something beautiful, of a mountain lake, of a sunny spring day, of her children. Oh God, her children! She felt miserable. How could she have left them behind. Now she was trapped here, in the hands of brutal killers with a dozen men who could go crazy at any moment. She might never see her family again. The feeling of powerlessness choked her. She had to somehow get out of this somehow. She looked around. Was there anywhere she could escape? At the front of the exit stood the guard with the machine gun. The man looked increasingly nervous and agitated. His gaze kept twitching and he stepped incessantly from one leg to the other. Perhaps it would only be a matter of time before he, too, went berserk. The only question was what he would do then. Go after the prisoners? Shoot wildly? Or would he run out into the storm like Björn did a few days ago? She prayed it would be the latter.

Only now did she notice that she was staring at the man. She quickly lowered her eyes.

For heaven's sake, don't provoke him, she thought.

The minutes passed agonizingly slowly. Linda tried to sink into herself, to block out the horrible background noise. But suddenly she heard the guard say something. First softly, then again, a little louder. It was a Russian word. She did not understand it. The man repeated it again. She did not dare look up. Who was he talking to? Linda heard a thump. Then another. She looked at the man briefly. He was banging his fist against the wall. Now he yelled something and raised his bloody fist in the air.

He's going to kill us all, Linda thought, trying to push herself very slowly with her legs further back into the corner of the room.

Matthew looked up at a small, round hatch above him that, judging from the plan, must lead directly to the deck of the ship. He had taken the elevator up one floor earlier and followed the lighted corridor to the middle of the ship. At a central intersection, like the one they had seen earlier at the very bottom of the ship's belly, a pathway led upward in addition to the four main corridors. On the side wall between two junctions were small rungs in the wall that could be used to climb up. Matthew put the charges and detonator in his jacket pockets and began the climb. He approached the hatch. When it was within reach, it began to pulse with warm, orange hues. Matthew touched the surface, and it took only a few seconds for the hatch to swing open downward with a low hum. Cold poured in and faint wind could be felt. There really had to be cracks in the ice up there. Matthew saw that there were also indentations on the hatch, large enough for him to put his foot in and push himself up. He turned around, put his left foot in one of the steps, grabbed the edge of the hatch, and pushed out with his legs. There was a handhold at the top, which he grasped to pull himself completely out of the opening. There was barely room to move up there, but he noticed a crevice next to him that he could possibly squeeze into. He only hoped he could get out again. But regardless, regardless, he had no choice.

He got down on all fours and crawled into the ice. Behind the narrow opening, the crevasses widened a bit, so Matthew soon made good progress. He heard the howling of the wind and then a crunch or crack. He did not let himself be distracted.

The tunnel in the ice led straight ahead for a few meters, then it rose. Matthew found a sort of fork, the left branch of which ended in a dead end after about five meters. Matthew placed one of the two charges, put the detonator in it, and crawled back. In the process, he tangled the detonator wire on the ground. The other branch led deeper into the ice. Matthew kept feeling cracks and depressions on the sides. He estimated that he must have already gone about twenty meters when the crevice became too narrow to crawl in. He sensed that it led even further—possibly even to the surface, from where a distinctly noticeable wind was blowing toward him. He stuffed the second charge into a crack and placed a detonator in it as well. Crawling backward, he laid the second detonator cable to the junction. There, he connected the two cables to the timer.

Matthew knelt in front of the small box for a short while and thought. How long had it taken him to climb up here? How far would it be back in the ship to the bow hatch? Was five minutes enough or should he take ten, instead? Were Anika and Loki already done with the launch preparations? He had to guess and hope. Then, he entered the countdown: 7:30 minutes. He took another deep breath in and out, then pressed the start button. With a soft beep, time began to run out. Matthew crawled backward through the crevasse as fast as he could, squeezing through the narrow passage and swinging his legs over the edge of the hatch. He slipped inside, sought secure footing on the side rungs, and then closed the hatch. With a juicy smack, it sealed itself automatically. Hastily, Matthew descended the rungs, then jumped down from the third-to-last one and rushed along the same corridor from which he had come earlier.

"I don't know if you can hear me," he roared. "But the detonator is armed. We have to be out of here in six and a half minutes!" He continued running toward the elevator. The doors were open, as if waiting for him. Once he was inside, they closed. There were no controls, and Matthew had to trust that technology would take him where he wanted to go. To Anika. But it didn't. Instead of going to the large engineering room, contrary to the arrangement, the elevator went straight to the bottom.

Matthew cursed. But he realized that there was nothing he could do. Maybe Anika had already disembarked. He walked along the corridor, which lit up in sections in front of him. At the intersection, he briefly oriented himself, then swung to the left, where the lights guided him. He ran and soon recognized a hatch in front of him. It was not the one through which they had entered. It had to be the bow hatch that Sigurdson had also used. Matthew approached it and it opened with a hiss. He stopped and peered out. "Anika?" he called. A fluttering echo came back, but no answer. Then, he turned and shouted into the hallway. "Anika, are you here? We have to get off the ship!" Then, he felt an increasing rumble under his feet. The ship was getting ready to take off. Where was she?

Loki's body lay lifeless in the closed stasis chamber. Anika looked at him with a pang of sadness. She knew that the process had succeeded and that the stranger now lived on in a different state, but still, she suddenly felt alone. The voice in her head had gone silent. His soul stone now glowed a bright green from the hollow in the apparatus.

She overcame her rigidity and hurriedly walked over to the console Loki had shown her earlier. She placed her hand on the silver-gray surface and heard Loki's words echoing in her mind again. "Homecoming," she thought.

The ship's response came immediately after. The display showed a cryptic string whose contents she couldn't identify exactly, but she knew from Loki that it was a countdown, and she didn't have much time. The hull of the ship began to vibrate. She took one last look at the stasis chamber. An automatic process had already begun to dissolve the body and absorb the organic components. She silently said goodbye and ran.

"Anika!" shouted Matthew again over the swelling drone. Should he go back and look for her? Or should he just run out and disappear through the cave? Had she already gone ahead? Matthew took a step out into the darkness in front of the ship. He looked at his wristwatch. It was just under two minutes until the blast. How much longer would the hatch remain open? He took another step back.

Finally, he heard footsteps in the hallway behind him.

Then, he saw her. "Hurry up!" he called to Anika.

She ran past him and jumped out of the ship. "What are you waiting for?" she shouted.

Matthew followed her through the ice tunnel to the rock face. They ran through the open rock door. Matthew stopped and tugged on it. It didn't move.

"What are you doing?"

"I want to close it in case the launch blows us away."

"Don't! No time to look for the mechanism."

Matthew saw the last dim light disappear. The ship's hatch must have closed. It was now completely dark. He let go of the door and felt his way along the wall to Anika. "The charge is about to go off," he murmured to her. "We've got to see about getting out of this tunnel."

They felt their way blindly through the corridor, which twisted several times. Finally, they saw a faint glow of light. It had to come from the burial chamber. They quickened their pace and stumbled into the chamber. They had no time to deal with the carnage they found. At that moment, they both felt a tremor as dust trickled from the ceiling. Success.

29

Boris Karlov sat in the darkness in Harry Stadler's office and tried to ignore the wild flickering that kept spreading in his field of vision. It seemed to him like a swarm of fireflies fluttering around inside his eyes. He squeezed them so tightly it hurt. He felt the last vestige of his self-control crumble, his rational thinking giving way more and more to an irrepressible drive—an archaic instinct. He wanted to prey. Karlov jumped.

Outside in the corridor, Smolski came toward him. He was screaming and holding his head with both hands. Karlov did not understand his words. He only felt an unbridled thirst for blood. Karlov dashed forward and pounced on Smolski. He wrestled him to the ground and bit his neck. He tasted warm blood and raw flesh. Only when Smolski's body went limp did Karlov straighten his torso again and looked around with a crazed look for the next victim.

A rumble echoed throughout and a thudding sound came from the ground. Karlov hardly noticed it. Then, gunshots mingled in with the noise. He stood and started walking very slowly toward the sound.

Mi took the wheel spider of the Jeep, swung out, and hit the window of the station kitchen with full force. It broke with a clang, but no one noticed. The sound was lost in the storm, shouting, and machine gun fire. Mi knocked away the shards all around and climbed in. No one was in the kitchen who could have spotted her. She crawled along the floor to the door and opened it a crack. Madness was raging in the dining room. She recognized one of the mercenaries lying dead near the exit with a knife in his chest. It was impossible to tell whether he had stabbed himself or been attacked. The men of the crew were all sitting in chairs or lying on the ground. They were shaking their shackles, some with faces contorted in pain, others screaming and growling. Two lay motionless on the floor. Mi hoped they were only unconscious. The bound women had moved as far away from them as possible.

It was time to act.

Mi scrambled out of the kitchen and then along the wall to the women. "Linda!" she called out, "I'll untie you, then you'll have to help me."

Linda Janssen looked at Mi aghast, tears in her eyes, whimpering softly to herself.

"Linda!" shouted Mi, shaking her shoulders. She took the silver implants out of her pocket and showed them to her. "We have to give them to the men; this will protect them."

Linda just stared at her.

Mi slapped her across the face.

The geologist shook herself and then nodded. "I'm so scared," she whispered.

"It's almost over," Mi assured her as she cut her loose. Then, she pressed half of the implants into her hand. "Just put them anywhere on your arm or hand. They go under your skin automatically."

Linda took the implants and crawled off.

The two women approached as unobtrusively as possible. Some nagged and grunted.

Thoralf wanted to snap at Mi but fell lengthwise with the chair he was tied to. Mi dropped an implant onto his arm. Almost instantly, it slipped through his skin. Thoralf calmed down after a little over a second.

Linda snuck up behind Björn, who was mumbling to himself, and slipped an implant into his hand. He fell silent and looked around in amazement.

They heard gunshots again from outside, along with bestial howling as if from an angry bear.

"Hurry up!" yelled Mi, rushing over to Juan Lopez, while Linda sidled over to Michael Ward. So, they tended to the other men as well. Once everyone had calmed down, they cut their bonds loose.

"Everyone, listen up!" shouted Mi. "We have to get out through the kitchen and make our way to the bunker! The women first. The Jeep's parked outside. The men need to grab the snowmobile and the snowplow."

"What about the soldiers?" asked Michael Ward. "We could overpower them now."

"They're long dead or have become wild animals. Sigurdson is outside with a machine gun, keeping them at bay until we're safe."

While Mi was discussing with Ward, Linda sent all the women to the kitchen.

"I'm going out to fight," Ward said.

"Me too," Thoralf declared.

Mi raised her hands in the air, perplexed. "Do what you want, but don't get killed!" Then, she ran through the kitchen door.

"What do we do now, captain?" asked Yevgeny Vostok for the second time.

Ali Zakayev tugged at his bushy mustache and exhaled heavily. "Are we still getting the same confused radio messages?"

"Yes, captain. Until just now. Then only rifle fire," said Vostok.

"Did you answer?"

"Yes, several times. But all that came back was loopy drivel. Now the channel is dead."

Zakayev went to the periscope and adjusted it to the settlement. There was not much to see in the blowing snow. He looked at the scene silently for a while, then, without averting his eyes, asked, "Do you feel it, too?"

Vostok cleared his throat. "With respect, Captain, this nagging unrest is actually getting worse. And things are just getting completely out of hand over there. We should get out of here while we still have our wits about us."

Zakayev turned toward him and nodded slowly. "Yes, you are probably right. There's no point in us putting ourselves in any more danger. It's not worth it. Make all the preparations for diving."

"I've already had the ship unhitched so we can get underway as soon as possible."

"Very well. If no one shows up here or sends a radio message in the next ten minutes, we'll leave." Zakayev turned back to the periscope and kept an eye on the situation outside. For a brief moment, he felt as if he saw a detonation up on the mountain. He blinked a few times, then there was nothing but gloom and blowing snow again. "Forget it, Vostok. We're diving right now."

Sigurdson crawled out of his cover behind a large container and ran to the entrance of the canteen. On the way, he tossed the machine gun to the side; it had become useless. The ammunition had long since run out and the return fire from inside had died down. He had finished off three of the bastards and would now send the rest to kingdom come—with his bare hands if necessary.

He stopped abruptly in the hallway. At the other end stood a beefy Russian with a devilish expression on his face. Sigurdson had seen something like that before—on the video from the mine. He eyed his counterpart. The guy was doing the same. His greedy eyes had fixed on him, like a predator smelling its prey. Saliva dripped from his bloodied mouth.

What was he supposed to do now? This berserker stood between him and the canteen. Had everyone already fled? Or were some still holding out in there?

It was clear to Sigurdson that he had to face this bear, which was certainly 20 kilos heavier than himself. After all, the guy had no weapon, just like Sigurdson. He still stood back there and waited, but not forever.

Sigurdson saw the door to the dining room behind the bear open very slowly. He recognized Thoralf.

The berserker didn't seem to have noticed.

Sigurdson's eyes snapped open, and he tried to tell Thoralf with glances, "Get out! Get lost!" He didn't want to put him in danger.

Thoralf looked at him uncertainly. Then, he disappeared into the dining room.

For a moment Sigurdson felt relieved, until Thoralf appeared again. He knelt and looked between the legs of the attacker. He made a gesture that Sigurdson did not understand. Then, he saw a large hunting knife slice through his legs and down the hallway.

The berserker turned around, but only saw Thoralf slam the door in his face. He howled.

Sigurdson sprang forward and grabbed the knife. "Hey!" he roared, drawing attention back to himself. "Yeah, I'm talking to you, asshole!" Sigurdson held up the knife. "Wanna play?"

The berserker let out a growl and started to move. He puffed like a steam engine that would roll down everything and anything in front of him.

Sigurdson felt every muscle in his body tense. He clenched the knife's handle, ready to ram it right into the guy's guts. There was no escape from this hallway. One of them would not leave it alive. A few more steps and he would be in range.

Sigurdson now also ran, left elbow first, to block the attacker and then stab him in the ribs with his right hand. But he slipped on a trail of blood, staggered, and almost fumbled the knife. Then, the berserker was upon him, grabbed him by the arm, and pushed him to the ground.

Sigurdson squirmed, thrust, and sank the blade deep into his kidneys.

The guy just but didn't seem to feel any pain. Sigurdson shook the handle but couldn't get it free. IT was lodged in his body.

He saw the sheer hatred in the man's eyes.

Matthew and Anika left the chaos and horror of the rock cave behind and ran out into the tunnel. They took the direct route to the exit. Soon, the outer lock came into view.

"When we get outside, run to the bunker," Matthew said.

"Are you not coming?"

"I'm going to the cafeteria."

"That's insane. Who knows what's going on there!"

"I have to. I can't let Sigurdson go up against these guys by himself."

"Then I'm coming, too."

"No, you're not coming. I'll carry you to the bunker and lock you up if I need to."

Anika stopped abruptly and stared at him. She wanted to say something, but the conflicting emotions inside her made it impossible for her to find the right words. She knew she was better off in the bunker and that there was no reason to put herself in any more danger. Matthew's face showed grim determination, and she didn't doubt for a second that he would make good on his words. "Okay," she said curtly, and strode to the airlock. She operated the opening mechanism and pulled it open. Wind blew in. On her way out, she had the impression that the storm was finally letting up a bit. "You don't have to carry me. I'm going voluntarily. But be careful. I'd like to see you again!"

Matthew pulled up the corners of his mouth into a faint smile.

At that moment, a singing sound mingled with the roar, drowning out the wind more and more clearly. They took a few steps away from the mine entrance, turned, and raised their heads. They saw a trail of light through the snow shower, rising ever faster into the sky.

"It worked!" exclaimed Anika. "He's on his way home."

Matthew looked silently at the sky and shook his head in disbelief. Then, he reflected. "It's not over yet. Go!" He squeezed her hand, then ran off toward the cafeteria.

Mi tried to keep the completely overloaded Jeep on course. Besides her, there were seven other women on board. In front of her was the snowplow, into which three other men besides Björn had squeezed. In the rearview mirror, she saw the headlights of the snowmobile with Jörn Svensson and Peter Eriksson. Still holding out in the canteen were Thoralf, Michael, and the rest of the men. Mi had no idea if they would be stupid enough to attack one of the mercenaries, but she wouldn't have had time to talk them out of it anyway.

A bullet whistled through the windshield, whizzed just past Mi's right ear, and struck the metal brace under the headrest. Mi wrenched the steering wheel and the Jeep slid sideways. She tried to brake and counter steer, but the car threatened to spin out of control.

Another shot rang out—this time in the side. Beside her, Linda howled and held her leg. Mi cranked the steering wheel wildly, but the Jeep lurched ever more violently. "Everybody get down!" she yelled. Then, the car crashed into a pile of snow. The unbuckled women in the back seat were thrown forward.

Another shot.

Mi tried to clear her head. Where were the shots coming from? She peered into the mirror. The snowplow had turned around and was behind her. She saw sparks flying from the roof. Apparently, Björn had driven between her and the shooters to provide cover.

"Is everyone okay?" exclaimed Mi.

The women sorted themselves out and climbed back into the back seat.

"I'm hit," Linda yelled.

"The rest of us are fine," she heard from behind.

"We have to run, as long as Björn distracts the guy," Mi said, "It's not far!"

She yanked open the door and dragged Linda out. "I'll prop you up." Then, taking cover in a snowbank, they ran off toward the bunker.

Björn's shoulder was bleeding. He had been grazed, but he suppressed the pain. Beside him, the others huddled as far down in the cab as possible. He backed up very slowly and tilted the snowplow to increase the cover for the women who had just climbed out of the Jeep. "They'll be safe in a minute," he muttered more to himself than to the others.

A shot shattered the pane on the left side. Björn winced. It was coming from back there at the shed. He peered through the half-broken window. The guy had entrenched himself somewhere near the rock wall and was protected from three sides.

The mercenary fired only single shots. Was it possible that he was running out of ammunition?

Again, a bullet slammed into the snowplow. This time, there was a loud clong. It must have hit the shovel. Suddenly, Björn had an idea. He backed up, straightened the shovel, and raised it like a shield. Then, he stepped on the gas.

"What are you doing?" he heard Juan call out beside him, completely in shock.

Björn did not react and only continued to accelerate. Shots clattered against the shovel. Then, Björn slid down as far as he could and operated the lever for the shovel. It lowered abruptly. Snow piled up in front of the vehicle. It pushed it right toward the shed. Björn had to guess the direction—he couldn't see exactly where he was heading.

He heard a few more shots, then a panicked scream, crunching of wood, and scraping of metal on stone. The snowplow rammed into the shed, pushing it against the rock. The impact sent Björn crashing against the steering wheel. Dazed, he remained lying over it.

Sigurdson gasped under the weight of the berserker. With brutal force, he pushed him to the ground. He knew his end had come. He had fought and lost. He only hoped that the monster would finally put an end to it and not torment him much longer. But the berserker hesitated. Sigurdson saw that his eyes were heavily bloodshot, twitching from left to right.

Then, he felt a rumble in the floor and heard a swelling sound from outside. The sound made his opponent let go of him and cover his ears.

Sigurdson could finally breathe freely again.

The berserker shook his head frantically. He stood up, ran full force into the wall, slid to the side, crashed to the floor, and doubled over. He emitted sounds as pitiful and pain stricken as Sigurdson would have ever thought possible. The hair stood up all over his body. Suddenly, silence returned. No more huffing and puffing. No more booming. Even the singing sound receded behind the whispering of the wind.

Sigurdson lay limply on the ground, closing his eyes and trying to calm his pulse. He felt more exhausted than he had ever felt in his life. His side stung with every breath, reminding him that he was miraculously still alive.

After a while, he heard the door open and footsteps approaching. Sigurdson jumped up.

"Lie still," a familiar voice said. He saw Matthew

leaning over him. "I want to examine you."

Sigurdson swallowed and tried to speak, but his mouth was parched. He coughed. Matthew pushed him down with gentle force. "Lie down. It's over. They're all dead and the ship is gone." He began to scan him for injuries. "You've got bruises, probably a broken rib, and bruises on your neck, but it's nothing bad. You'll be fine."

Matthew saw Thoralf and Michael come out of the dining room with a water bottle and a blanket in their hands. He waved them over. "Over here. It's alright now. We can wait out the end of the storm in peace."

Sigurdson greedily took a sip from the bottle, then fell into a dreamless black.

30

Lake Lutvann near Oslo, Norway
November 1

"So, if I understand what you're saying correctly, you still can't explain where this artifact disappeared to, Ms. Wahlgren? Or do you not want to contribute to the clarification?" Rasmus Nygård's gruff voice echoed through the sterile hall in the basement of the Norwegian Secret Service, surrounded on all sides by thick concrete walls. "Surely I don't have to remind you that you will face serious consequences if you lie to this investigating committee." He paused and twirled his mustache. Then, he followed up, "Or if you knowingly withhold anything from us."

Anika cleared her throat. "I have put everything I know on record. I have given my report and I have answered all your questions to the best of my knowledge. Those two weeks in Svalbard were the most fascinating and the most terrifying two weeks of my life. I wish we had had more time to explore everything and hadn't been victims of a brutal ambush. I take it you still haven't determined why we were attacked? Or who attacked us, for that matter?"

Silence spread.

"Good, then we're done here," Nygård said tersely, noisily closing the file in front of him. "You can go."

An armed guard opened a door at the far end and posted himself next to it.

Anika stood and looked again, one by one, at the five

men sitting there in front of her like judges, giving her stern looks. They had no sense of truth. Until just now, she hadn't been quite sure if it was right to keep quiet about what they had experienced inside the ship. But if she had reported the whole and unfiltered truth to those officials there, she would have been on her way to the insane asylum long ago. That was standard procedure. Anyone who told anything about aliens was declared insane. And the thing was, she couldn't even blame them. The story was unbelievable. Anika turned her back on the members of the investigating committee and left the hall.

A car was waiting outside the Secret Service headquarters on Lake Lutvann near Oslo to take her back to their hotel in the city. It was 4:00 p.m. and dusk was slowly settling over the land. Anika got in and the car. The snowy, peaceful landscape passed by the window as it drove off, and Anika felt herself gradually stripping away what had happened and leaving it all behind.

Thirty minutes later, in the lobby of the Oslo Plaza Hotel, she turned into the bar and settled at the counter. She ordered a large Irish coffee and took a sip. Comforting warmth spread through her stomach. She felt a warm hand on her left shoulder. She instinctively knew who it belonged to.

"Was it bad?" asked Matthew with a sympathetic smile on his lips.

"No, not really. Just awfully long."

Matthew nodded and sat down next to her. He ordered a beer. "They tend to be a little redundant with their questions. It must be some kind of spy quirk. Maybe they think if you tell them the same thing five times, you'll eventually slip up."

"I guess that's possible. But I think I ultimately told them what they wanted to hear. Even if they didn't seem particularly satisfied. They'll have to figure out the rest for themselves. I have no desire to be involved in a spy operation."

"Me neither."

The bartender brought the beer and handed it to Matthew, who then raised the glass and toasted Anika.

She sipped her coffee. "How are the others?" she asked.

"Everyone is actually fine, although some will probably be traumatized for a while. Only Sigurdson has disappeared. He was in the hospital yesterday for treatment, but there's been no sign of him since he was discharged."

"Do you think they moved him to Siberia?" asked Anika jokingly.

"Would that be worse than Svalbard?"

Anika laughed. "Probably not."

"I think he left voluntarily. I don't know what he's up to. I still can't read the man," Matthew said.

"Yes, but he was willing to sacrifice his life and stood up to that monster." Then, Anika was silent for a while, staring into her cup, as if she was mentally going over the memories of it all. "The artifacts?" she finally asked.

Matthew shook his head, his brown curls bouncing around. "They confiscated everything and locked them away who knows where. I don't think we'll see any of it again."

A saddened expression settled on Anika's face.

"But they don't have everything," Matthew said. He took Anika's hand and turned it palm up. He placed a small plastic box inside and closed his hand again. "It's kind of amazing. If it weren't for this, I'd doubt if any of it really happened at all."

"Thank you," she said curtly, and unobtrusively slipped the container into her pocket.

"My pleasure. I don't need it anymore. I just don't know if your idea will work." He looked at her indecisively. "But I guess it's worth a try. Do you want me to come with you tomorrow?"

"No, I'll handle it. Let's talk about something else. About surfing in the warm ocean, maybe?"

Matthew smiled. "Yes, that's a really nice idea. The only thing better than talking about it would be actually doing it. I'm leaving for South Africa in three days. Why don't you come with me?"

"You better be careful what you wish for. I might just take you up on that offer."

The next morning brought ice-blue skies and sun. It was bone-chillingly cold, but the air was of bracing clarity. Anika walked toward the Oslo Hospital on Ekebergveien in the Old Town. The complex of listed buildings radiated peace and quiet—an appropriate atmosphere for Norway's oldest psychiatric hospital.

She reported to the ward at exactly the start of visiting hours at 9:00 a.m. and was taken by an orderly to a large common room.

About half a dozen patients sat spread out at tables or on sofas. Some were playing board games; one woman was staring motionlessly out of the window.

The orderly led Anika to the back corner, where a bearded man sat in an armchair, looking around, absent-mindedly.

"Here he is, our professor," said the orderly. "But I don't think there's much point in talking to him."

Anika pulled up a chair and sat down in front of Henrik Oddevold. "Thank you very much," she said to the orderly.

Anika looked at Oddevold for a while, trying to figure out the state he was in. He seemed to look straight through her. Was this the same man that used to debate with her endlessly at conferences?

To her, it was as if he was moving his lips very inconspicuously, as if he were forming silent words in his mouth. Had he been drugged? If so, it still didn't seem to help very much. This was no way to live. Suddenly, Anika was sure that she had to try to help him, even if the result was uncertain. She looked around the room again.

The orderly was busy setting up a chess board on one of the other tables.

And so, Anika reached into her purse and pulled out the small, plastic box Matthew had given her the night before. She grasped the silver implant and gently placed it on Oddevold's wrist, which rested on the arm of the chair. She watched it slide through his skin without resistance. An agonizingly long second passed, during which Anika held her breath tensely. Then, Oddevold jumped up abruptly and inhaled aggressively, like a diver who had run out of oxygen underwater and struggled to reach the surface.

Anika also stood. She saw that the nurse rushed over in alarm.

Oddevold turned his head back and forth in irritation, looking around. He was obviously trying to figure out where he was. Then, his gaze fell on Anika and remained fixed on her. He eyed her as if in slow motion. "Ms. Wahlgren, what are you doing here?" He looked at the stunned orderly who was now standing behind her. "Where am I, anyway?"

Anika turned to the nurse. "It's alright. I'll explain everything to him."

The nurse tilted his head. After a while, he said, "Okay. But I have to call the attending." Then, he disappeared toward the wardroom.

Anika put her hand on Oddevold's shoulder. "Why don't we sit down? I think we have a lot to talk about."

31 – THANK YOU

Thank you to my family and friends, and of course, to all the readers, bloggers, and fellow authors who have supported me with this book, as well as all my other publications to date. Stay with me!

If you have any comments, critiques, or questions, feel free to contact me via email, on Facebook, Instagram, or through any other channel.

Mikael Lundt, November 2021

Printed in Great Britain
by Amazon